PENGUI
LIVES OF TH

Patricia Wendorf was born in Sor[...] the Second World War her parents moved to Loughborough, which is where she still lives. Her first two novels, *Peacefully in Berlin* and *Leo Days*, received excellent reviews, and the Patteran trilogy established her as a well-loved writer with a unique voice. Her last novel, *Double Wedding Ring*, which is also published by Penguin, was based closely on the history of her own family in Somerset.

PATRICIA WENDORF

LIVES OF TRANSLATION

PENGUIN BOOKS

PENGUIN BOOKS

Published by the Penguin Group
Penguin Books Ltd, 27 Wrights Lane, London W8 5TZ, England
Penguin Books USA Inc., 375 Hudson Street, New York, New York 10014, USA
Penguin Books Australia Ltd, Ringwood, Victoria, Australia
Penguin Books Canada Ltd, 10 Alcorn Avenue, Toronto, Ontario, Canada M4V 3B2
Penguin Books (NZ) Ltd, 182–190 Wairau Road, Auckland 10, New Zealand

Penguin Books Ltd, Registered Offices: Harmondsworth, Middlesex, England

First published by Viking 1992
Published in Penguin Books 1993
1 3 5 7 9 10 8 6 4 2

Printed in England by Clays Ltd, St Ives plc

For Melitta and Nigel

PART ONE

H E drove into the Deerpark just as I was leaving. I stood as I always did, beside the gate, looking back at the beloved place. On the edge of my vision I was absently aware of the small black van parked in the designated spot, and the tall thin boy who unfolded from it, a careful hand pressed to his midriff as if to protect an area of tenderness from contact with the steering wheel or van door. He began to walk towards the gate. His style was expensive, vaguely reminiscent of that of my grandsons. White chinos, black leather blouson jacket, white-rimmed sunglasses pushed high beyond his forehead, giving a surprised look to the oiled black hair that curled across his collar.

At his approach I stood a little to one side. He came slowly, stooping from hunched and bony shoulders. Now I could see the angular planes and pallor of his face; the luminous eyes that lacked colour in their iris. The frill of white wool showing at his neck must, I thought, be the collar of some designer-styled sweater. I stared at the top few inches of unclosed zip fastener and saw the frill begin to stir and move.

A thin wail rose up from inside the black leather. The cry was that of a very young infant.

I stood, indecisive, and watched him move away beneath the trees. Between the edge of the white chinos and the tops of his handmade Italian shoes, I could see the blue-tinged skin of his bare ankles.

Winter had been very mild. Cherry trees had bloomed in January; geraniums, left out in formal beds by absent-minded gardeners, had seen a second flowering in February. In April came the snow and frost. I sat beside a window in the village café and drank tea. If, I thought, I had been a different sort of woman, more courageous, I would have challenged the young man's possession of the infant, its exposure to the bitter morning. I stirred my tea and sought a reason for the presence of the unlikely pair in such a place, and after snow. A boy of seventeen or eighteen: I remembered the tautness of his features, the hard look of him that had precluded any critical comment from me; I recalled, uneasily, the blue skin of his feet. Briefly, I allowed his sockless state to become my main preoccupation.

From the café window I could see the car park. Even as I watched, the boy returned; the black and white shape of him was folded neatly back behind the steering wheel, and the van began to move, its bonnet turned towards the city.

It was not possible at such a distance for me to see, or not see, the frill of white knitted wool that must have been the baby's bonnet.

I left the café and returned to my house, which was not a home but a repository for things that I owned. It was the place where I slept and worked, from which I sent out letters and made phone calls. Widowhood had become as much a state of mind as a physical deprivation. There were a few aspects of my solitary condition that almost pleased me, although certain pointers needed to be watched.

Compulsive tidiness, unchecked, could lead to madness. Sometimes I would try to give an air of disarray to ordered rooms. Before leaving the house I would place an opened book face downwards on a table, my reading spectacles beside it. I often tossed a pair of mud-encrusted shoes across the kitchen floor; left my nightgown trailed across the bathtub, my bed unmade.

By these tricks I sought upon re-entry to prove the house

inhabited, even by me; but the dangers of compulsion were more easily recognized than cured. I had left the house that day at an early morning hour, having woken abruptly from a dream of loss. I came back to a scatter of mail behind the front door, dirty dishes in the washing-up bowl. I opened the letters. An unsolicited offer by my bank of a loan I neither wanted nor could afford. An invitation to address a meeting of retired Salvationists. A postcard from my son telling me of Spanish food and sunshine.

I switched on the kitchen radio, ran hot water on to greasy dishes. The local news, every hour on the hour, had nothing to say about the abduction of a tiny baby by a young man in a black van.

The Deerpark was open to pedestrians through all the daylight hours. Joggers came out from the city to run the paths that sloped among the bracken. Retired couples walked aged dogs on stretches where the turf was level. The ramblers' club came in anoraks and stout boots. The watchers of birds, binoculared and woolly-hatted, crouched beside the lake that was host to mallard and teal, tufted duck and Canada geese. On wintry days the herds of red and fallow deer seemed almost tame enough to touch. Certain areas of parkland were as familiar to me as the gardens of houses I had once owned; my proprietorial feelings about them unreasonable, but very strong.

The boy in the Bally shoes had been an intrusion; the infant zipped inside his jacket an anxiety I did not wish to own. My habit of walking was irregular, dependent on mood and need.

I returned to the park three days later, and there was the black van parked beside the gate. My approach was deliberately slow. I did not pass through the entrance but lingered, my gaze fixed on the wooded heights. The turning of my head was gradual; behind the windscreen of the van I could see the boy's inclined face. He was looking down into a sort of quilted bag, a feeding-bottle in his right hand. Fascination drew me closer, but so deep was his absorption that I stayed unnoticed until my shadow fell across him. He looked up and I saw again the pale glitter of his eyes, felt the fierceness that emanated from him. He placed the feeding bottle on the dashboard and lifted bag and body up to lie across his shoulder. The action had an easy practised movement; I was, momentarily, reassured.

With his free hand he began to wind down the window. 'Something you wanted?' he asked softly.

Immediately I felt foolish. The question direct was to be expected. Ladies of mature years should not presume to stare in at van windows, unless prepared to provoke challenge.

'Well – no –' I stammered, 'at least, not exactly wanted –'

'You've been following me,' he accused. 'I caught you at it once before.' The voice, still soft, was now undershot with menace.

I recoiled, but only briefly, then said with dignity, 'I never followed you! We just happened to be in the same place at the same time. I was surprised to see so young a baby –'

'Thought I'd pinched him, did you?'

'Not at all!'

'Yes you did. I could see it in your face.' He began to stroke and pat the quilted bag in the region where lay the baby's back and shoulders. His hand was broad, with prominent-knuckled fingers and short clean nails. His body rocked as he patted. His actions, motherly and unselfconscious, were so at odds with his fashionable looks that I smiled.

'He's your's, isn't he?' I asked gently.

The boy's face softened. 'Yeah – he's mine all right.'

'Does he have a name yet?'

'Jasper.'

'I like it.'

'Serena's folks can't stand it. They wanted her to call him Ashley or Julian. I reckon the wrong name can spoil your whole damn life. My father's name was Jasper.' The words came out awkwardly, as if he were unused to conversational exchange. Abruptly he began to wind shut the window. I felt myself dismissed, but did not at once walk away; the boy resumed the feeding of his son. The passenger seat held a carrycot decked out in pale blue. In it lay a packet of disposable nappies, a white shawl, a knitted yellow duck. The feeding bottle, I observed, was of the vacuum sort. I sought for but found no cause for criticism.

The weather changed. The short days of winter, which I loved, began to lengthen into evenings that were light and hollow. I planted pansies in tubs and window-boxes; I mowed the lawn, began the ritual cleaning of my house because these were the tasks performed by women of my age in the springtime. At times of exceptional unrest I would rearrange things, move furniture, books and pictures. In those days of early May I thought often of the young man and the baby, recalled the van, the leather passenger seat, myself looking in at the open window at the carrycot, the white shawl, the yellow knitted duck. I went into my sitting room that was used only when friends came to visit, and dragged at the heavy leather wing-chair until it stood close beside the window that faced the street. I moved a lamp and a low table to stand beside it, and stepped back to consider the effect. My dissatisfaction with the room, the house, became acute. I pushed at the chair until it stood again in its accustomed corner; replaced the lamp and table in their respective places. The reflected light from so much polished mahogany and leather, all my shining windows, was painful to the eyes. I put away the spray cans and the dusters, the aids to attainment of the perfect home. The kitchen bin, filled with rubbish, was left deliberately unemptied.

I came back to the Deerpark in mid-morning. Three weeks of sun, of light rains and warm winds had set a greenness upon turf and trees. I walked swiftly through the car park, noted the standing vehicles: the Landrover driven by the head keeper; the Mini from which an elderly couple enjoyed their view of granite rocks and ancient oaks; the bright blue Porsche; the Morris Minor that was almost an antique. My shoulders twitched in an involuntary shrug which meant that I had expected nothing; my pace increased as it always did when I sought flight from unacknowledged disappointment.

For an hour I climbed the tracks made by generations of red and fallow deer. I came up to a pinnacle of rock, sat down on the cropped turf and looked out towards the lake. My unfocused gaze did not at first take in the young man at the stream's edge who had started to skim stones into the water. I began to move downhill, stumbling on the uneven ground. As I approached the stream my pace slowed to a saunter. I walked to the bridge and leaned my forearms on the cool stone. My head was pointed carefully towards the deer herds on the hillside. I sensed his approach and sniffed the air for hostility; the rubber wheels had made no sound across the dry turf. A parasol, blue with a pattern of teddy-bears, was angled across the little pram. He came closer and stood for a time looking down into the water. It was not until I began to move away that he said, 'Haven't seen you out here lately?'

There was faint conciliation in his voice.

I said, 'I spring-cleaned the house.'

'Was it all that dirty?'

Now I turned and looked directly at him. 'No it wasn't!'

Today he wore shades of blue, jacket and trousers, shirt open at the neck, dark blue espadrilles, no socks; the effect casual but well cut. It occurred to me that he had dressed to match the pram. The idea was not too bizarre. On the day he had driven the black van he had worn black leather; the sunglasses now perched upon his hairline had rims of pale blue.

I said, 'How's Jasper?'

'See for yourself.'

I moved close to the pram and looked down on the sleeping child, who was also dressed in blue. He wore a cotton shirt and denim dungarees as if he were a manikin-workman kitted out to repair a water main or dig a hole in the road. His cheeks were pale with sleep; long lashes cast shadows on his plump face. The black curling hair was just beginning to grow in.

'How old is he?'

'Five months and two days.'

To cover the awkwardness we watched the baby instead of one another. I said at last, 'You're right, of course. Spring-cleaning is a stupid business. One of the last Victorian follies. I do it because my mother did it. My granddaughters will certainly be wiser.'

'Priorities,' he said. 'That's what it's all about. Getting them right. Doing the things you really want to.'

'Such as walking in the Deerpark?'

'If you like! It's the only way to beat them, you know. The only way to work the system.'

'For myself,' I said thoughtfully, 'I've never been too sure what the system is. I wouldn't know how to manipulate it in my favour.'

He surveyed me in a way that was almost insulting. 'Oh, I don't know – I'd say that for your age you don't do too badly.' He lowered his eyelids and laid the tip of his finger across his chin. 'Let me see now. Retired school-marm?'

I said, 'I don't have a Porsche standing in the car park.'

He looked like a hurt child. 'That's cheating. You saw me drive in.'

'No I didn't! But I can also make assumptions. The Porsche would seem to be your style, and blue seems to be today's theme.'

He said, 'Are you laughing at me?'

I began to walk away. Across my shoulder I said, 'You were wrong about my occupation. I never was a teacher. I have a job at which I work most every day.' I halted and turned again to face him. I saw his new assessment of me, his appraisal of the short white hair, my advanced years; the unlikely prospect of any paid employment.

He spoke around a small grin, 'So how do you pass the time?'

'I write.'

'As in poems?'

'As in novels.'

He said, defensively, 'I don't read books.'

'It's not obligatory.'

'Are you some famous author then? Should I have heard of you?'

I smiled. 'They seem to recognize me at my local library. I don't appear on chat shows. My name is not a household word.'

'You must be doing something wrong!' Now his interest was intense. 'You need some decent PR. I could put you in touch with this –'

'I don't think so,' I interrupted. 'Not my style, you see.'

At once I regretted the confidence, my loss of anonymity, however small. I glanced at my wristwatch but did not see the hours. 'I must be going,' I said, 'or I shall miss my bus.'

'You come here on a bus?' The shock in his voice was muted by contempt.

'I happen,' I said sharply, 'to like buses. I ride them almost every day. It's another of those odd habits I've got into. Like spring-cleaning.'

This time I walked away without turning back, leaving him standing beside the pram in his uncreased blue.

The double-decker was painted yellow. It moved with remarkable speed between the hawthorn hedges, the forsythia bushes and banks of celandines. Sometimes it met another of its kind in the narrow lanes. There would be a slackening of speed, a skilful manoeuvring by drivers, a final exhilarating rush as the buses, like jousting knights, endeavoured to pass one another without scraping paint.

I always rode on the top deck and, whenever possible, sat in the front seat. Riding at this height I was level with the tops of trees; my perspective of the world was altered. No bright blue Porsche, no limousine could give me this unique sensation that was part sailing, part flying, and always of escape.

My own experience of driving had been long ago and confidently inexpert. I had bowled across fields and down farm tracks on an ancient Fordson Tractor; had willed a battered van to climb impossible slopes. What, I wondered, had happened to all that insouciance, that reckless disregard for slipping clutch and outworn brakes? The world itself had been younger then, the War only two years ended, the summers longer. *Finian's Rainbow* had been the latest London

11

show. I had sung 'How are Things in Glocca Morra?' as I drove.

It was possible by minibus or double-decker to travel right across the county and beyond. I had my favourite destinations. Three cities, their libraries of reference a necessary aid, were just an hour away. There was a little market town for nostalgia; and the Deerpark for delight and solitude.

May was unseasonably warm. I bought a summer dress, cleaned last year's sandals. I opened windows through which dust and humidity sifted to dull the shine of polished surfaces. Hydrangeas flowered on the terrace. I repainted the wrought-iron table, set out sun-umbrella and lounger. The house settled back into its more normal state of lacklustre orderliness. The fine weather ended spectacularly with thunderstorms and heavy rain.

The post brought a card from Eileen, who was touring Russia. The weather in Moscow was warm and fine. Leningrad, being further north, was expected to be cooler.

In June the country lanes were deep green tunnels. The topmost branches of overhanging trees slapped hard at the upper windows of the double-decker. I dipped my head instinctively every time this happened. The ride to the Deerpark was timed to an exact twenty-three minutes. This morning's driver, youthful and heavily tattooed, a gold ring in his left earlobe, might well have learned his trade on the circuits of Castle Donington or Brands Hatch. The elderly bus shuddered and rattled up and down hills, stalled once on a gradient of one in ten, shed a portion of its rusted chassis in a hedgerow, and arrived seven minutes before scheduled time at the Deerpark gates. I thanked the driver on alighting; for what, I was not quite certain. A safe journey against all odds? For my speedy return to the beloved place?

The morning was cool and overcast. No recognizable vehicle stood in the car park. I began to walk the tarmac carriageway; at the point which would lead me up towards the Elder Plantation I took a grass path through the bracken.

He had dressed today for cooler weather, pale grey and scarlet, trousers and heavy-knit sweater, his shoes a soft punched suede. His forehead, without the pushed-up sunglasses, showed heavy lines; he was much older than I had at first thought.

He fell into step beside me without sign or greeting, as if we were a brace of foreign agents, trysting in a secret rendezvous. He should have worn a long black belted trenchcoat, I a Marlene Dietrich beret. One of us at least should carry a folded copy of *The Times*. As it was, we might still fit in to our imagined roles. The pram alone struck an incongruous note.

The thought brought on a twitching of my lips. I glanced up and saw the tension in his face. Just in time I bent my involuntary grin towards the sleeping Jasper. I said, 'He always seems to be asleep.'

'Don't you dare to believe it! He had me pacing the house until four this morning.' His tone was one of pride rather than complaint.

'You must be tired.'

'I'm OK. I sleep late in the mornings. It's Serena who needs the straight eight hours.'

'So you're the alternative mother?'

Surprisingly, he smiled. 'Hey,' he said, 'that's pretty good. I like it. The alternative mother.'

We sat down on a bench that stood beside a stone wall. The bracken fronds uncurled, May blossoms faded on the hawthorne trees, buttercups grew tall in shady corners. It was, I thought, a good year for daisies.

I rocked the pram, absentmindedly. 'My name,' I said, 'is Cathy Baumann.'

'I'm Roman — and that's a first name, not a nationality.' His gaze was fixed on the carriageway where a young couple walked, arms entwined. He asked, 'Written any good books lately?'

'I'm not working at the moment.'

He said, 'I bet you think I'm some sort of ponce. That I lounge about all day while my wife works for our living?'

'Nothing of the sort ever entered my head!' I spoke decisively, not quite certain what a ponce was.

'You disapprove of me though. You thought I'd kidnapped Jasper.'

I could not deny it. My arthritic fingers curled tightly around the handle of the pram, causing me pain. Forty years ago I would have thought him strikingly attractive. Now I was merely irritated by him, his vanity, the way he assumed that his company was welcome to me. Something in his voice again alerted me to danger.

'You mustn't,' I said, 'be so ready to believe that people are critical of you.'

'Serena says that I provoke hostility.'

'And do you?'

For the first time in our acquaintance he turned a smile upon me that creased the skin around his opalescent eyes and showed the perfection of his white teeth. He began to re-arrange the blanket on the pram, folding back the satin-bound edge from the child's small curled fists.

He said, 'Jasper rates me very highly.'

'Where are you parked?' I asked. 'I didn't see your van or Porsche as I came in.' I regretted the words as soon as they were spoken. I watched the open smile change to a triumphant grin. He sketched a low bow across the pram.

'Serena needed the Porsche, so we came in the van. Jasper reckoned you might not come if you knew that we were here. He advised me to park beside the pub. We reckoned that's one place you'd never visit.'

To describe the room as a study would have been pretentious. It contained a desk, a comfortable armchair, two walls of book-filled shelves, and a violet-coloured budgerigar in a white cage. Maps and pictures covered other walls; the window-sill held a row of green trailing plants. On a low shelf in a yellow folder lay a copy of my completed manuscript. Until the printers' proofs came in I would dust the folder every Sunday morning.

When the boy called Roman had asked, 'What do you do, then?' I had said 'I write'. It was a fact I did not readily admit. I had heard on a recent radio programme an eminent novelist, young, American, articulate, when asked to define his craft, describe it as a funny business carried on by sad and lonely people.

I sat down at the desk and stared at the scarred leather of its top; the new notebook, purchased ritually and always as the current novel was completed, lay underneath my hand. I opened it and reached for a pen. In large block capitals I printed I WRITE, then scored it through with several lines. Halfway down the page, in larger capitals I printed I WROTE, and embellished the statement with a little sketch of wreathed flowers. I threw down the pen, reached a hand towards the telephone, and then withdrew it. Six months ago my son had moved away, to a village on the far side of the county. His phone number, more familiar to me than my own, had changed. The altered digits would not, no matter how long I studied them, commit themselves to memory. In the time it took to find the pad that held his number, my resolve diminished. In this springtime of bitter winds and unexpected warm days, it had been easy to believe that I existed only in my own imagination. That I too was a fictional character based loosely on fact.

At the edge of the desk, secured by a springclip, lay a sheaf of bus timetables. Printed on distinctive, coloured papers, the smudged ink figures informed me of the options open to me on a Monday morning. I removed the clip and, with the ease of a practised solitaire player, I dealt the timetables fan-wise on to the brown leather desktop. The joker in the pack, a saffron-coloured sheet that was labelled DEERPARK. turned out, as always, to be wild.

The transport officials who decide such matters considered Monday to be a slow day for the travel business. The dark green minibus had a squat, unadventurous appearance; it lacked romance. The driver was middle-aged and careful. He halted at every amber traffic light, drove widely around cyc-lists, argued amiably with passengers about the weather and the price of tickets. I caught myself hankering for the stomach-clutching thrill of the ride on the ancient double-decker, for the tattooed, temperamental young man who made every journey as unpredictable as summer. I sat in my striped seat of brown and orange plush and watched the dusty villages go past the window. I conceded, reluctantly, that the use of a minibus by the travel company was well justified on Mondays. Between my town and the Deerpark entrance, only three passengers had embarked. This driver, who was solicitous of children and older ladies, implored me to 'Mind how you go!' as I stepped down. I did not thank him for the ride.

The early morning weather forecast had promised rain spread-ing from the south; in my handbag I carried an umbrella of the telescopic kind, even though the sun still shone. The maxims of childhood came into my mind. Better safe than sorry. Forewarned is forearmed. A stitch in time –

I entered the Deerpark by the side gate. Two weeks of fine hot weather had browned the turf. Foxgloves, pink and white, had grown tall since my last visit. I started to walk the river path and paused at the first waterfall. A dogrose bush, rooted precariously in a rocky crevice, leaned out across the water, its flowers trembling in the white spray. I could, I thought, now leave my house for extended periods of time without feeling any desire ever to return. That strong sense of place, and my own pivotal position in it, was quite gone, perhaps never to return. Lately I ate sandwiches in cafés, listened into conversations from adjoining tables carried on in ringing tones of resentment and outrage by young women against the men who were just arrived, already resident, or about to depart from their confused lives. I drank gritty hot chocolate or weak tea and waited for coherence in my own thoughts.

The signs of my distress were there for anyone to see, except that no observer had yet been permitted close enough to recognize them. Eileen, my friend, intelligent and disconcertingly perceptive had, before leaving for Russia, viewed me with surmise. At such times I had striven for normality, or whatever I considered to be normal. But how could I judge? There were the early morning hours when my own screaming woke me. I dreamed always of doors, closing finally upon me, or opening slowly to reveal unidentified horrors. My confidence, never strong, was gradually eroding. I wrote letters to relatives that were never posted. Dialled the numbers of friends only to replace the handset before the bell began to ring out. Life had started to silt up; sad thoughts accumulated and would not go away. I began to move carefully through

17

the days, aware that a single misplaced step could send me spinning out across the edge.

The hood of the blue pram came first into my vision, the parasol set fair above. He was dressed for summer, white shorts and T-shirt that bore a discreet red and yellow logo. His long thin legs were muscled and bronzed, his arms and face similarly tanned.

He said, 'Hi, Cathy!'

I said, 'Good morning, Roman,' and moved closer to the pram. Jasper was awake. I saw for the first time the soft grey of his eyes. I said, aware of the triteness of the words, 'My goodness, how he's grown.'

Roman smiled down on me as if I had bestowed a great gift. 'You really think so? It's hard for me to judge. He's beginning to sit up. He's got his first tooth.'

'How wonderful,' I murmured. How wonderful, I thought, to be able to take such delight in the cutting of a tooth, in a baby's elevation from prone to upright. I looked back at the dogrose bush rooted in the rocky crevice, and even as I watched, a sudden breeze caught the pale pink blooms and a dozen petals drifted down the waterfall.

Jasper also wore white, shorts and tiny T-shirt, the same quality logo embroidered on them in red and yellow. The fluffy duck had been replaced by a grey plush elephant.

Roman said, 'You haven't been out here for two weeks.'

'How do you know?'

'Jasper and I come every day.'

I said, 'I came most every day when I was writing. I think better when I'm walking.'

'So you've decided to retire?'

'Oh no! People like me don't retire; I shall just run down, like an old clock.'

'You believe in the work ethic.'

I smiled. 'I suppose I do. It seems to keep me steady. It's also habit-forming.'

He said, abruptly, 'I'm not a ponce, you know. I'm a house-husband.'

I turned the new phrase over in my mind. 'What exactly,' I asked, 'does that entail?'

In our progress across the turf I had, almost without noticing, taken the pram from him. We were back on the carriageway now. His hands were thrust into the pockets of his shorts; he straightened his shoulders, kicked at the stone that lay across his path, walked with an exaggerated swagger.

'It entails,' he said, 'more work than you would ever dream of. The amount of food and drink that three people get through – the washing and ironing, the shopping and the cooking. If it wasn't for the microwave,' he sighed, 'I just don't know how I'd manage.'

I remembered the farmhouse kitchen, the black, iron cooking range, the fire of which had needed hourly tending. I recalled the brick-built washing copper, which had also required a fire to heat the water. All that kindling and those logs, heavy buckets full of coal; my hands, raw in winter, barely healed up in the summer.

'Yes,' I said, 'housekeeping isn't easy.'

'In case you're wondering,' he said, 'Serena and I are in business together.' His offhand tone meant that he had wanted me to question him about aspects of his life, and I had failed him.

'How very interesting,' I murmured. 'I would love to hear about it.'

'We've got this chain of boutiques. Designer clothes for the young and upwardly mobile. She did three years of Fashion at the College of Art. I took a course in Business Studies.' He paused. 'When I was twenty-one I inherited some money. I trebled my capital in four years.'

Aware of my cotton shirtwaist dress, my scuffed white sandals, I said, 'I don't know anything about fashion.'

'Well, you wouldn't, would you? Your generation had the war and socialism, and hard times.'

'You make it sound unbearably dreary. I don't remember it that way.'

'Serena,' he went on, 'sees to the actual point-of-sales side of the business. She visits each shop at least twice in every week. I'm not too good with people. She's better at handling staff than I am. I do the ordering and buying, keep the books, deal with VAT and tax.' His swagger became more pronounced. 'I've got an eye for good design. I've never stocked a line that didn't sell like hot cakes.'

'You cater for both men and women?'

'His 'n' Hers. Male and female fashions that complement each other. It's what it's all about, isn't it, togetherness and all that?' He nodded towards Jasper. 'Serena's working lately on the father–son aspect. Could mean a whole new angle for us.'

I tried to imagine Jasper, sunglasses perched among his curls, his plump feet blue and sockless, a miniature blouson jacket of black leather zipped across his chubby body.

'My babies were dressed all in white up to the age of six months, after that pale blue and lemon. They wore matinée jackets and romper suits, and little silk shoes tied up with ribbons,' I said.

'Serena's working on some new designs for Jasper; a whole autumn range, including sportswear, is already finished. My favourite is the pale-cream tracksuit with a burnt-orange trim. There's a burnt-orange windproof jacket to go with it, and little cream leather trainers.'

'And how old will Jasper be when he attains this outfit?'

'Oh – seven, eight months.'

'And will you also be wearing pale cream and burnt orange?'

'Of course. That's to be our new marketing image.'

I said, 'An interesting concept, togetherness. It could, if taken too far, I think, become a little claustrophobic.'

He stared uncomprehendingly at me. 'It's good business,' he said, 'matched family outfits have been around for a few years now. We're lifting them above the Marks and Spencer range, that's all, and on to the designer level.'

Each long hot day of July was followed by another; rain fell on other places, but the Deerpark and surrounding country remained dry. The turf was now bleached to the pallor of wheat straw. Summer lay heavy on the Elder Plantation. Bracken had grown waist high, its fronds no longer tender but a strong, dark green. The first pale unripe fruits hung down from the mulberry tree that stood beside the Ruin. Harebells and thunder daisies appeared at the lake's edge. The waters of the River Lyn had slowed in places to a trickle over damp stones.

From its cage the budgerigar borrowed songs from the garden birds. He trilled like a blackbird, was repetitious as a thrush. Sometimes he mimicked the telephone bell, causing me to rush from bath or garden. His newest deception was to imitate the sound of running water. I had checked taps a dozen times before locating the sound deep inside the violet-feathered throat.

The budgerigars had been a Christmas gift from my brother. There had until recently been two of them in the white cage. I had fixed up a mirror and three swings, studied handbooks on the care of caged birds, protected them from draughts, fed them only the very best of seed. But for all my devotion, the female, less aggressive of the pair, had died. For a week the survivor moped and was silent, pecked at his seed without enthusiasm and forbore to echo telephone bells or running water. When brisk words from me failed to rouse him from grief I turned the radio to perpetual music and set it daylong beside the cage.

Very gradually the widower lifted up his head in song. Wagner, I noticed, had the greatest therapeutic value. The process of recovery was not yet accomplished, but I was hopeful.

The proofs arrived from my publishers on the first day of August. I removed the wrappings and placed the stack of printed pages on the corner of the desk; I plucked, pizzicato-fashion, at the wide green rubber bands that held them together. Proofreading was a task which did not grow easier with practice. Having written the book, my mind would then fall slack; I lacked the concentration necessary to check the finer points of its production. Sometimes, I became absorbed in the story I had written, and forgot to seek out typographical errors. I comforted myself with the thought that somewhere up in London, a professional proofreader was making good my own lack of expertise.

The job once begun, I worked in my usual haphazard but obsessive way. While others slept I marked errors with a red-tipped pen, brown moths fluttering around the lamp, the proofs spread out across the wide bed. In daylight hours I worked beside the terrace hydrangeas, the pages held down by a coffee pot and milk jug against the summer breeze. I felt like a sad mother who prepares her child for permanent adoption, wanting it to look its very best, but knowing that when the task is done she must relinquish all claim to it for ever.

The book was a long one. I checked it twice through, and

thought that it was as good as it was in my power to make it. I phoned my agent and publisher and made appointments for the following Thursday.

August continued to be hot and dry, the hollow days an echo chamber for my thoughts, the sun my enemy; the skin stretched tight across my bones, feeling as it always did in summer, one size too small to fit my body. This was my season of unease that had to be endured.

In the high fields that lay beyond the Deerpark, heads of corn and barley drooped with ripeness. In the lower fields dark smoke already billowed out from stubble-burning. I recalled another hot, protracted summer. Nineteen forty-seven. The harvest fields of Rutlandshire, Kurt throwing sheaves up on to the stack, his hair bleached by the sun to half a dozen shades of blonde, his arms brown.

Roman said, 'So how was London?'

'Awful.'

'But you delivered your book?'

'I delivered my book.'

'You've lost weight,' he accused.

'I didn't mean to.' I studied the long and skinny length of him stretched out upon the parched turf. Jasper sat beside him, tethered loosely into the baby seat that was his place of safety when travelling in the van or Porsche. Father and son wore matching shirts and shorts of a pale shade of biscuit.

We were in that area of park set aside for picnics, a sheltered spot furnished with rustic-style tables and benches. Jasper had been fed from tiny pots produced by Roman from a cool bag. The baby had performed his latest trick, that of drinking unaided from a two-handled cup, the overflow trickling down on to a Mothercare bib. The wiping of face and hands, the nappy change, were both swift and efficient. Father and son emerged from these ablutions in a pristine condition that I felt sure I myself could not have emulated. Roman assumed that we would walk together. He held a sated, sleepy Jasper out to me. 'Grab him while I fetch the pram!' I took the child, surprised at the solid weightiness of him, his placid acceptance of me. The soft skin of his legs against my arms, his head drooped across my shoulder, brought back times long gone, of my own sleeping babies. I turned thankfully towards the pram and lowered him into it. I gripped the ridged rubber of its handle and moved back on to the carriageway; as I walked, the tarmac surface became the lane that had led to the squat grey farmhouse, the pram my own: brand-new, navy-blue, coach-built, cream-lined and extravagantly sprung, so large that the baby within had looked unnaturally small. The illusion persisted until Roman came to walk beside me.

I said, 'I've tried so hard to be forward-looking, made my own rules, and kept them. But sometimes, just lately, past and present merge. I look at my grandson and see his father at the same age, and in that moment they become one person – and both of them are mine.' I had spoken quietly, but now said loudly, 'I don't want to do that! I really shouldn't do that!'

'I don't know,' said Roman, 'how it works – with families, you know.'

'But you must have –?'

'No. I don't have relatives. Only in-laws, and they don't count.' The closed expression was on his face, the antagonism that had in the beginning made me wary of him. In this mood he could, I thought, be dangerous for me to know. I sought for words that would restore him to his acceptable self.

'But surely, you and Jasper and Serena constitute a family?'

'Do we? I look at her sometimes and I don't know what she's thinking. Don't know what the hell goes on inside that head of hers!'

I acknowledged consciously for the first time the hint of foreignness that underlay his normal unaccented English. It showed up strongly when he was moved by anger, that trace of Middle European. I began to wonder about him, to emerge a fraction from my own self-absorption, to question at last his origins, his life, his Slavic cast of features, his unusual name.

We walked for a long time and in silence, past the Elder Plantation and the paths that led upwards through tall bracken. He kept a pace or two ahead; I took notice of the way he moved, loose-limbed and light, as would an athlete or a dancer. All at once he was a stranger, more remote than he had been at our first, abrasive encounter. But I had never been daunted by the unfamiliar. So often this rashness had brought about my downfall. I had made unwise choices in my life, had spoken careless words of invitation; had opened a door and let mischief in, knowing only too late what it was I had done.

I dug my fingernails into the ridged rubber of the pram handle, and began to walk a little faster. We had never before, I reflected, come so far along this carriageway together. As the Ruin came into view I said, 'You are, I think, a very troubled person.'

It was not what I had meant to say. The intrusive nature of the words dismayed me.

He slowed his pace, then halted. His face had the open vulnerable look of a small boy who had been chastened. 'I was beginning to think,' he said, 'that you would never notice.'

'You're not English, are you?'

'Whatever made you think I might be?'

'Oh, I don't know – one just assumes –' I laughed. 'Silly of me really. My husband came from the lands that lie on the far side of the River Oder. His accent was pretty heavy. Yours is noticeable only when you're angry or excited.'

'I'm flattered that my speech is good enough to fool even you,' he said.

Again he sketched the little bow across the pram that made me think of clicking heels and doffed caps. We took the long dry path across the turf that led towards the Ruin. The pram bumped a little on uneven ground.

'Shall I take him from you?'

'No!' I sought to moderate my fierce tone. 'No,' I murmured, 'I rather like to do this. We pushed our first grandchild, Kurt and I, in a little blue pram. Her favourite place was a duck pond. Kurt brought stale bread in a paper bag, and they fed the ducks together. When she thought he wasn't noticing, she nibbled on those dry crusts. It worried him. He said it reminded him of hungry children he had once seen –'

We found a bench in deep shade underneath an old tree. Jasper, his golden limbs splayed in the abandonment of sleep, twitched in some private dream, and then was still. I turned my gaze from child to father. Standing or sitting, Roman's long thin body arranged itself in postures of elegance and grace. It must, I thought, be a kind of gift, or the result of some intensive training? Tall people had intimidated me since childhood. I always felt more adequate when he and I were seated.

'So how,' he asked, 'did you come to meet a man from eastern Europe?'

'The war.'

'Which one?'

'Why – the Second World War, of course! My husband was a German. He was a prisoner-of-war in England.'

'There have been other wars since that one,' Roman pointed out.

'But not for me!' I said. 'Not one that counted.'

He turned to face me. 'I expect those wars counted for the people who were caught up in them. Korea, Vietnam, the Falklands.'

'But I don't have enough compassion to weep for the whole world! The only reality for me is the war that spoiled Kurt's life and changed mine.'

He turned his face away from me and gazed towards the Ruin. His tone was dismissive. 'History,' he said, 'that old war is history now. Adolf Hitler rates alongside Ghengis Khan and Nero. Oh, they've made some damn good movies about him! I wonder sometimes what the film moguls would have done for subject matter if it hadn't been for Hitler and his war.'

'That's what it means to you? A series of exciting war films?'

'I was born in 1961. Anything that happened before that date is sort of obsolete, not quite real.' He pointed back towards the Ruin.

'Five hundred years or fifty, it has no relevance for my generation. Young people fight other kinds of battles these days. Combat has a different meaning for us. To be truthful, my favourite videos are *Raiders of the Lost Ark*, and *Batman* and *Star Wars*.'

I stood up, attempting to rise in one fluid youthful movement, but a stiffened knee betrayed me.

He said, 'You shouldn't sit for too long. Damaged joints seize up fast when they're immobile.'

'What can you possibly know about such matters?'

'I know about them.' It was a statement. He did not qualify it.

I sat down again, unable to walk easily away, fearing to stumble in his sight. Down on the carriageway young families strolled together. There was usually a dog which chased a ball or retrieved a stick. Some of them glanced up towards the Ruin, the entrance gates of which were closed. Heat shimmered off the tarmac surface. It was cool underneath the tree. I looked up and saw that it was the mulberry, its fruits now ripened to a rich deep crimson. Some of the families wore matching outfits. When he talked about war, I thought that Roman had another conflict on his mind.

'Marriage,' I said, 'is a bit like a high-wire act. Climbing as far as you can dare to go. Jumping off into space. Trusting that your partner is still there and alert enough to catch you. Sometimes if you're wise you work with a safety net. Mostly you don't.'

He said, in a strange tight voice, 'I know what you mean.'

The weather broke, with slanted spears of rain hurtling from a dark sky and hitting the ground with such speed that the moisture could not easily be absorbed.

I awoke to daylight blessedly diffused by grey cloud; cold air poured through my open windows. I went out to the terrace. The storm was passing. Within hours the healing chill would spread up into my cranium, contracting the swollen cerebral blood vessels, restoring my reasonable self.

I went back into the house and stood before my desk. The pile of unanswered mail had risen like a soufflé and then toppled sideways. Tomorrow, I promised, or at least quite soon, I will see to all this. But not today.

I adjusted the calendar to show September, tearing the August days into confetti pieces. Friends, returning from holidays in western Scotland, had complained of mist and rain and chill winds. I had made plans to sell my house and move to Mull or Lismore. Something wrong with my mind, or my metabolism? To deny the sun was to deny life.

The date was the third; fiftieth anniversary of the Second World War. Black and white films on television. Errol Flynn and John Mills, tight-lipped and hard-jawed. Celebration, eulogy, xenophobia; the bitter past intoned by reverential commentator voices, more familiarly heard at Royal Weddings, or World Cup football matches. 'History,' Roman had said, 'obsolete, not quite real.'

There was a drawer in my desk, never locked but rarely opened, which held the mementoes of a man's life. There were a few diaries, a worn leather wallet, an English–German dictionary. There were also the letters. Every word he had ever written to me. The sight of the tall, sloping German script, unfaded over forty years, had yet the power to move me more than any photographed image of him. He had been a reluctant correspondent, his style terse. I shuffled through the frail sheets of grainy post-war letter paper. He always began with '*Meine liebste* Cathy' and ended with '*nie vergessender Mann*, Kurt'.

Accustomed as I was to my pale blue stationery, smooth and engraved with my name and address, the yellow sheets handled poignantly, more evocative than ration books, and plaintive as old songs. I imagined him seated at a table, writing the letter to me, tongue between his teeth as was his habit when concentrating, a swatch of blond hair fallen across one eye. He had written to me as a new husband, a lover; desperation threaded through his words, he was a refugee in his own country. I had re-read the letters only once since his death; the wallet I had left untouched. I opened it carefully now; even so the perished leather began to crumble in my fingers. I withdrew the scraps of paper; the first one dated December 1st, 1944. These letters began '*Liebe Eltern*'. I began to read, translating with a facility that I had believed lost. 'Since September 22nd I am a prisoner of the British. England is cold. It rains every day. We stay in the hut, sleep a lot and play chess. I am in good health but for frostbite on my ears and feet. Older *kameraden* are very sick, many were wounded before capture. Several have died since we were brought here. How goes it with you, and my sister and the children? I think of you often, also poor Papa in Russia. The British tell us we have lost the war. I knew this long ago, in France . . .'

December 25th, 1944
'*Liebe Eltern* – I write although there is small hope that you will ever read this. It is Christmas Day. We sing '*Stille Nacht*' and open our Red Cross parcels. It rains all the time. I think about you all . . .'

April 3rd, 1945
'The British tell us that the Russians hold East and West Prussia. Mecklenburg and Pommern are fallen, Berlin threatened on all sides.'

May 9th, 1945
'It is all over. The British Commandant says that Hitler is dead. It has stopped raining.'

I gathered up the scraps and eased them into the wallet. I reached for an empty box-file and labelled it 'Material concerning the life of Kurt Baumann'. Inside the file lay all his letters to me, the crumbling wallet, his Service Paybook. Last of all I placed the small grey document of release, issued in Münster in 1948, which had proclaimed him a civilian again. A free man in a divided land.

I reached for the springclip and played my game of solitaire with the timetables. Within the hour I was boarding the beige-coloured bus. The driver was well known to me, a large and quiet man who did not need to ask my destination. I thought, as I always did when travelling this route, how varied was the Leicestershire landscape, how dramatic was its change of aspect within the space of a few miles. Minutes later, and we were among rich and rolling farmlands; no rocky prominences here, no wooded heights, no medieval Deerpark. Already the trees had started to change colour, and mist lay thick in distant fields. I settled more comfortably into my seat. The turn of the year had always been my prime time; September the month when good things happened.

The ride to Melton Mowbray was timed for fifty-nine minutes; the town my final point of refuge. Once, at a time of crisis, I had found myself seated on this bus, ticket duly purchased, the journey halfway done, and I with no memory of ever having boarded, or consciously intending so to do. The episode, which should have alarmed me, seemed only to prove the reliability of instinct.

The beige bus was very clean, its floor swept clear of the detritus which accumulated on all other routes. I noted with approval the plastic box wedged beside the driver's seat, and the printed notice fastened to it which instructed passengers to PUT YOUR RUBBISH HERE. The road was busier than usual. Tuesday was cattle-market day. We slowed behind the tractor, the trailer of which was loaded high with hay bales.

An unlikely outpost of nostalgia was the bus station, unchanged in forty years. Here it was, on a wild November night, that Kurt had met my parents for the first time. I had stood in the tiny waiting room, gauging reactions, willing them to like one another. The prisoner-of-war patches, blue on the dark brown of his uniform, had hardly showed at all in the single gaslight. Later, on the telephone, my father had said, 'Bring him home at Christmas? Well, yes – if that's what you want.'

Happiness in those days had depended on deep preoccupations, like did the scarlet sweater I had knitted suit my colouring? My hair had its own foxy shade, perhaps blue would have been a wiser choice? I had asked for Kurt's opinion. He had not smiled. 'It is good that you can have so much nice clothes,' he'd said. 'It is not so in these days in my country.' He had never missed a chance to warn me, but I heard only the singing in my blood. I had worn the sweater which looked good with breeches. It made me visible from fields away, identifiable on the old green tractor. It always brought him to my side, no matter how slowly and reluctantly he came.

'You should be careful who you talk to,' the farmer's son had said. 'Fraternization with German prisoners-of-war is forbidden.'

I stepped down from the bus and began to walk towards the town park. I paused for a moment, as I always did, before the magical shapes and colours of the grouped trees. Kurt, who would not enter churches, had married me in Melton Mowbray, on a January morning. I turned from the park gates and into High Street. The building which had once housed the Register Office stood on a corner. I looked up at the windows; its façade was now the creamy colour obtained by experts on newly cleaned limestone. I remembered it shabbier, a little grimy, more endearing. The gold-leaf lettering on the glass proclaimed it to be a solicitor's office. The steep staircase alone was quite unaltered. I ventured to climb a few treads, and then, feeling foolish, descended to the street.

For an hour I wandered through the cattle market, pausing to watch auctions of sheep and cattle. Lunch as usual at the Anne of Cleves restaurant, and then back aboard the clean beige bus. It was a day that had been all my own, when Kurt seemed very close; in this town there were no distractions to hinder my awareness of him. After a day such as this I slept long and deeply, and awoke feeling temporarily healed.

Included among my mild eccentricities was an avoidance of newsprint. I rarely read magazines or watched television newscasts. Current events, the agonies of the world, came muted through the radio which stood on the kitchen windowsill. It was on a visit to the library that the headline caught my attention.

A copy of *The Times*, dated September 26th, the paper folded to overseas news:

MORE SWIMMING THROUGH
HOLE IN THE IRON CURTAIN

As the flow of East German refugees from Hungary to Austria continues at a small but steady rate, more disgruntled and desperate East Germans are making their way towards Hungary's hole in the Iron Curtain by swimming the Danube, the border between Hungary and Czechoslovakia ... 87 East Germans braved the swift and chilly waters under cover of darkness at the weekend, bringing to 345 the number in the past two weeks who swam to freedom.

It was, I told myself, no more than a brief item on an inside page; but printed in a respected newspaper not given to overstatement or hysteria.

Three days later, and on this occasion my reading of *The Times* was not accidental. Front page. From our own correspondent in Bonn.

MORE GERMANS FLEE TO EMBASSIES

More East German refugees continued to pour into the West German embassies in Prague and Warsaw yesterday. With about 2,200 camped in the grounds of the gracious Lobkowicz Palace . . . conditions are said to be deteriorating rapidly . . .

Czechoslovakia is refusing to listen to appeals from Bonn to let the refugees go . . . more and more refugees are now choosing to cross into Poland to wait for freedom.

The refugee issue is clouding preparations for the country's fortieth anniversary festivities on October 7th.

Ten years ago and I had been there, travelling through East Germany, witnessing those celebrations. I recalled the railway station at Marienborn, the posters positioned at intervals up and down the platform. The slogans in yard-high letters, the illustration of a clenched fist, the index finger pointing sky-wards. The words 'Thirty Years' Anniversary of the D.D.R. 1949–1979'.

I remembered the Border, the watch-towers and land-mines; the strips of mined earth fortifications cunningly de-signed and efficiently manned. Only armed guards and *Transportspolizei* had been allowed to approach the Berlin train. The unmuzzled Alsatians had been urged to sniff and search underneath each carriage, the train itself had been searched from end to end and from top to bottom. The most desperate of its citizens had no longer attempted to escape from the DDR by this route; even I, while proffer-ing my dark-blue British passport, had felt an unease that was very close to fear.

A morning in late September, cool and golden. The sun, low in the sky, was kinder now; on such a day my sons had been born, and for me ever afterwards it was to be autumn that signified birth and new beginnings, never springtime. I sorted through the pile of correspondence at last and answered more urgent letters. The budgerigar, sitting beside me in his white cage, was illuminated by a shaft of sunlight. He was plump again, his feathers sleek with health; he did his blackbird imitation and then I could no longer tolerate the room, the house.

The black van stood in the Deerpark car park. I crossed the road and began to walk towards the café; the rustic seats and tables stood inside the forecourt; a party of cyclists drank coffee in the sunshine, their racing machines propped against the fence.

I sat at an adjoining table and ordered Darjeeling tea. I knew that Roman and Jasper were waiting for me by the park gates, colour-coordinated, linked by style, immediately identifiable as father and small son. The cream tracksuits with burnt-orange trim suited their dark looks; they made a picture marred only by the Mothercare bib worn by a dribbling, teething Jasper.

'We came on Tuesday and you weren't here. Where were you?' The hurt in Roman's voice, his aggrieved air, at first amused and then annoyed me. He was, I thought, displaying the selfishness permitted only to the young or the very old. I had, for no good reason, come to expect better of him.

'I went to Melton Mowbray.'

He considered for a moment. 'We don't have an outlet there.' He spoke with a finality which doubted the existence of a town so disfavoured as to lack one of his boutiques.

'Well you wouldn't, would you?' I heard the acid in my tone and was not ashamed. 'Not your sort of place at all.'

His strange pale eyes narrowed under heavy brows. He said, with surprising insight, 'You spend a lot of time dwelling on the past.'

'So what else can I be sure of?'

I knew that what he said was true. The root of my melancholy, the restlessness, my bedrock of reliable desperation, was due entirely to the way my head now turned back across my shoulder. No wonder I stumbled through present days seeing no future.

'There was a time,' I told him, 'when I had it all to come, warm and safe in the hollow of my hand. Love and babies, playing at housewife in a frilly apron, pushing out the brand new pram. At twenty-one I thought never to grow old. At sixty-one I seem to have arrived at a destination I never intended to set out for –' I saw his uneasy looks. 'Forgive me,' I murmured. 'I'm not good company today.' I studied him more closely. Against the rich cream of the tracksuit his skin had a greyish pallor, and there were dark marks underneath his eyes.

'Bad night?' I asked. 'Oh, I remember teething troubles!'

Roman shook his head very slowly as if that small effort was too much.

'So what is it?' I asked. 'You're not happy, are you?'

Once again I regretted the question as soon as it was spoken, but he had just allowed me to voice my own dilemma, and fair was fair. We began to walk the carriageway. I took the pram. Between the fashionable baby and his stylish father my tweed skirt and anorak looked ordinary; I would never be mistaken for Jasper's nanny. I glanced up and sideways at Roman's profile, his jutting jaw and bunched fists.

'Business troubles?' I inquired. He did not reply. I studied Jasper, who sat among a menagerie of soft toys; tigers and lions filled the pram while he crooned to himself and soaked the Mothercare bib. He looked cheerful and healthy. Which left only Serena.

Roman said, 'My passport just ran out. I've had Jasper included on my new one.'

'Oh,' I said, 'well that will be handy when you go on holiday.'

'It will be handy,' he corrected me, 'if I should leave Serena and wish to take my son with me.'

'But you can't do that. You can't separate a baby from his mother.'

'And why not? You said it yourself. I am the alternative mother. How could I go away and not take him with me? He hardly knows her.'

I thought this might well be the truth, but even so, such precipitate flight was not to be encouraged, far less condoned. I sought for the in-words that might sound acceptable to him. People in the soap operas seemed to need interminable discussions of their problems, the line most often repeated in these dramas being 'Darling – we must talk!'

'Have you,' I ventured, 'talked to Serena about your problems?'

'It's not that easy. I was the one who set up this whole situation, forced it upon her if you like. What's even worse – I don't know how to change things. Supposing she was willing to back-track – I have no alternatives to offer.'

Unsure of exactly what it was about which he complained, I guessed wildly. 'I think I see what you mean. Jasper is here. A fact, a presence.'

'What makes you think it's got anything to do with Jasper?'

'Well, hasn't it?'

He paused, one hand upon the pram, forcing me to halt. His shrug was an exaggerated movement that lifted his shoulders level with his earlobes; his other hand spread widely, palm upwards. There was a comic element about him that tempted me to laughter.

He said, 'Our greatest problem is that she is English and I am not.'

'That,' I said, 'would seem to be unalterable.'

'She's also more experienced.' His tone was gloomy. 'Anything I've done she can always top it. Better, faster, more efficient, in bed or out of it, Serena has the whiphand.'

'Not the best basis for a marriage' – I smiled – 'if what you say is true?'

'I'm not a liar!'

'I'm sure you're not. But I happen to be the mother of sons, remember? A tendency to exaggerate is not the sole prerogative of women. Perhaps things are not as hopeless as they seem?'

'They're worse.'

He was determined to suffer and to be seen to suffer. These confidences, I thought, had been gathering for quite some time. I remembered the day he had accused me of spying on him. Perhaps his only means of making contact was through hostile exchange. Fists first, smiles later.

'How did you come to meet Serena?' I inquired.

'I ran over her with the Porsche.'

'What a novel introduction!'

'Well – to be accurate, I knocked her down on a pedestrian crossing. It was only her handbag I actually ran over.'

Genuinely curious now, I asked, 'Was this absentmindedness on your part?'

'I'd had the odd bump before,' he admitted. 'The magistrate got very nasty. I explained that I'd only had the Porsche for a few days and was not quite used to handling it. The old swine disqualified me for two years.'

I said, 'So what about Serena?'

'Well – after the court case I took her to lunch. The cast was off her foot by that time so she was able to drive me.' He grinned. 'They say adversity brings people together. We got very close in a short time.'

We were almost level with the Ruin. Slanting sunlight warmed the ancient brickwork. Shadows stretched farther now than in the springtime. We moved without consultation to the bench beside the wall, but I was resolved to walk by myself, to hear no more, and did not sit down.

Jasper, eyes drooping into sleep, slumped back against his pillow. I pulled the blanket close about him and raised the pram hood. The actions, tender and remembered, weakened my resolve. I sat down, one hand upon the pram, rocking it, and asked, 'So what happened next?'

Roman, when invited to confide his deeper anxieties, seemed unable to begin. The mulberry tree had shed several leaves, the bracken had changed colour, its fronds crumpled into brown lace. White birds swooped above the lake. When he spoke, the trace of Middle European had hardened to a definable accent. Polish? I thought. Definitely Slavic. It set him apart, pinned my interest to his words.

He said, 'She was in a relationship with somebody else. It had seemed to be a permanent thing but something went wrong. She never said what. She talked a lot about caring for this man. He hadn't offered marriage but she didn't want it. So she said. I think this man had hurt her very badly. She talked about him just that one time. I never knew his name.' He paused. 'She is very beautiful woman. I am very jealous person.'

'Oh – jealousy,' I said. 'Now that is something I can understand. It's the most powerful and destructive of human emotions.' I smiled. 'When I was young I couldn't stand to see Kurt smile at any other girl.'

'So you know what it feels like.'

He sat, shoulders hunched against misery, one hand laid lightly on the sleeping child. The physical contact between father and son was maintained at an almost constant level. On only one occasion had I been permitted to hold Jasper; at all other times I was allowed to look but not to touch. It was possible, I discovered, to feel angry with Roman and yet sorry for him, both at the same time. I said, 'The child means a great deal to you.'

'He is my life!'

I discounted one-third of the drama of his answer; after all, his origins were Slavic. What remained was still unarguably disquieting.

'It can,' I said tentatively, 'be a mistake for one parent to monopolize a child at the cost of the other.'

'I do not monopolize. I read it in the childcare books. It is called bonding.'

'I've heard about that.' I sought for lightness. 'A duckling who has lost its mother will follow the farmer's wife's green wellies – and never know the difference.'

'It is not a joking matter.'

'Forgive me. I really *do* want to understand. When my children were young, a great deal was talked about maternal instinct. You either had it – or you didn't. The role of the father was hardly ever mentioned.'

He said, 'Serena does not have maternal instinct. She cares nothing about bonding.'

I spoke reflectively, feeling my way towards appropriate words. 'Sometimes,' I said, 'it is the child who chooses. There will be an affinity, a kind of recognition between a baby and the parent to whom he will give his eventual devotion.' I paused. 'I watched it happen once. A long time ago.'

Roman said, 'I intend to leave Serena and take Jasper with me.' The words were defiant, delivered on a sideways glance.

In the silence that followed he waited for me to dissuade him. He was, I began to suspect, a player of games. My sympathy ebbed. For the first time in my acquaintance with him I experienced a sneaking sympathy with Jasper's mother. It was, I recalled, a peculiarly painful exclusion, that of second place in the affections of one's own child. It was a thought I did not care to dwell upon.

I said, without premeditation, 'I'm going away. I may be gone for quite some time.'

'You sound like Captain Oates walking out into the blizzard.'

'I have relatives in East Berlin. It's ten years since I was there. I need to see them.'

Roman said, 'You're the only person I can talk to.'

I stood up, and this time the knee joint did not fail me. 'Don't do anything foolish,' I said, 'while I'm away.'

'This is all a bit sudden, isn't it? Why Berlin – and why now?'

He was not owed an explanation of anything I planned to do. 'You wouldn't understand.'

'Try me,' he said. 'Perhaps I will understand it better than you think.' He paused. 'I was born in East Berlin.'

Of course, I thought, and wondered why I had not seen the truth. He must be a defector, or the son of a defector. It explained so much about him, his lack of family, his air of isolation. I waited for him to continue but he turned his face away towards the lake.

'Then you must know,' I said gently, 'about the changes that are taking place in Eastern Europe. About perestroika and glasnost?'

He lifted his shoulders in the familiar disowning gesture. 'I take no interest in these matters. I am from travelling people. I have no country.'

'But you do know about them,' I persisted. 'You watch television. You read newspapers.'

He nodded.

'I have family and friends,' I said, 'in West and East Berlin. People who are very dear to me. There are many reasons why I need to see them. I've planned to go so very often – but it takes courage.' The admission, spoken aloud, took me by surprise.

'Will we see you before you go?'

'But of course! I shall need to make arrangements, book flights, talk to people.'

'Things are pretty bad between Serena and me,' he said.

I answered him carelessly. In my mind I was already landing at Tegel airport, looking out for a sight of Melanie's smooth blonde head, her welcoming smile.

'Try a little give and take,' I told Roman. 'You'll find it works wonders.'

The persistent house, like an unloved dependant, nudged daily for my attention. A bathroom overflow pipe began to drip water into the garden. The central heating, when switched on after months of disuse, performed inadequately. Doors and windows, which had opened freely in the heat of summer, jammed in the October dampness. I decided to ignore it all.

With the growing coolness of autumn days my thoughts changed direction. Unaccustomed to anticipating further than the events of the next hour or day, the proposed visit to Berlin appeared vast and unattainable; its planning stretched away into infinity, as unmanageable as mountain peaks. There was the publication of my latest book in November, and the promotion of it. I would need energy for that. There was the house which I had ceased to cherish. There was also the matter of Martin, my son, to which, if I was being thoroughly honest, I had never yet faced up.

I thought of Jasper, beloved of his father, estranged already from his mother long before he had uttered his first word or taken an unaided step. Then I began to think about Martin, who had also been beloved of his father; who had never turned to me at times of unhappiness or sickness. Martin, whom I had frequently antagonized and alienated without ever meaning to do so.

Martin was a renovator, an improver. He would purchase a house that required attention, work on it for a year or two and then sell it at a profit. His family, meanwhile, lived tolerantly with sawdust and a measure of disorder, as new windows replaced old ones, kitchens and bathrooms were refitted, driveways were relaid and gardens redesigned. By nature restless and energetic, he was happy only when employed on complicated projects; when achieving self-imposed goals. I knew that he was capable of love and kindness; in the role of father he was relaxed, assured, devoted. I observed with awe and admiration the camaraderie, the joking respect that bound Martin to his two children. It was from Kurt that Martin had learned how to be a parent. Too much closeness between mother and sons was, I had always believed, a bad thing.

Paul, my elder son, whom I had always understood, the child who had long ago brought me wild flowers from the fields; with whom I shared a sense of what was grave or funny, now lived many miles away. He came as often as he could, but I did not reproach him for his absence.

When Martin had arrived bearing cards and gifts on my most recent birthday I had said, complainingly, 'You hardly ever come here.' I should have anticipated his swift change from smiles to anger.

'Well, you never visit me!' He was almost shouting.

'I come when I'm invited,' I said quietly.

'And what,' roared Martin, 'if I waited to be invited here, to your house? I would wait forever.'

For a moment we confronted one another, both knowing that what he said was true. But Martin's anger, like Kurt's, was never prolonged. Because of the day the rift was closed. We parted warmly. But I was left uneasy.

I telephoned two days later. 'I might,' I said uncertainly, 'come over to see you?'

'You don't have to make appointments.'

'I know – I know. It's just – well – I expect you must be busy with the house extension.'

'I have just,' he said, 'taken half the roof off.' Martin laughed unexpectedly, and at once my grip on the handset eased. 'I'll be here all day,' he went on. 'I'm expecting delivery of roof beams. You can help me unload the lorry.'

I arrived to find roof beams stacked neatly in the long shed. Nervously, I climbed a ladder into the extension, was shown the architect's plan, the areas designated for three new bedrooms and a bathroom. Martin talked about plumbing and electricity, the fitting of a staircase, his thin face animated, his hands expressive.

I, understanding little that he said, wondered at the provenance of all this manual dexterity and felt proud.

He insisted on driving me the five miles to my home, though I said I could quite well take the bus. On a quiet country back road I fixed my gaze on his fingers, long and spatulate, resting lightly on the steering wheel.

'I'm going to West Berlin, to see your father's family,' I said. 'You don't remember them, do you? You were eighteen months old when we last met them, in Dietkirchendorf.' I paused, my glance lifting to his face. 'I would like you to come with me.'

I saw his jawline harden, his fingers tighten on the wheel, and could not imagine what his thoughts were, or what might be his answer. A lifetime of propinquity with father, brother, husband, sons, had given me no insight into the workings of the male mind. Before he could answer one way or the other, I said, 'Only if you want to, of course,' and at once felt panic at the prospect of being alone with him for some extended period of time.

'Think it over,' I said, 'but don't take too long. I shall need to make involved arrangements. It might,' I added, 'be rather nice if Maraid came with us.'

I liked my daughter-in-law. To travel as a threesome might be easier, wiser.

Events in East Germany, which a week ago had been reported in a single column found deep within the paper, now began to fill a half page, to merit front-page notice. I stayed faithful to *The Times*, believing in its factual statements, the Biblical veracity of its information.

The library, just a short walk from my house, provided daily copies of the weightier news-sheets. Every morning found me seated at the readers' broad polished table, among the retired gentlemen who sought gardening tips and stock-market prices.

In these first days of October Martin came to see me. He said nothing about the proposed trip, forcing me to ask, 'Have you thought about my suggestion?'

'Yes, I have. I would like to come. In fact, I'd like it very much.'

'And Maraid?'

'She's starting this new job. It's important to her, the kind of thing she's always longed to do. She's keen to come, but she'll need to clear things with her boss.'

I studied Martin. The springy tension of him was, as always, disturbing. I felt as edgy and uncertain of him now as I had when he was three years old, liable to break free from my restraining hand, reject my mothering ways, and dart into danger.

'It will be nicer for you if Maraid can come,' I said.

Martin nodded. He said, 'The news from Berlin gets livelier every day.'

'It's perfectly safe!' I hoped this was indeed the case. 'We shall keep well away from any demonstrations.'

'Oh, I wouldn't mind observing the odd demo.'

I saw the glint in his eye, remembered his youthful enthusiasm for lost causes. But he had never been there as I had; had not yet seen the border crossings, the strips of mined earth, the guard dogs.

'Maraid and I,' I said dryly, 'would rather not be doused by water cannon, or carted off by the *Staatzpolizei*.'

'Hard to imagine,' said Martin, 'a secret police force dressed in jeans and T-shirts, mingling with the population. They call them "Stasi", don't they? I read that the borders are all closed. The people are trapped in their own country.'

Already, I thought, although he speaks no German, he is learning the emotive words.

'Your cousins have lived all their lives under such repressions,' I pointed out. 'You won't get mixed up in any sort of protest, will you?'

He grinned. 'Well – you never know that, do you?'

'You have dual nationality,' I warned him.

He said, 'How nice for me.'

The cream and burnt-orange tracksuit showed up clearly in the autumn sunshine. Roman sat beneath the mulberry tree in the shadow of the Ruin. Jasper crawled among the dusty bracken, moving crablike on all fours, but mostly shuffling backwards on his bottom.

I sat down. 'He's getting very dirty,' I observed.

'I'm testing his suit for washability.' Roman's tone was distant. I let the silence grow between us. He said at last, 'Didn't expect to see you here again. Shouldn't you be in East Berlin?'

'We fly on the seventeenth.'

'Will your son go with you?'

'Yes. We shall meet my sister-in-law; people of pensionable age still have free access to the West. But as for a reunion with my niece and nephew – well, that's another matter. It has not been possible for me to see them since 1953. They were children then. Now they have children of their own. It's important that Martin should get to know his German cousins.'

'So you think that it matters where and what a person comes from?' asked Roman.

'Of course! The place of birth is not important; what counts is blood, generations of inherited characteristics: the genes.'

'Ah,' he said, gazing at Jasper, 'the genes.'

I awaited his confidences, but he turned the conversation back to Berlin. 'I read this morning that the first East German refugee trains have reached Bavaria, they're pulling into Hof at intervals of thirty minutes. Today,' said Roman, 'Gorbachev will be in East Berlin for the Fortieth Anniversary celebrations. That could be the trigger that sets the country on fire. If Gorbachev refuses to back their Communist regime, then Erich Honecker will be a dead duck!'

I said, 'How well informed you are. One might almost think you had a special interest?'

I waited for his response, but he bent to retrieve and dust off a less-than-pristine Jasper, and would not be drawn further on the subject.

I had never been a regular watcher of television, but now I sat each evening, rapt before the small screen. Every newscast began with the latest pictures from eastern Europe. A thousand people marched in Potsdam. Police helicopters hovered over crowds in Karl-Marx-Stadt. Three thousand protesters had blocked the streets of Halle. There was trouble in Magdeburg. A candlelit vigil for imprisoned demonstrators had continued for a week in the church of the Gethsemane, East Berlin.

The Stasi, it was said, armed with truncheons loaded with ball-bearings, had been seen to club people to the ground. In one week, wrote *The Times* correspondent in Dresden, the mood of hopelessness, which led thousands of East Germans to flee the country, had changed to one of defiance. In the streets of Dresden women and children were trampled underfoot by riot police, who beat individuals mercilessly. There was widespread use throughout the country of water cannon and police dogs. I made a call to West Berlin. On the eastern side, said Melanie, the number of border guards had been quadrupled all along the Berlin Wall, in case of an attempted mass breakout of the East German population.

The lethargy that had possessed me since early springtime had not departed. There were times when I was able, briefly, to lift a corner of the disabling ennui, to feel a stir of enthusiasm, a flash of passionate commitment. In such a moment I bought another notebook and packed it, unsullied, between my camera and passport. I listened to German language tapes, carrying the small machine from bathroom to kitchen, picking up keywords and phrases unheard, and unused, in the past ten years.

On October 10th Erich Honecker warned his countrymen that they risked bloodshed through military intervention. The crossing-points between East and West Berlin were closed. The mass exodus of young skilled workers through Poland

and Hungary brought a warning from the Russian leader. To delay reform any longer would be dangerous, said Mikhail Gorbachev. On October 11th the tension eased. Demonstrators were allowed to make their protest unmolested. Churchmen were said to be hopeful. Like an interceding pilgrim, I made daily visits to the Deerpark, muttering prayers to a deity in which I did not altogether believe.

The River Lyn ran low between its banks after the dry summer. The trees showed every shade of leaf from palest lemon to deepest bronze. Among the deer herd, the older stags had shed their velvet; the rich red coat of summer was already darkening for winter. The ritual of the rut, complex and dramatic, had begun, the stags defending their harems of hinds.

I avoided Roman. Unwilling to be drawn further into his problems, I came as late or early to the Deerpark as bus schedules would allow. I sat on the dry turf beneath an ancient oak, my back supported by the tree's bole. On the far side of the river, in fields from which the public were excluded, the rut approached its climax. Stags postured and looked threateningly at rivals. The does wore complacent, almost simpering expressions. A stag, separated from his fellows, came walking slowly down the path towards me. He stood so close that I could see the rolling of his yellow eyes, the burnished antlers. My involuntary movement set the animal to instant flight; I watched him leap at the place where the river narrowed and rejoin a group of grazing does. I thought about the coming journey, about proximity, seven days spent in the unremitting company of others. I had guarded my solitary state; believed that at too close quarters people did damage to one another. I valued old friendships, the spontaneous, uncomplicated love of grandchildren. My sons, I thought, never really saw me as a person; they awarded me their rueful affection and almost certainly prayed that I be no embarrassment to them. My inadequacy in close relationships was never greater than when in the company of my children; which was, I reflected, a little strange, when compared with the easy exchange between Roman and myself. But Roman meant nothing in my life, he was not a son. I could say anything to him.

Periods of time spent in the company of Martin could, I thought, be counted back in minutes, the odd half hour, a rare protracted day, but even that was long ago. Well, I was not complaining, was I? I had no right, since the space between us had been made through mutual and unvoiced collusion. I closed my suitcase, snapped locks, tied labels, felt a pulse of fear and wondered yet again what in hell's name we would find to say to one another on the drive down to Heathrow; on a flight of two hours; in a week spent in his father's country. My avoidance of Roman in these last days had been unkind. You, he had said, are the only one that I can talk to. Things are pretty bad between Serena and me. I had not encouraged further revelations but had studied Jasper, who was Roman's image, and felt a stab of pity for the excluded Serena; things, I had thought, are also pretty bad between Martin and me. My son and I are strangers to one another. He too was exclusive to his father. In my mind they were always bracketed together. My last sight of Roman had been a blur of cream and orange tracksuit bright against the dying bracken, a cheerful and dishevelled Jasper clasped tightly in his arms. I had experienced again that curious shift of the mind, the superimposing of one image on another. Just for that moment Roman and Jasper had been Kurt and Martin, indivisible, linked forever in my sight. It was then that the visit to Berlin had become inevitable.

The drive down to Heathrow, which I had dreaded, passed easily in conversation. Maraid, who was employed in the most caring of all professions, spoke of patient after-care, the responsibilities of her new posting, the City hospital from which she worked. I studied the elegance of Maraid, the dark hair and pale skin, the hazel, almost golden eyes, and wondered, as I always did, that someone of such striking looks, of such sophistication, should have chosen to work among the sick and dying. It occurred to me now that, in all the long years of our acquaintance, I had never experienced this degree of proximity to Maraid, this unavoidable togetherness. Martin, silent at the wheel, negotiated lane changes and other dangerous motorway manoeuvres which I chose not to witness.

I turned towards my daughter-in-law and was further disconcerted; I remembered the lighthearted, lovely girl who had married Martin, and could not quite equate her with the serious and charming woman who now sat at my side. I stared at the back of Martin's neck, at the Harris tweed of his jacket collar. He has nice ears, I thought, a well-shaped head. His face was reflected in the driving mirror, the heavy brows over deep-set blue eyes, the long straight nose, the clipped moustache above a mobile mouth, the brown brushed-back hair. He bore no resemblance to the blond and restless child of my inner vision.

Maraid's thoughtful glance made me wonder how I myself might be regarded. Mothers-in-law were a music-hall joke, a notorious hazard of matrimony. But I do not intrude, I told myself. I have never been intrusive. The grandchildren are my weakness, but even in that area of love I am habitually wary, careful always to avoid possessiveness, to stay within my limits.

At Heathrow airport Martin attended to the checking-in procedure while Maraid found a table in the coffee shop, and joined the queue for light refreshments. My usual absentminded passage through a busy airport was this time reassuringly marshalled; I buttered a scone and drank scalding coffee. Maraid went away again to change pounds into Deutsche Marks, her tall figure moving swiftly through the crowds of people, self-assured and fashionable.

I wondered if Maraid and Martin found me dull. What I had to say on any subject could be of little interest to them. They so clearly lived in a wider world, understood the workings of video recorders, of telephone answering-machines, of computers and word processors. My own place was at the scarred desk in the book-lined room, the violet budgerigar beside me in his white cage.

Martin crumbled the scone between his fingers, poured a second cup of coffee. He said abruptly, 'I don't remember Germany. I know my aunt and cousins only from photographs. I don't speak German.'

The confident relaxed appearance that he wore when driving had altogether left him. He looked vulnerable and younger now.

'It won't matter,' I said. 'I can translate for you.'

'But I'll feel so inadequate. I should have learned at least a little of the language.'

'There wasn't time! I gave you very little chance for any sort of preparation. Don't worry about it. It truly will not matter.'

He looked at me with Kurt's deep-set blue gaze. 'I don't think you understand how important this visit is to me. Aunt Christina – she's my father's closest relative – I've seen pictures of her – she looks exactly like him.' Martin wadded scone crumbs into solid pellets and pushed them around his plate. I felt my heart contract with pity for him. I recalled the ordeal of my own first meeting with Christina after Kurt's death, the shock of that amazing physical resemblance. I longed to reach out a hand to the restless fingers across the table, but such gestures were unknown between us. I would not add embarrassment to the discomfort he already suffered. I should have known the degree of significance that he would attach to this visit; if I had failed to be aware of such a predictable reaction, how many other signals from Martin had I overlooked?

Our flight was called. On the long walk out towards the aircraft he recalled my fear of moving walkways and escalators. As we approached the slithering belt I halted. Martin's fingers, firm and inescapable, clamped above my elbow.

'It's all right,' he murmured as he propelled me forward. 'I won't let you fall.'

The plane lifted off through heavy cloud into brilliant sunshine. Drinks were ordered, the plastic box of assorted snacks which, when travelling alone, I tended to ignore, was opened now with curious pleasure. Maraid and Martin admitted to extreme hunger; none of us had eaten breakfast. We buttered rolls and opened packets and smiled conspiratorially at one another; the journey took on the feel of an illicit party, as though this was a time stolen from the span of life. Perhaps, I thought, after all my misgivings, it would not turn out to be an absolute disaster.

Maraid began to talk about the children, who were, of course, no longer children. Matthew, still at school, was already taller than his father. Liese, a student nurse, was to spend the week of her parents' absence at home with her younger brother. The freezer had been stocked with their favourite meals, spare keys left with a neighbour. Maraid's father was always available in case of need. 'But they will manage beautifully, of course,' said Maraid. 'They are such good and responsible children. So very adult.'

I knew this to be the truth, and wondered again how this

miracle had come to pass, and what was the secret of their successful parenthood.

Martin, from his window seat, peered down from clear skies as the cities and farmsteads of Lower Saxony slipped away beneath us. I noted his rapt gaze and wondered briefly what his thoughts might be.

Ten years ago I had chosen to come to Berlin by the slow, more romantic overland route. I had boarded the boat train at Nottingham station, taken the overnight ferry from the Hook of Holland. I recalled exactly the long dark-green train which would, should one wish to go there, eventually deposit the traveller in Warsaw or Moscow; I remembered the dark-red leather carriage seats, the antiquated inefficient heating, the unappetizing menu presented by the dining car attendant. It had been a journey taken out of great need, and heightened by a sense of drama contained in that emotive word – Berlin. I had gone to meet my sister-in-law Christina, whom I had not seen for twenty-six years. A meeting I had feared for many reasons: my spoken German was not fluent; I would need to cross the Berlin Wall; I had been unsure of my reception by Kurt's sister.

I had not had, as it turned out, any cause for worry. We had met underneath an almond tree, sat together on a bench in the gardens of the Pergamon Museum in East Berlin. Christina had greeted me with love, had called me '*Liebe* Cathy – *liebe schwester*'. No one had ever called me sister; no one since Kurt had spoken to me with affection, or claimed me. Tomorrow we would meet again; even now Christina would be making preparations for her journey from Dresden to West Berlin.

I fastened my seat belt. All around me the smokers extinguished their cigarettes; there was a sudden stir and bustle in the aircraft preparatory to landing. Martin's face had an absorbed expression, as if he would commit to memory this aerial view of West Berlin. Beneath us the rose-red and golden-ochre of old restored buildings sat reassuringly among the chrome and plate glass of new tower blocks, the silver gleam of Tegel Lake, the trees on almost every street, the grey divisive Wall.

The aircraft dipped and circled and began to fall swiftly towards the city. I saw the hexagonal outlines of Tegel Airport, felt the single bump that proved a faultless landing.

Martin turned abruptly from the window, his features set with an inner concentration. I recognized with shock that for the first time in his life I knew with certainty what his thoughts were.

I unbuckled my seat belt and flexed my stiff knee joints, preparatory to rising. My movements were mechanical, my actions automatic, my mind locked irretrievably into memories of Kurt. I waited for the ache of loss, the familiar regret that he had not lived long enough to share this final lap with me. My gaze met that of Martin; a pain shared, I now discovered, was not quite a pain halved. But the agony, when it came, was this time strangely muted.

Martin and Maraid stood beside the luggage carousel, baggage trolley at the ready. When my suitcase did not readily appear I felt certain that my misrouted clothes were at this very minute flying onwards towards Helsinki or Cairo. I would spend the coming week imprisoned in the dark, straitjacket suit, the shiny court shoes, the frilled blouse.

'Why,' I moaned, 'do I always buy black suitcases that look exactly like a million others?'

Martin spoke kindly. 'Yours has got a red address-tag fastened to the handle. Look – leave it to me. I'll find it for you.'

I wandered away feeling carefree and cosseted. It was very

pleasant, rather like childhood when parents had dealt with the practicalities of life. A door opened briefly in a far wall. I glimpsed the waiting people, saw Melanie's smooth blonde head, and the silver curling hair of the tall man at her side. I waved and Melanie waved back. The door closed; I stared at its shiny yellow painted surface. On previous visits it had been only Christina, Melanie and me in the apartment on Mechner Strasse. But seven years ago Melanie had married an Englishman: Ryan Barry, who had settled in West Berlin, was employed by the British Administration in the City. Theirs had been a romantic courtship; Melanie had written happy letters. I had been happy for her.

It was only now, seeing them together at the barrier, that I conceded the actual presence of Ryan. The apartment was his home. I closed my eyes and tried to place him among the pale blue velvet chairs and sofas, the towering antique cabinets, and could not. It was equally hard to imagine Martin and Maraid relaxed in that room of formal grandeur. I myself had always preferred the kitchen, with its cushioned bentwood chairs and smells of spices and herbs.

Coming back to any place carried risks of disappointment. I could, I thought, have come here by myself. It would not have been extraordinary. Isolation is my habit. Talking to Roman about Berlin had been my first mistake. Giving voice to thoughts was an irreversible process, like setting free a flock of trapped birds. I had gone on to compound my rashness, issued invitations, used rare words like 'us' and 'we'.

I turned back towards the luggage carousel and saw Martin reach dangerously outward to grab a black, red-labelled suitcase. Maraid snatched at a pale-green bag as it threatened to sweep past her. The two of them exchanged congratulatory smiles. The baggage trolley was now stacked with our full tally of possessions.

I started to walk back towards them. They were so tall, they had such long arms; they did not anticipate disasters. Martin smiled at my approach; I noted the whiteness of his knuckles as he gripped the baggage trolley and began to move towards the exit.

'You have the passports and the tickets?'

'I have the passports and the tickets.'

'Right!' he said. 'Let's get this show on the road!'

The journey from Tegel Airport to Lichterfelde was made in convoy. I travelled with Melanie in her small car. Martin and Maraid rode in the larger car with Ryan and the luggage. The drive across West Berlin was, as always, swift, efficient, and confusing. Place names, immediately memorable, hung above the streets at every intersection. I began to anticipate them. Reinickendorf. Wedding. Wilmersdorf. Schöneberg. Steglitz. I had a sense of homecoming; I allowed it to overwhelm me, was moved briefly to ridiculous tears, as if I were some late-returning German exile.

Melanie said, 'It's been such a long time –?'

'I know,' I answered. 'Things happened. Each time I planned to come, oh, something came up.' I spoke ruefully. 'I've turned into the sort of woman who writes novels for monetary gain. It's proved to be very time-consuming. I've given it a lot of thought just lately. I just might not bother with it anymore.' We halted at a red light.

Melanie said, 'I think that would be a pity. I enjoy your novels.'

I said, 'I have a sense of urgency about this visit. A now or never feeling. Ten years of absence and – wham! – there I was, inviting Maraid and Martin to come with me. Asking you to arrange a meeting with Christina and her family. I thought I had forgotten how to be impulsive.'

Melanie said, 'Things are very tense here.'

'I know. I've read the papers, seen the television newscasts.'

'Christina arrives in Berlin tomorrow afternoon. We shall meet her at the Botanischer Garten S-Bahn station. On Thursday it is arranged that we all go over to East Berlin. The family will travel down from Dresden. A table has been booked in the Hotel Unter den Linden. We shall be a luncheon party of eleven.'

'But that's wonderful! More than I had ever hoped for.' I paused. 'The border crossings will be open?'

'Oh yes. They were closed for only a short time. Things are back to normal now.'

We swung into Hindenburgdamm. I recognized shops, and cafés, and anticipated precisely the sharp turn into Mechner Strasse. From Ryan's car Martin unloaded cases on to the cobbled pavement. For a moment we stood together beneath the trees, a tableau of five people. Now there was time for proper introductions.

'Meet my son and daughter-in-law,' I said.

Ryan smiled, shook hands, and lifted a suitcase. We followed him into the apartment building. He turned the keys easily in the complicated series of locks that had always given me so much trouble. I stepped past the carved oak door and believed at last that I had truly arrived. I thought of the coming pleasures that were solely mine. Tomorrow I would walk alone in Lichterfelde. I would think about Kurt. If my perception should be keen enough, I would sense his shade walking with me, at my left shoulder. Tomorrow.

PART TWO

PART TWO

THERE were areas of Berlin which in autumn had a country aspect. One-third of the city was made up of lakes and forest. Away from the glitz and roar of Kurfürstendamm and the Europa-Centre, the air was soft, the sky a high and hazy blue.

On Mechner Strasse the acacia trees glowed like lamps in the October sunshine. Underfoot the fallen leaves made puddled gold on the uneven cobbles. This quiet street of apartment houses had the ambience of an older, more dignified Berlin. On the balcony of Number Seventeen, late summer flowers trailed a final shower of colour; beyond the petunias and geraniums, behind the glass doors of Melanie's sitting-room, Maraid and Martin planned with Ryan their first morning in the city. I stood in the street absorbing the strangeness. I thought fleetingly of Roman who at this moment would be walking with Jasper in the Deerpark. I too began to walk, stiffly at first, and then less painfully. By the time I turned into the broad thoroughfare of Hindenburgdamm I was moving easily in what I thought of as my normal amble. I called at the Berliner Bank, changed travellers' cheques, replying without hesitation to the teller's queries. The German words came back quite easily sometimes.

The adjacent antiques shop still held the same style of dark carved chairs and tables, rococo mirrors and gloomy oil paintings. The stock seemed hardly to have changed in the ten years of my absence; perhaps, I thought, the shop was just a cover; the owner might make his living in a more exciting and sinister way?

In Berlin, city of spies and intrigue, how easy it was to

imagine dramas in the lives of others. I saw my reflection in a gilt, cherubim-encrusted looking-glass, and hardly recognized as mine the white hair stylishly curled, the dark-red suit worn only for London visits to my agent or publisher, the smart black court shoes – dressed like this, Roman and Jasper would pass me by without a glance or nod.

I moved along, taking care to avoid the edge of the broad pavement which in this city was reserved for cyclists. A school-boy rode past, his sandalled feet pumping at the bicycle pedals, a multi-coloured satchel flapping between his shoulder-blades, his blond hair blown into a quiff. I paused to stare into a toyshop window. The games displayed bore German names which had no meaning for me. If Kurt and I had stayed in Germany in 1948 I would have known those games and toys; a boy like the cyclist with the blond quiff might have been my grandson. But we had not stayed. Kurt's sons had grown up to be Englishmen, Midlanders, and Martin felt inadequate today because he could not speak or understand his father's language.

I had forgotten the white-painted café that stood on the corner of Handel Strasse. The doors stood wide open to the mild autumn morning, the smells of baked *apfelkuchen* and fresh-brewed coffee not to be passed by. I trod the carpet of the old-fashioned café, sat down at a lacy-clothed table beside swagged blue-velvet window curtains. An elderly waitress took my order; at adjoining tables people spoke a rapid Berlinese of which I comprehended almost nothing. I settled back into my chair, sipped the scalding aromatic coffee. Nottingham or West Berlin, it seemed to make no difference; I began, as was my habit when seated in cafés or restaurants, to evaluate my situation. The island of my single table, my obvious preoccupation, always ensured me privacy among a host of people. I did not understand why a certain clarity of thought should be available only when in a public place and hemmed about by strangers, but was grateful for it.

I had slept long and deeply in the little room that had been mine on previous visits. Over breakfast the arrangements of the day had been discussed. Melanie had needed to shop, I to visit the Berliner Bank. Martin and Maraid had opted to explore Berlin with Ryan. At two o'clock that afternoon, Christina would arrive from Dresden.

I drank deeply of the cooling coffee. The elderly waitress approached. '*Noch etwas für die Dame?*'

'*Noch eine Tasse Kaffee, bitte.*' The coffee came and this time the saucer held a gratuitous biscuit. I wrapped my fingers around the cup's warmth as if it were already winter. My mind turned back to yesterday's arrival. I had been naively unprepared for changes, had cherished a memory of Melanie's apartment, of the room that resembled a miniature European salon, and expected to find it exactly the same. I had followed Maraid through the tiny hallway, my daughter-in-law had paused on the threshold, lifted her gaze to the high moulded ceiling and tall windows, and then looked down to the pale parquet floor and rich rugs.

Maraid had turned to Melanie, had said in a hushed tone, 'This is a most beautiful room.' I recalled the stab of pure pleasure I had felt, as if some possession of my own was being genuinely praised. I felt grateful to Maraid, for her good taste and discernment and the voicing of it; and most unexpectedly for her presence in Berlin. We drank tea and talked about the journey, about the semi-roofless state of Martin's house, about Maraid's important hospital posting from which she had begged a few brief days in order to be with Martin and me.

I sat with them, yet apart; once content that the four would get along together, the tension in my body had eased, my grip on the teacup lessened. I began unobtrusively to look about me. My impression on entering the room had been of change. Now I was able to detail differences. The sofas and armchairs were no longer covered in blue velvet but in an attractive heavy cream-coloured linen. The most intimidating of the towering antique cabinets had been removed. In its place stood tiered equipment: a stereo double-deck music centre, a compact disc player, a television and a video recorder. Many shelves held books with English titles; an answering-machine stood beside the telephone, business files were ranked beneath it. Handsome hand-built shelf units in a pale wood reached from floor to ceiling. Behind the glazed doors I glimpsed a collection of fossils, beautifully displayed. A desk held a computer. The room had lost nothing in its reformation; it had gained since the coming of Ryan the warmth and comfort of a shared home.

The café was beginning to fill up. All around me vacant tables had been taken, people studied menus, wine was ordered. Traditional German food was served here, heavy roasts with dumplings and rich sauces. *Sauerkraut mit Eisbein. Schokoladenpudding.* The waitress hovered; the table was required for more lucrative customers. I nibbled at the biscuit, still unwilling to depart. At last I rose, paid my bill with the small unfamiliar notes, and slipped the light coins given in change into my jacket pocket. I came out into the sunshine of Hindenburgdamm, and began to walk slowly back towards Mechner Strasse.

Martin had hardly slept but did not feel tired. He was conscious this morning of an excitement which he did not altogether trust or welcome; a more acute awareness in all his senses, of living on a keener level. Like most Englishmen he was not good at emotional encounters. High feelings among men in the English Midlands were acceptable only on the

Leicester City football terraces, or more decorously at Trent Bridge cricket fixtures. He would sometimes join in a heated political discussion across a pint of mild and bitter at his village local. He cared passionately about wildlife and endangered species: was a member of the Royal Society for the Protection of Birds. Martin had been known when very much younger to raise both voice and fists in anger. But today he believed himself to have mellowed; he had for some time now cultivated a calm and uninvolved approach to life.

Driving with Ryan and Maraid through the golden morning, he attempted to relax the stiffness of his facial muscles, the tension of his shoulders; to listen and respond.

'I thought,' said Ryan, 'that we might begin by looking at the Reichstag. It was almost burned down in 1933, and again in 1945. The structure is in the style of the Italian Renaissance. By 1957 only the shell remained reasonably intact. It was then restored by the authorities at a cost of a 100 million Deutsche Mark. People here have sometimes questioned the wisdom of spending so much money on such a doubtful project.'

Martin remembered early childhood, sitting with his father watching television, a jerky black-and-white film that showed the Reichstag burning. He had observed his father's stillness, had asked, 'What is it, Dad? What does it mean?'

His mother had gone into the kitchen to clatter dishes and saucepans. His father had said, 'It means nothing now. It's better burned down.'

The sky above Berlin was the same shade of hazy blue that was over Martin's home village in mid-October. He thought about his son and daughter. Matthew would have walked the dog before catching the school bus. Liese would be tidying the kitchen after breakfast, phoning interminably to friends. The plumber should have arrived by now to install piping for the new bathroom.

Ryan said of the Reichstag, 'We'll have to park some distance from it, but the slow approach is quite dramatic.'

They began to walk. Maraid took Martin's arm; her warm fingers clasped his cold hand. In spite of the Harris tweed and Aran sweater, in spite of the sunshine, he felt chilled.

'Perhaps I ought to phone the children,' said Maraid.

'Better not until this evening,' he said. 'That was our arrangement with them.'

Maraid turned back to speak to Ryan. Martin heard the murmur of their voices. He heard Ryan say, 'The actual building remains unused for the most part. The West Wing contains an historic exhibition called "Questions about German History". They hold the occasional conference here, I believe.'

Martin came first to the flight of stone steps. He looked up at the resurrected Reichstag, studied its grey bulk, the pocked and bitten pillars. He laid his finger along the scar made by a bullet.

Ryan said quietly, 'There are many buildings in Berlin where the bullets are still embedded in the stonework.'

Martin thought about the final storming of this building, the armies which had swept over and around it; the gunfire, the fear, the smell of burning flesh. His hand went out again to the unfilled bullet hole. Who needed an historic exhibition in the West Wing?

'The Berlin Wall,' said Ryan, 'if straightened, would measure one hundred and five miles. It's of reinforced concrete, stands ten to thirteen feet high, and behind it, on the eastern side, stands yet another formidable Wall. In the hundreds of yards of no man's land that lie between are the watchtowers and the dog-runs. At night, every inch of it is floodlit.'

Martin listened as if his very life depended on the knowledge. All at once it was important that he know about these matters. He should have known them long since. He began to walk the raised platform; he saw the tidy memorials to those who escaped the East only into death. He stood, bunched fists thrust deep into his pockets. He stared at the watchtowers and the guards stared back at him.

Over there was the land he had always believed to be his father's home. A place of deep winter snows and impenetrable forest. Another country, where his Aunt Christina and his cousins lived, unbelievably imprisoned. He wondered if the white storks still flew from Africa to nest on the roofs and in the chimneys of the village called Mechtenhagen. They arrived, so his father had said, on the first day of spring, coming back year after year to the same nests. The males came first. When the females flew in, their presence was greeted by a great display of bill-clattering and clapping. The storks fed on mice and frogs and insects. Of all his father's stories this was the one most favoured by Paul and Martin. But that was a long time ago, in another life, before the war that brought division, isolation. He came back into the present.

'The German words for the Wall,' said Ryan, 'are *Die Mauer*.'

Martin muttered it softly. It had a sinister sound. He studied the amazing construction of it, the graffiti laid upon graffiti. It had a certain brilliant obscene fascination for him.

He had almost stopped smoking before leaving England; now, quite unconscious of his action, he lit the emergency cigarette that he always carried in his jacket pocket.

My understanding of the German language was passable; I could not for some reason often bring myself to speak it. In recent weeks I had studied dictionaries and grammars, had purchased cassettes of a BBC language course called *Deutsche*

Direkt! I carried in my handbag a German translation of the poetry of Emily Dickinson, which I recited aloud on the top deck of the bus that travelled to Melton Mowbray and Nottingham. The poetry had done nothing to rouse the German words that lay ten years dormant in my mind. *Deutsche Direckt!* had informed me on how I should request a full tank of petrol or a tyre change, how to book a hotel room with private bathroom; and instructed me on how to find my way about the city of Cologne.

Perhaps, I thought, in such a situation it was easier to be Martin, of whom no linguistic skills would be expected, unlike myself, who had been around the language for more than forty years with only minimal results of fluency. On every visit I had resolved to do better, and on each occasion shyness or some kind of nervous block had kept me silent, or at best allowed no more than a stumbling response. In the coffee shop at Heathrow Airport, I had said to Martin, 'I can translate for you.' On the short drive from Mechner Strasse to the Botanischer Garten S–Bahn station, I began seriously to doubt my ability to keep that promise.

Christina was waiting for us at the station entrance. She wore a plain grey skirt and a toning jacket of pale checks. Since her heart attack two years ago, Christina had grown thinner. Her hair, as white as my own, curled softly around a face that had lost much of its high and handsome colour.

Parking in the station forecourt, said Melanie, was not permitted. There was not time for proper greetings. A swift grasp of hands, an exchange of words and smiles, and Christina was belted securely into the front seat of the car, her suitcase stowed. Within minutes we were driving again on Hindenburgdamm, and then swinging sharply back into Mechner Strasse. Once more the little tableau of yesterday's arrival was repeated. This time six people stood together under the acacias; for a moment we gazed at one another, and then Christina's arms were outstretched. There was a swift hug for Melanie and Maraid, a sheen of tears as her embrace enfolded me. She turned last of all to Martin, and it was him to whom she clung as if she would never let him go. It was Martin for whom her tears spilled over.

In other times I had coveted the table. It was circular and large, with carved pedestal feet and a gleaming inlaid surface. Today, it was covered by a protective pad and embroidered linen cloth. We sat around it at the meal's end. Melanie talked with Maraid and Martin. Christina and Ryan spoke quietly together. I drifted, as was my habit, on an ebb and flow of memory. The visits made here in the years soon after Kurt's death were imprinted on my mind with all the nostalgic power of sepia photos pasted in an album; like dried flowers laid between the pages of a book. I had travelled once in mid-December, taking ferry and train. A Force-9 gale had blown up in the Channel, but I was never seasick. I had booked an outside cabin, had sat wakeful through the night beside the porthole and had watched the lights of passing ships. On my bunk had lain the large black suitcase, safely within view. I had thought about Kurt, making this same voyage in 1948, released from his time as a prisoner-of-war in the English Midlands, to return to his devastated homeland.

In the morning I had boarded the long, dark-green train. It had snowed from the Hook of Holland right through to Zoo station, West Berlin. I had viewed the winter landscape with delight, loving the whiteness and lavender-tinted shadows, the invigorating cold. On that particular arrival Christina had been waiting for me in Melanie's apartment. There had been so much that I had wished to say, meant to say. But as always, when I was face to face with Kurt's sister, the German words, carefully chosen and rehearsed, would not pass my lips.

On Sunday we had driven out to Grünewald, walked and slid on the frozen lake. We drank hot spiced *glühwein*, bought from an enterprising vendor who set up his stall beside the lake's edge. By midday the lake and its surrounding woodlands were filled with people. Babies and small children, cocooned in brightly coloured woollens, were pulled on little wooden sledges by their parents. Most of fashionable West Berlin society, it seemed, had come to walk on the Grünewald lake that Sunday in their ankle-length fur coats, tinted glasses and high, tooled-leather boots.

I came slowly back into the present. Beyond the glass of the balcony doors I could see the tops of the acacia trees, shrouded now in autumn dusk. I became aware, on either hand, of earnest conversation; of Melanie's almost faultless English, spoken to Maraid and Martin in that lilting accent that made musical the most mundane of observations.

I did not at once take in that the exchange between Ryan and Christina was in rapid fluent German. But of course it was! What else would they be speaking? They were discussing the political situation, the growing unrest behind the Wall. So why had I never thought of Ryan as speaking the language of the land? Melanie had once mentioned in a letter that he was taking lessons. I had also taken lessons, wrestled with the intricacies of grammar and pronunciation. Five sessions at winter evening classes had not yet enabled me to speak my heart and mind.

Ryan spoke with an accent similar to my own. Well, of course he would. We were both English, weren't we? I listened, sat straighter in my chair, was amazed and then disproportionately delighted at what I heard. Unlike myself, Ryan did not seek unsuccessfully for tenses and declensions, for ultimate perfection. He spoke confidently. He was by nature and profession a communicator, and what he had to impart was considerable and sufficient to put me to deep shame.

Martin was also listening to Ryan. I said, 'They're talking about tomorrow's visit to East Berlin, about your meeting with your cousins.'

Melanie said, 'Do you remember anything about them, Martin?'

'Not really. I was eighteen months old. Paul was three, he recalls far more than I do.' He smiled. 'You know how it is with these old family legends. When you've heard something for the sixteenth time you're not sure if you actually remember it, or only think you do. But, in fact, there are one or two things –' He looked at me, eyebrows raised. 'Easter eggs? Hidden in the hotel garden under bushes and behind trees? Dad said it was a German custom.'

'Yes,' I said.

'There was something else. A stick? A cricket bat? You tried to take it from me several times, and I wouldn't give it up?'

'It was a wooden spoon,' I said. 'You found it on a rubbish heap, a filthy mud-encrusted object. You would not be parted from it. You were by far the youngest and the smallest of the children. You used it as a weapon to thwack your brother and your cousins.'

I turned to Christina; fists clenched, breath shallow, I began to speak my heavily accented German. I talked of that long-ago Easter in Dietkirchendorf, the Easter eggs, the spoon, the intractability of Martin.

Christina laughed. Oh yes, she recalled every detail. Hadn't they photographed him, belligerent and tiny, brandishing his treasure?

Martin joined in the exchange. Maraid had questions of her own. I started to translate, stiffly at first, and then scarcely without effort, roving from English into German and back again.

Melanie had left the table; now she returned, a wooden spoon held aloft. She handed it to Martin. 'Tomorrow,' she said, 'you must take it with you to the East. We will see if your cousins also recollect the past!'

It was time for the early evening newscast. Ryan pressed a switch and the image of the presenter came up on the television screen. The West German media style was less formal than that of the BBC. This newsreader wore a grey and white loose-knit sweater over an open-necked blue shirt; he stood in a relaxed pose, his delivery made without the aid of notes. The only hint of tension, of excitement, was in his voice. I translated swiftly for Martin and Maraid.

'The East German leader, Herr Erich Honecker, has this day resigned from his position as Head of State. Herr Egon Krenz has been selected to replace him.'

Ryan touched a switch and the TV image faded. For a moment the silence held and then a cheer went up around the table. All eyes were turned towards Christina. Her voice was angry.

'Krenz will be no better,' she said. 'He is one from the same stable as Honecker. Nothing will change.' She spoke with the hopeless conviction of one who had grown up under Nazi rule, who had experienced a further forty-four years of life in a Communist state.

'But surely,' said Melanie, 'it is the power of the people that has toppled Honecker. Things are changing, Christina! On Monday evening 120,000 people marched and demonstrated in Leipzig – and were allowed to do so without intervention.' She fetched wine and glasses, determined to make this an occasion, a celebration. A toast was raised to the downfall of the man who had resisted change. As we drank Melanie cried out, 'Oh – but this wine is terrible, it's so sour! Please leave it. I'll fetch another bottle.'

Christina smiled. 'No,' she said, 'let us drink what we have here. Sour wine is quite good enough to see off Erich Honecker!'

I woke early on that Thursday morning. I sat by the open window and watched the sky grow light above Lichterfelde, drank Earl Grey tea and enjoyed the draught of cold air on my head and face. I attempted to think about the coming day, the events of which would be unprecedented and traumatic. But my mind slid away to a September morning in the Deerpark, seated underneath the mulberry tree, Jasper in his pram drooping into sleep, Roman hunched in misery beside me.

'I have family and friends,' I had said, 'in West and East Berlin.' At the time I had hardly registered the blankness in his eyes, his sudden wary stillness. I thought about it now. Perhaps it was not, after all, my threatened absence from his life, his temporary lack of a shoulder to cry on, that disturbed him, but rather the mention of my destination. The single word – Berlin.

Recalled in the heightened mood of this particular morning, I now recognized the tungsten hardness at the core of Roman. I had known a few implacable men in my own life, none of them English. Englishmen I found to be, on the whole, amenable, open to persuasion, tractable. In Roman I sensed the same vein of intractability that had been Kurt's strength, and ultimately his weakness. 'If you won't bend a little,' I had once told him, 'then you will surely break.'

Martin, too, I had observed, found compromise a kind of failure.

In the case of Kurt, strength of mind and body had been necessary for survival. Born into a farming family, he had worked as a child in the hay and harvest fields alongside his parents. At the age of thirteen he had already left the village schoolroom to walk all day behind a team of horses. At the age of twenty his education was completed in the gunnery classes of the Naval Training school at Kiel. If he was intolerant of intellectual pretensions, of what he saw as the self-indulgence of soft urban living, then it was not too surprising.

But what kind of childhood, what early experience of life, had welded Roman's backbone? The mystery of his origins, the danger inherent in my friendship with him, my unwise but growing attachment to the baby Jasper, would have to be faced on my return to England.

I could, I thought, have sent a holiday postcard to Roman – views of present-day Berlin – had I known his surname and his address.

The Friedrich Strasse U–Bahn station was a crossing point for pedestrians into East Berlin. It had an echoing, vault-like quality, many flights of greasy stone steps and a peculiarly sour smell. Nobody sauntered here, nobody lingered. At intervals the rumble of trains drowned out all other sounds. Metal barriers, reminiscent of cattle pens or sheep runs, channelled into categories all those who wished to cross over to the East, each section being clearly labelled for citizens of the DDR, for citizens of West Berlin, for citizens of Western Germany, and for all other Foreign Nationals.

Martin's first impression was of confusion; Foreign Nationals was the longest and most unruly of the four groups. The long straggle of assorted nationalities and races had no notion of orderly queuing as the British understood it.

Melanie said, 'Well, this is where we have to separate. See you on the other side!' The native Germans, he noted, passed swiftly and in orderly fashion through their checkpoints. Among the Foreign Nationals he observed a disturbing amount of elbowing and queue jumping. Martin took up a firm position behind his wife and mother, arms outstretched to span the barriers, insulating them marginally from the party of jostling Dutch schoolchildren who ate ice-cream and spilled Coca-Cola while their worried teachers took a head count.

The East German guards were neither young nor particularly martial. They had the creased and crumpled look of family men who had overslept and failed to find clean shirts that morning. He had not anticipated kindness from them and yet, as the line of Foreign Nationals grew longer and more rowdy, the guards moved along the barriers calling out the elderly and the young parents who held crying infants, allowing them to move up to the head of the queue. The businessmen and salesmen who wished to enter East Berlin were identifiable by their briefcases and rolled umbrellas and their impatient aspect. Already, another twenty or more people had joined the line. A young man with a briefcase was advancing through the press of people with a sly sideways movement which had so far gone unchallenged. Maraid, who had also noticed this manoeuvre, looked a little fearfully at Martin. 'Don't worry,' he confirmed, 'he won't get past me.' He assumed a nonchalance he did not feel. In this place and at this moment he thought he might well sell his soul for a cigarette. Again he had been lying wakeful into the early morning hours; when he slept it was to dream about his father, not as he had been in his last illness but strong and youthful, his great voice roaring out across the fields to call the cows home for milking, or to summon the horse called Ginger, who was old and cranky and disinclined for work.

In the dream Martin rode that horse again, he and Paul perched high up on the broad back. He had a view of the cut hayfields, dog-roses in the hedges, the river running brown and fast between green banks, the black and white cattle grazing. His mother had walked beside the horse, her long rusty-coloured hair lifting in the breeze, her face habitually anxious, her eyes unfocused. The world, thought Martin, had always required of his mother a greater effort of concentration than she was capable of making. He studied her now, unnaturally smart in the red suit and black shoes, and therefore unfamiliar to him. Since she spoke the language of the country it had been agreed that she should be in charge of papers. The three dark blue passports were already in her hand. She looked drawn, unusually pale. He said, 'You OK?'

'Only hungry,' she said. 'I couldn't seem to eat any breakfast.'

Martin had also surveyed without appetite the platters of cold ham and sausage, the baskets of warm and fragrant rolls, the board of unfamiliar smoked cheeses. Three cups of strong coffee had been as much as he could manage. He had envied Maraid. This morning she wore a patterned dress of muted golds and browns, and looked relaxed and rested. She had smiled understandingly across the table at him, sensing his tension, and he thought how good they were for one another. He had noticed with surprise how well Maraid and his mother got along together. He had decided long ago that they were totally disparate; seeing them now, deep in conversation, he realized how much alike they really were.

He moved closer to them. His mother said, 'I believe the River Spree runs right above this U-Bahn station, I read somewhere that there are bulkheads that keep the water out. In 1948 your father swam the River Elbe after dark. He crossed over to the East without papers to visit his mother and Christina. It was a terrible time. Manfred and Ria were little children; their grandfather had died in Russia; their father was missing on the Eastern Front. There was hardly any food. The Russians were in military occupation.' She paused and looked around her. 'Well, they eat a little better these days, but there is still this obscenity – this *Mauer*!'

Martin thought about his father, swimming the River Elbe by night, his clothing rolled into a bundle and held above his head. This was a story never previously mentioned in his hearing. He said, 'I didn't know about any of that. Wasn't it a risky thing to do?'

'Illegal entry into the Soviet Zone would almost certainly have resulted in his instant deportation to Russia. He was young and fit and strong. German prisoners-of-war had been treated well in England. There were stories of what happened to those who were foolish enough to return behind the Iron Curtain – but he hadn't seen his family for over five years –' she hesitated '– and of course he needed to confess to them that he had married in England; that he had married me.'

'So what happened?'

'He stayed hidden in his mother's house for ten days and then he grew reckless on the journey back to West Berlin – well, you remember how· he was, always loved to take a chance. He was stopped by Russian officers, on a railway station. The only document he carried was his English Certificate of Marriage which he had taken over to show to his mother and sister. The Russians must have been impressed, because they let him go!' She smiled. 'There's a certain irony in that, if you think about it.' She shuffled the blue passports.

'But for my marriage lines I might have lost him altogether, and you would not be here today.'

The important young businessman had advanced through the queue by several yards since Martin had last spied him. He edged closer, the briefcase held shieldlike across his chest. People glowered as he sidled through and around them, but not one of them made any attempt to halt his progress. Martin assumed a relaxed stance, feet apart, his fingertips resting lightly on either metal barrier, lips stretched in a small smile. The young man spoke in a heavily accented English. 'Please excuse me,' he said politely.

Martin said, 'No. I will not excuse you. You must wait in line like everybody else!'

'But I have an appointment in East Berlin. It is urgent that I cross at once. I have to be there at eleven.'

Martin shook his head, then leaned forward so that his face was only inches from that of the other man.

'We all of us have important appointments in East Berlin,' he said softly, 'and you will stay right where you are, chum.'

The queue, which had not advanced for many minutes, suddenly surged forward. Now it was their turn to stand before the glass-sided cubicle, to be scrutinized by a seated guard, their faces matched to passport photos. Through a slot in the glass his mother pushed the D-mark notes that were the price of their admittance to the DDR. The stamp came down three times on separate passes and they were through. As they began to move away the guard leaned forward in his box. He called out, *'Halt! Ein moment, bitte!'* Maraid and Martin halted. Cathy returned. There was a brief exchange of rapid German, and two D-mark notes were slid back through the slot.

His mother rejoined them, smiling and waving the returned notes. 'He wanted to know,' she said, 'if I was a pensioner in

England. He must have noticed the colour of my hair. When I said I was, he apologized for overcharging me. Old folks, it seems, even foreign ones, pay less to enter the DDR.'

As they finally walked away Martin glanced back across his shoulder. The young man who had been in such a hurry to get through, now relieved of his briefcase, was being marched off between two tall guards.

Beyond the narrow door that admitted us to East Berlin, Christina, Melanie and Ryan were waiting; I walked quickly, my fragile calm disturbed by the prolonged separation from them, by a conviction that the magic meeting-hour of eleven o'clock was already past. While still in England I had imagined every possible failure of this plan, from the crashing of our aircraft, to incapacitating illness; or what seemed almost certain, the civil disobedience of the East German people, and escalation of their unrest into bloodshed, even revolution. We came out from the dank chill of the crossing-point into hazy golden sunlight. I saw how Martin's casual air served only to accentuate his inner turmoil. He's as tight as a drum, I thought; like me, he is ready to fly apart. We do not either of us stand up well to anticipation. We are about to meet Kurt's niece and nephew, I told myself; Martin is to see his cousins. I remembered the snapshots; worn, black and white pictures Kurt had carried always in his wallet. My sister's children, he had told me proudly in those first days of our courtship, and I had smiled at the images of the small blonde girl and her plump baby brother. Later on, there had been other pictures. Ria and Manfred, holding prayer books, grave-faced at their confirmation ceremony; and after that, Ria in her wedding gown, Manfred in the uniform of the East German Navy. Kurt studied the photos for a long time, his careful face showing no emotion. I had found frames, had hung them on a white wall that caught the sunlight; had made of them a family gallery displaying only Baumanns.

As we crossed the expanse of the station forecourt I heard a clock chime. Martin said to Maraid, 'Right on time! I was beginning to think, back there, when we stood in line, that we might be late.'

Punctuality was a virtue in Martin that still surprised and pleased me. I had learned only lately that he invariably did those things that he had said he would do. But then again, when I thought about it, he always had. It was I who had not appreciated him.

From the street a group of people stepped on to the forecourt. They moved slowly at first, as if uncertain, and then all at once very quickly, so that their few final steps were taken at a run. I was clasped, almost lifted off my feet, in the arms of a very tall man, only to be released into the tight embrace of a slim blonde woman. I gazed up into their smiling faces, again saw in my mind the tiny fairhaired girl and her baby brother; the young bride, the earnest-looking sailor of the photographs that still hung on my bedroom wall. '*Tante* Cathy!' they said, and I at last knew recognition. Yes, I thought, of course that is what I am. I am their English aunt. I am part of their family. I was embraced by Inge, Manfred's wife, and by Simone, their daughter. Last of all came Britta, Ria's daughter, who spoke English. 'We are,' she said, 'so happy to see you, *Tante* Cathy!'

'I am so very pleased to be here,' I replied.

The Hotel Unter den Linden was, by East German standards, opulent and rare. The luncheon table for eleven people had been reserved with a degree of difficulty unknown to the visitors from England. We entered a foyer furnished with thick carpet, deep soft sofas, and arrangements of fresh flowers. The lighting was subdued; piped music, only faintly audible, murmured alternatively Strauss and Mozart. Recalling time spent in other DDR hotels, I marvelled at the western-style luxury, and wondered where the listening devices were concealed. I wondered also at the ease with which my mind assumed such a suspicious stance, then decided that in the present political uproar, and considering the rage of the people against the *Staatspolizei*, it could hardly matter any more. The secret police force of this country could not, industrious though they were, arrest everybody.

Manfred had brought roses for the ladies of the party, long-stemmed and perfect blooms of deep pink, just emerging from the bud. It was the kind of courtly, very German gesture that Kurt would have made.

'I should have brought flowers,' Martin whispered to me.

'Englishmen,' I whispered back, 'don't do that sort of thing. No one would expect it of you.'

At first we formed small separate groups around the glass-topped coffee tables. I sat with Ria and Christina, showed them photographs of Paul and his family, spoke German uninhibitedly and badly, and failed to worry about it. We were joined at intervals by Melanie or Ryan. On the far side of the foyer Martin and Maraid talked to Manfred and Inge, their words translated back and forth by Britta. Ryan began to photograph us all. I also produced my camera.

The separate groups came together, Manfred gestured to gain Martin's attention. From his pocket he withdrew a snapshot, black and white, a little curled around the edges. He said to Britta, 'Ask him if he remembers the time when we were children in Dietkirchendorf – how he hit us with a wooden spoon?'

Informed of the question Martin said, 'Tell Manfred that I don't remember, but my mother does.' From his pocket he produced the wooden spoon that Melanie had given him, and held it up beside the snapshot image of himself. The cousins laughed uproariously together. I felt tears start in my eyes. Martin, who all his life had rejected public expressions of physical affection, was now being lionized and fêted, arms laid across his shoulders, his hands held by his cousins' daughters. I found it an oddly gratifying sight to see my son so unavoidably encompassed, so swamped by love. I watched his flushed and smiling face, his look of pure pleasure, and felt a sharp, almost bitter envy of him. All at once it was no longer enough for me to be the visiting English aunt, a connection through marriage; I ached to be as Martin was, linked to them inevitably by blood, by a shared ancestry.

We were summoned by a waiter to a long and beautifully appointed table. The food was of a quality not obtainable in the shops by the ordinary citizens of the DDR. In this place, I suspected, it might be possible on demand to be served with delicacies unobtainable in East Germany, like fresh orange juice, bananas even! I ate very slowly and was never to be able, afterwards, to remember what it was that I had ordered. I would not forget the silver centrepiece vase of yellow roses that matched exactly the yellow tablecloth and napkins of heavy linen. I would not forget the faces present at this meal: Melanie and Ryan, happy and relaxed in the company of old friends; Inge, delicate and pretty, in appearance too young to be the mother of nineteen-year-old Simone; Maraid, smiling and nodding, heroic in her efforts at comprehension; Martin, who pushed the food around his plate, but hardly ate a mouthful; Ria who, in maturity, had attained the same kind of ageless beauty as that of her mother, Christina; the young and serious faces of Britta and Simone.

My gaze came last of all to Manfred, who, because of his profession – which made him an employee of the State – had never been permitted to have any contact with me. His letter of condolence, written to me on Kurt's death, must have been a grave risk deliberately taken. His presence here today, and that of his family, meant that something had changed. Perhaps he no longer cared. I observed him closely, seeking signs of Kurt, but there was no physical resemblance. Manfred had the dark hair and the eyes of Ernst, his father, that tall and sad-faced soldier of the tattered snapshots in my album, pictured long ago with his small children before his return to the Russian Front and a presumed death.

I began to concentrate quite fiercely on the plate of food that lay before me, as if the cutting up of meat, the impaling of vegetables on my fork, was of prime importance. It could all, I thought, have been so very different. I would not have blamed Kurt's family if they had been wary, if they had at first withheld their trust of these unknown and foreign visitors from England. In my own life I had found that acceptance must inevitably be hard sought, that love must be earned. There was always a price that must be paid. From my seat by the window I could see the grey monolithic buildings lining the Unter den Linden, and beside them the rows of half-grown lime trees planted to replace the original trees that were chopped down for fuel in the bitter winters of the war years.

In the short walk from the Friedrich Strasse Bahnhof I had sensed an atmosphere of recklessness, of anticipation. It was in the air, in the way that people moved and spoke. Surely, I thought, the little plastic cars, the Wartburgs and Trabants, now moved at increased speeds; voices were louder, eyes no longer watched and calculated. There was a sense of great events about to happen. I found the change, loaded as it was with risk and danger, unbearably moving. Ten years ago, a family meeting such as this could not possibly have taken place. To have gathered publicly, in the dining-room of an expensive East Berlin hotel, would have been unthinkable. Christina and I had always met clandestinely in railway station buffets, in a secluded corner of the Pergamon Museum, our voices pitched deliberately low. But how was it to end? Would this present insurrection be put down by tanks and bullets? My thoughts became chaotic, fragmented. I tried to do what I always did in restaurants in England, but here the people were impossible to categorize. A multiplicity of languages were being spoken; I caught a phrase or two of Polish, of Russian, a snatch of what I guessed at as Hungarian. Girls teetered past the table, dressed in long fringed skirts of brightly coloured cowhide and high-heeled shoes. A great deal of leather and diamonds were being worn by both men and women; the total effect was a bizarre combination of cowboy American and flashy central European. The faces were of equal interest, dark and intense, splitting occasionally into loud uninhibited laughter. I caught the gleam of yellow gold from teeth and neck-chains. Many of the younger men looked remarkably like Roman. I had decided before leaving England that I would not think about him, would not dwell on problems that were not my own, or dissipate my sympathies. I found it disturbing that here, where I had thought it would be easy to forget him and his troubles, my concern could still be triggered by a type of face, a gold-rimmed smile.

My plate, which I had absentmindedly emptied, was reclaimed by a silent, almost surly waiter. A sweet, which I did not remember ordering, was set firmly down before me with that take-it or leave-it air that reminded me of English restaurants in the war years. The waiters were not German; they were polite but inattentive. It was a standard of service that would not be acceptable in a hotel of similar repute in England. The very notion of service, I supposed, was a capitalist indulgence.

The clatter of my spoon into the empty compote glass brought me back to an awareness of the moment. My gaze roved around the table. I saw that already a measure of close contact had been achieved, but something else was growing here between the cousins: a warmth, an emanation of emotion, a kind of radiance that was not dependent on the spoken word. Once again, I longed to share this new involvement, this love. But I knew that my emotions would remain, as they had always been, subterranean, unfathomable and secret.

Plans were made to walk out in the sunshine. People rose, chairs were pushed back from the table, a drift began towards the glass doors of the hotel entrance. I stood apart. I pointed my camera at the row of metal barriers that stood on this eastern side of the Brandenburg Gate. Today I felt impelled to record the barricades rather than the architecture. The Wall, seen from this side, was blank and grey. Graffiti was, after all, a western expression of a nation's freedom.

The family began to walk in groups, very slowly, along Unter den Linden. I did not join the animated clusters, but walked a little ahead and to one side, turning at intervals to photograph them. There was a time, I thought, when this wide boulevard had been as fashionable and famous as the Champs-Élysées or the Mall in London. It had been possible once, long ago, to travel its length unimpeded, to stroll underneath the original lime trees that led up to the magnificent Palace of the Hohenzollerns. The remains of that palace had long since been demolished to make a Soviet parade ground. But the statue of Frederick the Great had been refurbished and restored to its rightful spot, as had the State Opera House and St Hedwig's Cathedral been refurbished, although I chose not to photograph them. I recorded instead Manfred and

Maraid walking arm in arm together, Martin and Ria and Britta, Simone with Christina. We came level with the building known as *Neue Wache*, a former Prussian Army guard house, now labelled as a 'Memorial to the victims of fascism and militarism' and paraded past regularly by the soldiers of the East Berlin Regiment of Guards. These young men, standing at attention on either side of the broad entrance, had a curiously unreal appearance. I was tempted to reach up and tweak the waxen cheeks beneath the helmet; instead I passed into the gloom of the great hall, where burned an Eternal Flame beneath the faceted glass of a cut-crystal block. The sudden change from light to darkness caused the prisms to blur; I tried to read the inscription, and made out with difficulty that beneath the Flame lay the ashes of an unknown soldier and a resistance fighter; included also were twenty urns of blood-soaked soil from the battlefields of eastern Europe. I turned away, stumbling a little, and as I sought the sunlight I saw Christina, her features drawn and unusually anxious, begin to use the inhalant spray that eased the pain of her angina.

A short walk brought us into the Marx-Engels Platz and across Marx-Engels Forum to the Nicolai quarter. In this urban square the reality of socialism was to be seen. Here were small exclusive shops, filled with leather goods and furs, jewellery and designer-garments, and patronized only by tourists or the well-paid hierarchy of the Communist regime. Here also were wooden benches grouped around a restaurant entrance. Manfred and Ryan fetched lager in tall glasses. I sat beside Christina and watched a little colour return to my sister-in-law's pale features. I took Christina's hand and held it. No words were needed. On either side of us the Baumann cousins spoke and laughed together. Poses were struck, cameras clicked; the sun, slanting lower now across the great grey buildings, caught and held the colours of the scene. Fixed always in my mind would be the crimson sheen of Ria's blouse, the cream of Martin's Aran sweater, the lustre of Maraid's dark hair. Away to the left, I had a glimpse of people gathering together, a small crowd that did not carry the distinguishing guide books and the Leicas; a group which was causing a new alertness among certain casually attired young men.

Manfred also saw the stir and movement, and began to gather up the lager glasses. He returned them to the restaurant in some haste. A slow amble, he suggested, back to the Friedrich Strasse Bahnof? He and his family must, he said, catch the train back to Dresden at four-thirty. His face and tone of voice implied that the Alexander Platz was no longer a safe place to be.

We came back to the forecourt of the Alexander Platz station. Childishly and without hope, I willed the laughter to continue. I recalled the morning hours, the way we had run towards each other; our collective, almost comic disbelief that this meeting was actually achieved. The goodbyes were mercifully swift. I watched them walk away, turn back to wave, then vanish from my sight. Now came the threat of tears, held in check through all that magical day; for a minute or two I struggled for control. Was Dresden, I wondered, any safer than Halle or Leipzig? At the Friedrich Strasse crossing-point, I submitted the three British passports for examination, and was nodded back, quite casually, into West Berlin.

As we walked out towards Ryan's parked car, the significance of the day began to seep into my consciousness. The Wall, the checkpoints, still had a permanent, unmovable appearance. What hope of freedom had those gatherings of unarmed people against the accumulated power of an entrenched regime?

Later that evening West German television described a massive demonstration, taking place at that very moment, said the commentator, in the Alexander Platz, in East Berlin.

There had never passed a day in which I did not think of Kurt. In those first bereft years I explored every twist and turn of the twenty-seven years of my marriage to him. I had used mercilessly the benefit of hindsight; had set down with devastating clarity and painful truth the record of our time together. I did not quite believe in death. In the first months of widowhood, my arguments, my conversations with him had been spoken in a quiet voice. I had walked, muttering, in isolated places: in parks in winter, in the cemetery, along a river path. Sometimes I wept. More often anger had sent me striding mindlessly from one village to another until, exhausted, I had sought a tea-room and, when rested, had caught a bus back to the empty house, then laid myself down, but not to sleep. And so are habits formed, escape routes tunnelled, despair allowed to set a pattern for the future. This ritual of mine, of walks, of cafés, of bus rides, of sleepless night hours, had first been forged in grief; I clung to it now because familiarity meant safety. And oh, how much I needed to feel safe!

Conversations with Kurt were no longer spoken diatribes of pain and anger, but rather a reasoned dialogue that went on inside my head. I talked things over with him, explained my present life. One area alone lay beyond our scope of consultation. I had told him of the publication of my first book: 'This is something that won't interest you. It's of no real importance; it just sort of happened after you went, like flu or a broken leg. It's what I do with the small part of me that still functions without you.' Kurt would, I thought, have eyed with suspicion the row of books that now bore my name. What he would have respected was my unguessed-at, hardly credible ability to make money by the mere putting down of words on paper. I lay awake in the darkness, the window of my room pushed wide to the cold air of the October night, to the rustling sounds of falling leaves down in Mechner Strasse. The night sky above Lichterfelde was pale with the reflected glow from Steglitz and the distant Ku'damm. Today I had been very close to Kurt. The dialogue between us as I walked on the Unter den Linden had been so easy that I knew beyond doubt that at some time he too must have walked there. I slept on the thought and did not dream.

Martin had found a shop on Hindenburgdamm that sold his brand of cigarettes. His resolution not to smoke had been rapidly eroded by the stress of recent days. Hitherto unknown emotions, the battering of his mind by the unfamiliar, had caused him to need urgently the easement of tobacco. Here in Berlin he found himself forced hourly into re-evaluations; of the past, of people. In the three days since his arrival, he had come to know intimately the bushes and the flowers, the paths that bisected the apartment gardens. On this fourth morning he came slowly down the stairs, the after-breakfast cigarette unlit but in his hand. Already the white mist of early morning was melting before sunshine. The garden trees, beech and lilac, sycamore and birch, shed casual leaves upon his head, falling one by one, as if determined to prolong the sweetness of the season. He halted, lit the cigarette, and drew deeply on it. A man like himself, he thought, did not indulge in self-analysis. Women coped better with all that sort of thing; seemed even to enjoy it. Even so, when emotions were heightened, when happiness was tangible, when memories crowded in, a degree of introspection would seem to be inevitable. There had been moments yesterday, in East Berlin, when, astonishingly, he had looked at his mother and guessed what she was thinking. He drew carefully on the half-smoked cigarette and began to walk the garden paths. Late flowers bloomed in sheltered corners; familiar to him by their shapes and colours, yet he could not name them. He had not grown up with gardens, but in the wider freedom of wild pastures, of growing crops. The summers of his childhood had been lived in hayfields; he remembered the sweet scent of it, the slow turning of the hayrake. He recalled the harvests of those years, gathered in without the benefit of combines. He had ridden with his father on the tractor, had known that field mice and rabbits crouched trembling in the last few feet of standing crop. When he pleaded for their reprieve his father had indulged him. Martin had jumped down from the tractor, had stood at the edge of that last square of uncut corn or barley and shouted, clapped his hands, and watched the wild and furry scamperings towards the safety of the distant hedgerows.

An inch of cigarette remained; he held it pinched between his thumb and fingers. Last night's demonstration in the Alexander Platz; thousands of people crowded together in that small square. He threw down the cigarette-end and ground it hard beneath his heel. He would, he thought, have liked to be there with them.

On the very edge of the control-point known as Checkpoint Charlie there is a street of tall and shabby buildings. The last house in the row is a museum. In what was once the Sunday-best front room of a Berlin family there now stands a counter packed with leaflets, souvenirs, books about the Wall and those who escaped across or beneath it. The cost of entry was DM 3.50. I bought tickets for myself, Maraid and Martin.

Every inch of wallspace was taken up by photographs and posters. *'Es geschah an der Mauer'* was the theme – 'it happened at the Wall'. The stories and pictures were familiar to me. For Maraid and Martin the crowded displays that told of fear and desperation were as new and strange as had been their first sighting of the Reichstag building, of the Eternal Flame that burned in *Neue Wache*. Maraid, visibly distressed by what she saw, held on to Martin's arm. I left them, standing together in the claustrophobic silence. Slowly I began to climb the twisting staircase. Certain exhibits merited a whole room; I studied the hot-air balloon in which two young families had escaped from the DDR in 1979, the mini-submarine in which a young man crossed the Baltic Sea to find refuge in Denmark.

From an upper window I could see the checkpoint, that collection of prefabricated shacks that was as notorious and unreal as the Black Hole of Calcutta or the Golden Temple of Amritsar. The glass-walled cabins looked quite ordinary, I had seen their like in garden-centres; but people had died here, spies had probably been exchanged, international games of cat-and-mouse played out by politicians.

I descended to the street, where I was joined eventually by Martin and Maraid. We bought scalding coffee from the stall that stood before the Haus am Checkpoint Charlie. We photographed each other, one foot set illegally across the white-painted line that marked the division of the city. Of what we had seen in the little museum, we said not one word.

Tegel Airport, which on arrival had seemed vast and busy, appeared on departure to have contracted to a single checking-in desk, a narrow waiting area with insufficient seating and a busy duty-free shop. I joined Maraid among the perfumes. I bought a large flask of Fiji for Liese and aftershave for grandsons whose shaving was, as yet, no more than a token gesture towards manhood. The concentration I brought to these transactions was quite disproportionate to their importance, as if by such means I could enforce normality. I returned to sit with Martin. His eyes were as expressionless as glass, he seemed disinclined for conversation. I no longer wished to know what he was thinking, my own thoughts were enough this morning. Better never to have said hello, if goodbye was so much torture; better for me to become reclusive, buy that crofter's house on Lismore, become an islander excluded from the world by sea and storm.

I had said my goodbyes to Melanie and Ryan. Well, that was all right, we would meet again, in England or Berlin. With Christina it had been quite another matter. We had gone back with her to the Botanischer Garten S-Bahn station, riding in a taxi the driver of which spoke a fascinating, fractured sort of English. So must I sound, I thought, when I am speaking German: quaint but sincere.

We had talked, in evening conversations, of a visit by Christina to my home in England. Next June. When the days were warmer. When the terrace roses and hydrangeas were in flower. Martin will meet you at Heathrow. Stay a month; spend the summer with me. In an instant I had planned a season. We could visit the half-completed house of Martin and Maraid; ride on buses, take short strolls in the Deerpark. I would show Christina all the places Kurt had loved, take her to the farm, walk the old fields, say to her, 'In this spot your brother passed the happiest time of all his days in England.' I would plant more flowers in the terrace urns, buy one of those garden chaise-longue things so that Christina might rest. Kurt had taken little white tablets for his angina, dissolved underneath his tongue; they had not always worked. Fifteen years on, and Christina had an inhalant spray, the effects of which were instant, magical. It would be safe; I knew about sick hearts, and Christina's illness was under tight control.

The S-Bahn train had been on time; the doors slid back and Christina had stood for a moment, looking like a picture framed in cream-painted wood. Briefly, the grey skirt, the jacket of pale checks, the white curling hair, had blurred in my vision. I had taken Christina's hand, had said urgently, '*Bis Juni — ja?*' The doors of the train had slid together; Christina, seen through glass, had seemed at once remote, unreachable. We had waved until the train was out of sight. Until June.

Ten minutes into the flight, seat belts unbuckled, and with West Berlin already slipped away beneath us, the first drinks were served. The plastic trays were brought: roll and butter, potato salad, smoked meats and cheeses, and an hermetically sealed slice of apple cake. I picked at the food in the way that annoyed me when other people did it. It was at this point, inappropriately, fork in one hand, paper napkin in the other, that the first tears slid down behind the tinted lenses of my glasses. I hated to weep, found no release in it; it only made my head ache. I clenched the fork hard into my palm, bit my tongue, curled my toes inside the smart and shiny shoes. I glanced sideways. Martin, busy with his meal, had noticed nothing. Maraid, in her window seat, looked down and observed the last outskirts of the city of Berlin. I felt the tears roll down my face to soak the collar of my blouse.

Back in Berlin it had been yet another mild and sunny morning. Down in Mechner Strasse the acacia trees shed the last of their leaves; we had sat around the circular table and drunk tea from Melanie's delicate rose-patterned cups. In

crystal vases, Manfred's roses had stayed fresh, not a leaf
crumpled or a petal fallen. Our suitcases had stood ready in
the hall. Ryan would drive us to the airport. It happened
only rarely in life that plans were fulfilled, hopes realized,
wishes granted. As each perfect day had passed I had waited
for the snag, the hitch; it never came. Time without flaw.
Not an awkward or uncomfortable moment. '*So viel liebe,*'
Christina had said. 'So much love.'

Beside me, Martin said quietly, 'Would you like a brandy
– or something?' I shook my head. I blew my nose, surrepti-
tiously repaired my make-up, drank the bitter British Airways
coffee. Maraid reached out a hand and touched my hand. The
dark shadow lifted, the premonition of approaching sadness
slid away.

The skies above London were overcast. Heathrow on a
Monday morning had a feel of foreignness, an alien look; I had
no sense of homecoming. Maraid at once telephoned the
children. Martin bought a newspaper and turned to the back
pages. Nottingham Forest, he reported, had done well on
Saturday. Leicester City had played a disastrous game, a total
washout.

The car smelled of new upholstery and faint perfume. I
wound a window down and the air, rain-laden and cool,
signified as could nothing else that this was England. I picked
up Martin's newspaper and saw that there had been an earth-
quake in San Francisco. A man, still seated in his car, had
been buried for ninety hours beneath the Oakland freeway.
His rescue was described as a miracle, his medical condition
critical. In Rome, the Pope had beatified a French nun. In
southern Italy the tusks of an elephant, dead for a million
years, had been found in a coalmine.

In East Berlin there had been another weekend demonstration. A young demonstrator was reported as saying to an East

German Politburo member, 'You tell us what to do, when to do it, and how to do it. Why should we bother to listen to you any more?'

PART THREE

MY house, upon re-entry, was cold; it had a musty smell. I had long suspected dry-rot, rising-damp; imagined mushrooms proliferating in the cellar. I attempted to let in fresh air. I tried to push up the window sashes then remembered that the cords were broken. I switched on the heating. The boiler flame ignited, but almost at once a thudding sound came from the airing-cupboard which housed the pump. The noise grew louder. I ignored it. I unpacked my suitcase, tried not to think about gas explosions, threw dirty washing into the machine, hung up garments on hangers, set my shoes back in a neat row. The disturbance in the airing-cupboard called for alarm, but my nerve held. I wandered through the rooms, traced my name in dust on the mahogany surface of the dining table, watered a wilting fern. The violet budgerigar, safe in his white cage and fed by a neighbour in my absence, regarded me with bored indifference, as was his habit. I went out to the terrace. The hydrangeas had withered in their pots, their great globes of pink and blue turned to dirty beige, their leaves falling at my touch.

I went back into the house through which a gentle warmth was spreading; hot water now flowed into washing-machine and bathtub, and the noise from the airing-cupboard had diminished to an occasional shudder. The budgerigar jumped, chuckling, from perch to perch.

I lay in my bed and waited for sleep. My favourite photographs of Kurt, that of the young man in the uniform of *Kriegsmarine*, of the grandfather who held Paul's first child in his arms, looked down on me from the pale walls. So I went there, I told him. So I went to Berlin, but you know all about that. Now, here I am, back again. Something happened, you know? I'm not sure yet what it was, but something definitely happened. Martin and I are getting to know one another.

The telephone rang. I reached out a hand, lifted the receiver, said cautiously because the hour was late, 'Hello?'

Martin said, 'Everything OK with you?'

'Yes,' I said, 'everything is fine.'

'Well, that's all right then. Just thought I'd make sure you were settled back in –' He paused. 'I also wanted to say thank you.'

The pull of the Deerpark was very strong, more insistent than I had ever known it, as if a will more powerful than my own exerted some magnetic force upon me.

For almost a week I watched the double-decker buses pull away from bus stops on their way to Melton Mowbray, to Nottingham, to the forest heights wherein lay the Medieval Park. In those days I answered letters, telephoned friends, did a token dusting and polishing of rooms I used. Since my absence from it I was more keenly than ever aware that the house and I did not fit one another.

Since Kurt's death I had moved three times; on each occasion I had meant to make a home, to create a garden for my old age. I no longer returned the packing crates provided by removal firms, but stacked them in the cellar, just in case. This vagrant irresponsibility caused concern among family and friends. Even to me, my restlessness appeared excessive. A long dull Sunday spent alone and beside the television screen in my small dark sitting room was the final pressure. On Monday morning I rose early, packed sandwiches and a thermos of coffee in a satchel, put on walking shoes and raincoat, and studied the bus timetable although I did not need to. It was all a part of the pleasure of anticipation, the prospect of escape.

My delight in the yellow double-decker on this particular morning was childlike; it equalled snow at Christmas, marzipan in chocolates. I climbed as ever to the top deck, claimed the front seat and breathed in the smell of stale cigarette smoke, toed to one side the weekend litter of empty Coke cans and crisp packets, and slid back the windows. The rush of air was cool and fresh upon my face. White rags of cloud hung low across the hills, banks of thicker cloud massed darkly in the region of the Deerpark. My spirits lifted. I took pleasure in the little villages, their roofs and pavements damp from early rain, their gardens filled with berried bushes, Michaelmas daisies.

Already I could feel the carriageway tarmac smooth and level underneath my feet, the easement of stiff knee joints as I stretched out into a regular rhythmic stride away from traffic hazards, away from the dark containment of my house. As I stepped down from the bus, the driver said, 'Rain coming.'

'I know,' I said contentedly. 'And it's getting colder.'

I had successfully suppressed all thought of Roman and Jasper; or so I thought; but the very act of walking through the car park brought their images so vividly to mind that my actual sighting of them when it came was almost anticlimactic.

They were no longer colour-matched and style co-ordinated. Roman wore what looked like a flying suit in dense black cotton, a one-piece garment, all slanting zips and cunning little pockets. Jasper's outfit was also warm and multi-zipped, but a brilliant scarlet. This departure from their usual mirror-image of each other alerted me as could nothing else that in my absence a balance had shifted.

I saw as I came closer that Roman's hair was streaked artistically and improbably silver. Bleached spiky curls now nestled between black ones on his forehead and above his ears. A single silver earring of a heavy and intricate design dangled from his right earlobe, giving him an unfinished, lopsided appearance. I regarded him in silence and spoke only to Jasper, who rewarded me with a seraphic smile. I bent to touch the child's plump hand, his cushiony fingers, his soft cheek. For a moment I felt a piercing sadness that he was not a grandchild, that I had no claim to him.

Roman said, 'So you're back then.'

I did not look up. It had happened before, this feeling of withdrawal when I had not seen him for some period of time; this frisson that came close to fear.

I straightened up but did not look in his direction. 'A week ago,' I said.

'Well, you certainly took your time coming out here –'

'I was not aware,' I interrupted, 'that I was under any obligation.'

'Ah-ha! So who rattled your cage in East Berlin?'

Now I looked up; if I could have reached his face I would have slapped it.

'Nobody,' I said tightly, 'rattled my cage in East Berlin. The whole visit was a wonderful experience.'

His tone expressed a degree of boredom that came close to insult. 'You'll have to tell me all about it – sometime or other.'

We began to walk; I took possession of the pushchair as if I had never been away. Roman kept a few strides ahead balancing on the edge of the carriageway, as if he was not really with us. We were on the path that led up to the Ruin when he spoke again. 'You look different,' he said, 'not so up-tight.'

'You're a little altered, too.'

He put a hand up to his hair and swung around to face me. 'You don't like it, do you?'

'No. I don't like it.'

'Why not?'

'You have,' I said slowly, 'the most beautiful hair I have ever seen. I see no good reason why you should have bleached it and glued it into spikes. It makes you look like a demented hedgehog.'

He laughed. 'That's not a bad description of the way I feel.'

So that, I thought, is what this is all about.

'I like the earring.' I sought to distract him from introspection.

He brightened. 'It is pretty special, isn't it?' As he spoke he unhooked the silver from his earlobe and placed it on my outstretched palm. I stroked the exquisite chasing, the inset amethyst and pearls.

'What happened to the other one?'

He turned away, his shoulders bowed; he at once appeared older and yet vulnerable. When he spoke the trace of accent in his voice had deepened. 'The other one is – was – in the possession of someone in my family. An heirloom, I think you call it. They belonged originally to my great-grandmother.'

He had never before spoken about his family, and I had the sensation of one who treads on eggs. I said, riskily, 'I would guess that this is gypsy jewellery. I've seen pictures of Zinte women wearing earrings similar to these.'

'How very clever of you.'

'Oh,' I smiled, 'in my line of work one amasses vast quantities of useless information.'

We came up to the bench beside the wall. I sat down, while Roman stood, hands in pockets, looking out towards the lake. Jasper, in his nest of blankets, slept. It was, I thought again, as if I had never been away.

'So how was Berlin?' His tone was grudging. I knew that he meant East Berlin although he did not say so. He sat down, stiffly and awkwardly, lacking his usual grace of movement.

'There is not very much to tell. It's what politicians call a volatile situation. I'm fearful for my niece and nephew and their families, for my sister-in-law who has a heart condition. Leaving them was one of the hardest things I've ever had to do,' I said.

He stared at me, his pale opalescent eyes opened wide. 'But why should it matter so much to you? You're an Englishwoman. You live safely and cosily in England.'

'It matters to me,' I said quietly, 'because, if he were here, it would have mattered very much to Kurt.'

'But,' he burst out, 'you can't live like that! Your husband's dead, you can't go on carrying torches for him. Dead is dead. Finished. No concern of yours anymore. What about your own life?'

'A good question. One that must occur to a great many widowed women of my generation. We mostly stayed at home and brought up our children. Any other activities were regarded as hobbies – working for pin money was what men called it.'

Roman regarded me with surprise and a degree of interest he did not often show. He spoke kindly to me. 'It's not just your clothes and your bus rides, is it? You're an altogether different species.'

I moved towards the pushchair where Jasper still slept. I bent close, studying his face, the sweet curve of his cheeks, the small straight nose, the firm lips. He smelled of soap and some expensive baby fragrance. Everything about him indicated careful nurturing and forethought. In the three weeks of my absence he had altered, his summer tan was fading; he was, in fact, quite pale. I reached out a tentative hand and smoothed the thick black curls back from his forehead. The bruise spread all along his hairline. A very recent bruise, dark and ugly. The shock of it startled me to silence, my fingers splayed fan-like just above his head.

I straightened up; the concealing curls tumbled back into their usual position. I expected to find Roman's gaze fixed on me, and felt an unease that came close to guilt, as if I had been caught reading someone else's letters. But Roman was already halfway down the track. He called back across his shoulder, 'Hey, come on, Cathy! It's going to pour down any minute now!' He waited for me on the carriageway.

Roman straightened Jasper's blanket, tucking the small hands carefully beneath it. He pulled up the pushchair's hood and fastened the clear plastic cover across the still-sleeping child.

I said, 'Shouldn't he be awake at this time of the morning?'

The closed look was back on Roman's face.

'He's cutting double teeth. I had a bad night with him.'

'He's very pale.'

'He's always pale when he's asleep.'

I seized the pushchair and began to walk briskly towards the car park. Roman lagged behind, his shoulders hunched. He caught up with me as I approached the black van.

'I wanted to talk to you,' he said. 'I mean really talk. I need your advice about something.'

I looked at my watch. 'Sorry,' I said, 'I'll have to go now, my bus is due.'

'I could give you a lift.'

'No, no. I couldn't put you to all that bother. I don't live in your direction anyway.'

'Tomorrow, then. I'll be waiting for you in the café. Your bus gets here at ten-fifteen.' From his pocket he pulled the pale blue timetable of the Forest Busline. 'I always know what time you're likely to turn up.'

I walked away, leaving him beside the van. He shouted after me, 'What's all the hurry? Bus isn't due for another ten minutes. See you tomorrow, eh? In the café. Just *be* there!'

The transition from autumn into winter was hardly noticeable. November came in mild and rainy. Children built Guy Fawkes bonfires; strange sounds continued to come from the airing cupboard each time the central heating unit began its cycle. I made a note on the telephone pad of the Gas Board's emergency number. Having once decided that I would not think about it, the fact of the bruise was the only thought that filled my mind. I should, of course, have taxed Roman with it, demanded explanation. It was the coward in my soul, the craven, that had restrained me; and I had misjudged him once before, had seen him as an abductor of infants. The most I could do, or perhaps the least, was to keep a watchful eye.

The café opened later in autumn; my arrival coincided with the laying of clean cloths on the rustic-style tables, with the first fragrance of percolating coffee, the sweeping-up of fallen leaves from the entrance porch.

'I'm waiting for a friend,' I told the waitress, and then began privately to question the accuracy of this description of Roman. He was, I concluded, more like an obligation; even so, my involvement with him had a curious inevitability, and there was always the child. The relief I felt on their safe arrival at the café was the most disturbing factor.

My gaze went straight away to Jasper. He was sitting upright in the pushchair; he waved a striped plush tiger at me and made greeting noises. There was colour in his cheeks; he smiled his toothy smile. The turning over of one's heart was surely a physical impossibility, and yet that was exactly what I felt. Roman was more difficult to read. Again he wore the zipped black outfit, but topped off by a matching baseball cap that concealed completely his two-toned hair. The single earring had also disappeared. I at once felt more at ease with him, more able to see him as responsible; as a father should be. He lifted Jasper from the pushchair and placed him carefully into the high chair provided by the café. His handling of the child this morning was cautious to the point of nervousness; or was it, I wondered, a performance to impress me? He was like an actor, always on stage. I could not rid myself of the frightening suspicion that he was not quite real; that from my loneliness of spirit I had conjured him up from the glossy pages of magazines like *Cosmopolitan* or *Elle*. Or was his tender handling of Jasper a necessary kindness? Were other, more extensive, bruises concealed by the little scarlet suit?

Roman, when contrite, was almost irresistible. This morning he was solicitous, hanging up my raincoat and umbrella, insisting that I take the seat beside the window which offered the best view of the Deerpark. He ordered coffee for two, warm milk and biscuits for Jasper. He removed the baseball cap to reveal a head of hair that was once more uniformly black.

He shrugged at my surprised look. 'Well – it did look pretty silly. You were absolutely right.' Implicit in the words was regret for his behaviour of the previous day. I poured coffee into thick cups and learned that Roman, predictably, took his black and without sugar. I added cream and sugar to my own cup, selected a biscuit and then pushed the plate towards him. The small domesticity of it all, Jasper beside me, shortcake in one plump hand, feeder-cup in the other, made my fears of yesterday seem groundless. On the other hand, meeting like this by appointment and within walls established my attachment to these two in a way I had not anticipated. In the Deerpark our meetings, although not always accidental, could be made to seem so. By this means I had preserved a certain freedom for myself. Now, even if we had not actually broken bread together, we had broken biscuits. The thought made me smile.

Roman said, 'This is nice. We should have come here sooner.' His eyes, intelligent and watchful, challenged me to disagree. 'We might even be a family, on an outing together.' He did not say we looked like mother, son, and grandchild, but that was what he meant.

I said, 'How is Serena?'

He was not often disconcerted; I observed the slow contraction of his facial muscles, the hardened jawline. But when he answered his voice was noncommittal, as if he spoke about a seldom-seen acquaintance. 'Serena? Oh, she's OK. Our paths don't seem to cross very often these days.'

I searched for the words that he would be likely to comprehend. 'You're not chasing some other girl, are you? You're not into a new relationship?'

He leaned urgently towards me across the table; his grip on my upper arm was fierce and unexpected. 'You don't even begin to understand, do you?'

He released his hold; whatever anger he had felt began to seep away, leaching all colour from his face. His pallor alarmed me. 'I think,' I said, 'you had better talk to me about it.'

'Not here.'

'Very well. Let's walk, shall we?'

I watched him as he lifted Jasper from the high chair, wiped the child's mouth and fingers and strapped him back into the pushchair. His movements were controlled, careful;

he would, I imagined, always be meticulous in what he did. I left the café and crossed over to the car park, glad to be back in the cold moist air. He caught up with me as I came into the Park. I took the pushchair from him and saw again how his hands at once were thrust deep into his pockets, as if in relief that a burden had been momentarily sidestepped. Joggers passed us on the carriageway; I watched them out of sight, the jewel colours of their tracksuits showing bright against the dun shades of the hillside.

I said, 'Well then –?'

'Yes,' he said. 'Whatever I say you're bound to think badly of me.'

'Try me.'

'Let's get one thing straight. There is no other girl, no relationships – nothing!'

He stretched out his hand and tapped the pushchair's hood. 'Twenty-four hours a day, seven days a week. Doesn't leave much space for dalliance, does it?'

'But surely Serena –?'

'No. As I've said before, on a scale of one to ten for mother love, Serena would score two.'

I said, 'You could afford professional care for Jasper – a well-trained nanny?'

'No!'

'But why not?'

He did not answer straight away. When he spoke his accent became more Slavic than it had ever been. 'The first months and years of a life are very important. Would you not say so?'

'Yes. I would say so.'

'Then consider. What is the first thing you can remember?'

I said, without needing to think about it, 'A quarrel. Raised voices. Myself very small. When I cried the shouting stopped.' I paused. 'Other things. A field where cowslips grew so thickly that the hillside seemed bathed in perpetual sunshine.

A hedgerow favoured by snails, their shells wonderfully whorled and patterned. Gypsies coming and going in the lane; the bowed shape of their wagons. Myself, crying in the night after frightening dreams.'

'You see,' he shouted, 'good and bad things! I want Jasper's first memories to be all good. I want him to remember this place; trees and water, the deer feeding in the bracken, and me always with him. A father should be first in a boy's life. Who knows what a nanny might put into his mind?'

I said, 'You don't much like women, do you?'

'Perhaps it is the women who do not like me.'

I smiled. 'I can imagine that a great many young women would find it no strain at all to love you. But there are moments, I agree, when you are not particularly likeable.'

I glanced nervously at him then, but Roman was never offended by plain speaking. His only sign of distress was the hunching of his shoulders in the familiar pose of melancholy. My footsteps slowed until the pushchair and I were almost stationary. This time I had expected candour from him, a clear statement of his troubles. Instead, he was doing what he always did – tempting me down paths of argument that led away from his main grievance, whatever that was. I halted on the carriageway and observed the long black shape of him walking on against the grey skies. This really, I told myself, could not continue. There was urgent business of my own to which I should be attending. But my change of pace had alerted Jasper; he stirred beneath the plastic hood, looked up at me and smiled in the sweet and trusting way that is exclusive to small children. I could just make out the yellowing edge of the bruise beneath the dark curls. I began to walk; Jasper settled back against his pillow. The trouble, I thought, was partly of my own making. I had this reluctance to question people; to probe, I believed, was ill-mannered, to be intrusive was to run the risk of being considered prying. People, I had always maintained, if they really wanted to confide, would do so of their own free will. But not Roman. I was aware of a growing lassitude within myself; wondering about him used up more emotion than I could comfortably spare. I increased my pace until I drew level with him. Breathless but resolute I asked, 'Where exactly do you live? I don't believe you ever told me.'

He said, with no sign of resentment, 'In an apartment, above our main boutique in the middle of the city. It's not ideal for Jasper, but our capital is tied up in the business — and anyway — Serena loves it.' His tone changed from bored to curious. 'I thought you knew all this? I'm sure I told you.'

'No,' I said, 'I didn't know.' Emboldened by his words I asked, 'Don't you think that if I knew a little more about you it might be a help?'

The stance he now adopted was deliberately informative, as if he mocked me. 'Well now, let me see. I live with my wife and child in this unbelievable flat which is situated in an exclusive mall in a nearby city. We have Laura Ashley wallpaper and squashy sofas, all flowery chintz and scatter cushions. We have antique pine, and arrangements of dried flowers in little wicker baskets. In the kitchen we have genuine old butchers' marble counter-tops, and a lot of antique wooden implements and kitchen gear that Serena tells me are known as 'treen'. Our child's room is unreal. His wallpaper already leads him to believe that rabbits wear waistcoats, that bears wear pinafores and slippers, that small animals live in furnished accommodation in hollowed-out oak trees.'

'Where's the harm in that?' I asked mildly. 'I would hardly have called Beatrix Potter subversive.'

The rage he turned upon me was controlled, but only just. 'By the time I was five years old I had lived in a dozen countries. Animals, to me, were creatures to be feared, respected. Bears danced on the end of a chain for a crowd's entertainment. Rabbits were for the pot.'

'Yes,' I said slowly, 'well, I can see how all that would affect your view of life.' I willed my face to remain still and calm; in my mind I felt a powerful quickening of interest, a surging of excitement. There were other questions I would like to ask him. Which countries? What about his parents? Most important of all, what misadventure had brought him to an English deerpark on a wet day in November to confide the anguish of his soul to a stranger?

I said, 'The realities of life for most of us become apparent all too soon. It does no harm to defer them for a few years.' I pointed at the striped plush toy in Jasper's arms. 'After all, you haven't given him a live tiger cub to play with, have you?'

Roman's laughter was harsh, but at least he laughed. 'All right, all right! So I get a bit uptight about some things.' He paused. 'It's being so much on my own.' The admission did not come easily from him. 'Brooding – you know? I do a lot of brooding.' He smiled down at me and the smile was Jasper's, trusting and open and quite impossible to disregard. Now I thought I saw what I had missed, and my belated insight into his condition shamed me.

'You're lonely,' I said wonderingly. 'That's what it all comes down to. Isolation. Lack of contact with your own kind. Although,' I added, 'I don't suppose that house-husbands are too thick on the ground for company in Leicestershire.'

'Too right they aren't! I tried joining groups – but the other mothers gave me funny looks and didn't speak to me. I used to take him to town parks – he loves the swings – but I got snide remarks like, was I on shift work? And how nice that I always seemed to have so much free time? In the baby clinic they treated me like I was some weird species. I was given longer sessions than the other mothers. I got them all: health visitors, social workers, paediatricians! I don't go there any more. Why should I? I check up in the child-care books. He's absolutely normal for his age. There is nothing they can tell me that I really need to know.'

I said, 'Perhaps it's you they need to check on? Your state of tension?'

He swung round to face me and said, 'Don't get me wrong. I set up this whole scenario; it's what I want, the way I planned it.'

'I'm sure it is what you want. What you couldn't have planned for was your own needs. How long is it since you and Serena had an evening out together? When did you last have a couple of hours when you were free to do anything you wanted for yourself? I suspect,' I went on, 'that your evenings and Sundays are taken up with managing your boutique business?'

He nodded.

'What about a babysitter?'

'We tried it once. She was very young, she brought her boyfriend. We were burgled one week later. End of story.'

'Somebody older then? Someone like –'

He smiled. 'Like you?'

We had walked much further than was usual. The end of the carriageway was in sight. Grey stone walls marked the boundaries of safety for red deer and for humans. Beyond them traffic sped dangerously through narrow lanes.

So here we are, I thought, arrived at last at the point to which he had, all along, almost certainly intended to bring me.

'I could have him with me for a few hours every week. If that is what you really want,' I said.

113

'I would appreciate it.'

'Very well then!' Having made the offer of assistance I found it easy to be decisive about future plans. 'But not immediately. I have a hardback publication coming up early next month. It will take me away for ten days at least. When I come back –'

'We'll still be here, waiting for you.'

The publication of a book and the necessary contact with people who arranged such matters had become familiar to me in recent years. So familiar, that this time I hardly registered the absence of the routine phone-calls and letters which informed me of dates, events, my required presence in distant towns and cities. On my return from Berlin I had half expected to find word from London. Two and a half weeks to countdown, and I grew uneasy at the continued silence. But former publication days had always gone smoothly, hadn't they? I recalled signing sessions; ten previous occasions made easy by thoughtful publishers. Once I had appeared in the shop window of a prestigious London store, twice in a village bookshop and, more recently, in the West Country town where, of all places in the world, I felt most at home. Better not start phoning London and chivvying people, I thought. I did not wish to gain a reputation for author interference or prima-donna delusions. In any case, my natural inclination was to trust in the infallibility of others.

On Wednesday I visited Eileen. We talked about winter plans; the twice-monthly visits made together to the Recorded Music Society, a possible December trip to the Lincoln Christmas Market; a weekend in Paris to visit art galleries, often discussed but never achieved.

'And when,' asked Eileen, 'is your publication date?'

'November 19th. Or at least, that's what they told me.'

'But that's just over a week away!'

'I know. I suppose I ought to get in touch.'

'Do it tomorrow,' said Eileen firmly. 'First thing in the morning.'

My reluctance even to dial the London number was a measure of my unease. From his cage the budgerigar observed me, his head sagaciously inclined. Eileen had shown me an article in the *Observer* which described the confusion visited upon authors by the recent changes in certain publishing houses. I punched out the digits, made the connection, inquired if I might speak to my editor.

'Oh – sorry,' said the bright young voice, 'I'm afraid she is no longer with us. She left at the end of September. Perhaps I can help you?'

I had known that my editor was leaving, but had believed, mistakenly it seemed, that this amicable and efficient lady would remain in the office at least until Christmas, until after my publication. Shocked, but not wishing to sound pushy, I said, 'Well – it's like this – I've got a book coming out next week, and so far there's been no word from your office about events. There's usually a couple of signings, local radio broadcasts, newspaper interviews – you know the sort of thing.'

'Ah,' said the girl, but more thoughtfully this time. 'What did you say your name was?' I told her. 'Mm-mm,' the voice, no longer bright or thoughtful, became flat and noncommittal. 'You really need to speak to Hepzibah. She's our new person in this office. But she's not here at the moment. Perhaps you could call back?'

I agreed that I would do so. I replaced the handset with a tiny crash of irritation. The budgerigar, who did not like loud noises, ruffled his feathers and looked aggrieved.

'There was,' I told him, 'something rather worrying about that conversation.'

I turned my back upon the telephone and began to rifle through *The Times* in search of the section labelled Overseas News. Since my return from West Berlin I had invested in a daily paper. Part of each day was spent in the comparison of radio and television newscasts with newspaper reports. I was probably as well informed on the German situation as any British politician. Political unrest continued to escalate, East Berliners massed in the Alexander Platz shouting 'Egon Krenz – here we come!'

'Trust our policy of renewal,' answered Krenz. 'Your place, dear citizens, is here. Do not leave our homeland. Each one of you which leaves is one too many!'

Other marches, said *The Times*, had taken place that weekend in Leipzig, Dresden, Magdeburg and Rostock. It was in Rostock that the State Police had their Stasi headquarters, and the population of that town, I read, were now calling for the disbandment of the hated Stasi.

No word had come from Christina since our parting in West Berlin, but there had not been time, I told myself. A phone call from Melanie had confirmed that she and Ryan had also received no news from Dresden. But, as Melanie said, postal and telephone communication between East and West had almost broken down.

The mellow weather had returned. The sun, slanted low across the land, gave light but little warmth. My euphoria, legacy of the magical Berlin days, had seeped gradually away; what remained was the new, unspoken understanding between Martin and myself, and my fear for Christina to which I could not put a name. My anticipation of the winter days was as keen as it had ever been. Summer offered no challenge; I had always suspected the heat and sunshine, the indolence of warm days, of easy living. Now in November I looked forward to small adventures, forays into adjacent counties, visits to book fairs and antique markets. By travelling to Leicester, I had just discovered, it was possible on a change of buses to extend my journeys into Lincolnshire, Warwickshire, to reach within the day Stamford, Peterborough, Northampton even.

The new notebook, purchased for the novel which I could not write, still lay where I had thrown it months ago, at the far edge of my desk. The time was not yet right; I doubted that it ever would be. Talking to Roman about the past had altered the pattern of the present. I had not yet found the courage to confess to my publisher and agent that there was no new book in preparation. I had a sense of waiting for momentous events, of impending change.

Martin phoned that evening; I answered his greeting with a quickening of the heart, a warmth of tone that must, I imagined, still be as novel to him as it was to me. The subject of conversation came around inevitably to Berlin.

'Things are coming to a climax!' He spoke with the enthusiasm of one who was too young to remember the bad days of the Cold War. 'From day to day, hour to hour, the people are becoming stronger. Krenz won't hold them back much longer.' I recalled the spring of 1953; tanks in the streets of East Berlin, the shootings, the reprisals. 'Insurrection' they had called it that time.

I said, 'Martin – I'm so frightened for them. It could all go dreadfully wrong.'

'It won't,' he said. 'This is not a handful of people protesting, it's most of eastern Europe.' I could sense his smile. 'It's been a long hot summer. It's left you a bit on edge – it always does. I'll be over to see you at the weekend.'

I replaced the handset, but gently this time. Tomorrow I must telephone London, seek out Hepzibah, be firm, decisive.

The room, like the evening, was growing dark; I leaned back into the leather armchair, did not switch on lamps. Roman had accused me of living in the past; it was not altogether true. More accurate would be to say that I was never too firmly fixed in the present. It required a particular set of circumstances to take me all the way back. Memory, I found, could be revived by happenstance: a snatch of song, a scent, a certain kind of morning, an emotive phrase. My father had used Martin's very words back in 1947. 'It's been a long hot summer,' he had said, 'no wonder you're on edge, stuck in that office full of old folks.' My father had understood my determination to escape. He, in his turn, had also made a few memorable departures. My mother had, from the very first word, set her face against the project.

'You?' she had said. 'In the Women's Land Army? You won't survive the first week. As for a winter working in the open fields –'

I had been a small and skinny child. In spite of Virol and Parrishes Food, and bottles of red-coloured tonic from the doctor, my arms and legs remained sticklike, my shoulder-blades protruding through my gymslip like the burgeoning of angel's wings. My father had described me as 'vinnied', which in Somerset means 'blue-veined'. My mother was surprised at my continued survival. Because of my frail looks I never learned to swim or play games. No one had expected it of me.

1947 had been the year of my rebellion, my nineteenth birthday, the signal for a first move towards independence. I would never know what perversity of mind had led me to the Women's Land Army recruiting office. With the war already two years over I could hardly claim patriotism. My stated reasons varied according to the questioner. To my mother I said loftily, 'It's in my blood – a love of the country. You come from a farming family. I'm just a throwback.'

To friends I said more honestly, 'I'm fed up with labouring at the Ministry of Labour.'

My father it was who said, 'Try it. You can always come home if you don't like it.'

I had found the uniform attractive; the recruitment posters showing a rosy-cheeked land-girl clutching a small white lamb to her green woollen jersey appealed to my sense of the romantic. I imagined myself, riding high on laden harvest wagons, gathering eggs in a wicker basket, stroking new-born calves.

I took the train to Leicester on a thundery afternoon in early August. The application forms were in my handbag filled out in my best Civil Service script, my hair brushed, my dress neat, my sandals whitened. Before announcing my intention to family and friends I had made sure that the Land Army in 1947 was still urgently in need of young women of willing spirit and an open mind when it came to performing unpalatable tasks.

The Land Army office was housed in a large Victorian villa close by the railway station. The Recruiting Officer was middle-aged and plump, her yellow hair set in ridged waves, her cheeks pink. After five minutes of probing conversation and a close study of the application form, the lady smiled a condescending smile.

'It would seem that you have an excellent position in the

Civil Service. I feel that you would be most unwise to leave it.'

Deliberately obtuse, I chose not to acknowledge the drift of this remark. 'I would prefer,' I said, 'to live-in with the farmer and his family. I don't care for the idea of hostel life.'

The Recruiting Officer looked doubtfully at me. 'We prefer our girls to be a little more robust.' She tapped the form. 'You say here that you have never suffered any major illness?'

Remembering schoolmates who had fallen to the scourges of diptheria and tuberculosis I said, 'I was saved by Virol and red flannel. I've hardly ever ailed at all.'

A silence fell and lengthened. But I, who had spent the last two years behind a similar desk, employed in the business of directing people to jobs of national importance to which they had no desire to go, was not intimidated. I leaned back in my chair; my hair had grown very long that summer, I could feel the weight of it across my shoulders. Short would be better, I decided, under those natty little felt hats that were Land Army issue; very short, in fact.

The blonde lady fiddled uncomfortably with her double string of matched pearls. The 'county' accent intensified. She said, 'You will, of course, need to pass our medical examination.'

I nodded.

'Take this green form to the address printed on it. Our doctor sees prospective candidates between three and four o'clock. Meanwhile, I suggest you think long and hard about your future prospects.'

The doctor, employed by the Land Army to confirm that recruits were unlikely to collapse when lifting milk buckets or driving tractors, was young and good-looking. He asked me at once, in a practised unromantic manner, if I would meet him in a local bar that evening. His speech, I thought, was rather slurred. He accepted my refusal without rancour, and reached across the narrow desk to clasp my left wrist. After a few seconds' contact with my pulse he abandoned my hand, took up his pen and scrawled his name across the green form.

I said, surprised, 'Is that all?' He was, I concluded, very drunk, although his manner towards me had not been improper.

Now he leered, 'What else would you like me to do, eh?'

I stood up, grabbed the form and backed away. My experience of men had been limited to long walks and cinema visits, first with a lay preacher who also played the organ in his church, and lately with an effeminate young man who talked a lot about his mother.

Seated once more before the Recruiting Officer, the urge to complain about the doctor was very great. I studied the piece of paper in my hand. All I had wanted was his signature; any complaint I made about his thoroughness would be bound to invalidate the green form. Why muddy the waters?

'Passed A1,' I said, unable to keep triumph from my voice. The Recruiting Officer began to twist individual pearls upon the necklace string. I now recognized this to be a bad sign. Rejection by the Land Army was something I had never thought of; now that acceptance seemed in doubt I knew that to be a land-girl was my sole ambition.

'Are you absolutely sure that this is what you want? You are not, I am bound to say, the usual sort of girl who applies to join us. In fact, of all the applicants who have ever come before me, I would describe you as being the least likely!'

'I really do know what's involved,' I said. 'I'm not afraid of hard work or getting dirty.' Why, I thought, I had never so much as flinched when changing the inky typewriter ribbon on my Imperial machine at the Ministry of Labour.

'I just don't want you to do anything that you will later regret. You have such a good and safe career – it does seem such a pity.'

'But I want to do something else. That is why I'm here.' The urgency in my voice caused the pearls to be abandoned for the pen.

'Very well. But I suggest that you aim for poultry-girl or market garden. The work is less arduous.' A drawer was pulled open and a file consulted. 'We have a placing in Cambridgeshire that might suit. Poultry-girl, to live-in with family. It's a very isolated spot, two miles' walk to the nearest bus stop. No electricity, no laid-on water. How do you feel about oil lamps and pumps?'

I had no experience of either, but nodded cheerfully; I had an altogether different exclusion on my mind.

'I won't have to work with German prisoners-of-war, will I?' I asked.

'It's highly unlikely,' I was told. 'They're all being repatriated anyway. There are very few still left in England.'

My papers, I was told, would take a week to process. I was to return on the following Monday, bringing with me a large suitcase. Uniform would then be issued, and all arrangements finalized.

On September 22nd, 1947 I travelled into Cambridgeshire, confident in the possession of a book found on a second-hand stall entitled *Keeping Hens in Wartime*. Also tucked into my suitcase was a tube of handcream and a bottle of liniment for the relief of aching joints, pressed upon me by my mother.

*

The morning phone call to London was not reassuring. Hepzibah remained elusive.

'I'm afraid she won't be in the office until Monday.' The bright young voice was remote, unconcerned.

'Perhaps I might speak to her then?'

'Yes, of course.' A note of irritation came clearly down the line. 'But you really have no need to worry. I'm quite sure that everything's in hand.'

As soon as the connection was cut I knew that I should have been assertive, demanding, even angry. I thought regretfully of the long and trustful years with my former editor. I had never been good about meeting new people, getting on with strangers.

My dreams that night had been confused but happy. I had wakened with the feeling of other years still in my mind. My triple anxieties, of East Berlin, Jasper, and the unresolved publication, were overlaid today by the aura of that golden autumn of 1947. The farm must still be there, tucked into the hollow underneath the hill; such places were forever, as immovable as churches. I remembered my first sighting of it, and with the memory came a longing to return. I had noticed lately that the girl I had once been had an increasing tendency to re-emerge through the overlay of years. I consulted a timetable and discovered that the Peterborough bus, which left Leicester at nine every morning, was routed to take me as close to the farm on which I had worked as a land-girl as it was possible to reach by public transport.

The Peterborough bus was warm and well-sprung, with plush upholstered seats and clean floors. The driver wore a white uniform-shirt with dark blue epaulettes and a company tie. His driving as he negotiated the traffic of Leicester's suburbs was smooth and skilled. On my scale of awards this eastern busline merited three stars.

The November day was cool and quiet; now we were coming into country that was exactly as my mind had stored it: gently rolling wolds, the farmhouses and outbuildings shrouded in a white mist, old trees and hedges. The route wound in and out of adjacent counties, skimming the edge of Rutlandshire, dipping briefly towards Cambridgeshire; a landscape in which villages were few. I saw a pony eating apples from the low branches of an orchard; great golden stacks of rolled straw; for a mile or two the rich red earth of the potato fields of Lincolnshire; the tender green of fields of half-grown cabbage.

Then all at once, around a corner unexpectedly, dramatic in black and white, I read the name of the village in which Kurt had once been detained.

I rose abruptly and moved towards the driver. 'Will you drop me here?'

'You've paid as far as Peterborough. I can't give you a refund.'

'I know. It really doesn't matter. I've just remembered something that I have to do in this place.'

I left the bus and began to walk. When I reached a high point from which it was possible to see clear away to the horizon, I remained for a long time, absolutely still. Somewhere among these fields and hills had stood the huddle of corrugated huts and latrines, the cookhouse and the officers' quarters, the guard house and the barbed wire of Prisoner-of-War Camp Number 186.

It had taken twenty years of marriage before Kurt had found it possible to speak about those years. Oh, I had asked him.

'Tell me,' I had said, 'how did you feel? What did you

124

think? Did you still believe that Germany would win the war? Were you glad when they captured you in France?'

He had turned away, retreated into silences that I could not endure. In the end I had learned to accept the limits that he set, had recognized in time the trespass signals in his eyes, and known my place.

It was in the third year of his illness that he had said, 'It's hard to believe that one's father is dead when the news arrives two years after the event.'

When he finally trusted me enough to speak his sorrow I had not known how to answer him, could only say, 'That must have been awful for you.'

I walked back into the village. In the pub I found a quiet corner by a window. I ordered sandwiches and soup. In my head Kurt's voice still spoke.

'It was a Sunday in November, 1946. We were taken out from the camp to work on farms on every weekday. On Sundays we washed our clothes, darned our socks and cleaned our boots. Church service was at eleven. Afterwards our Pastor handed out letters. There was never post for me. I no longer looked for any.' Kurt paused. I waited. He said at last, 'It was a postcard, covered in my mother's tiny writing, and in pencil. She said that in November 1944 a printed card had reached her from England telling her that I was a prisoner-of-war. The first letter from me did not reach her until July 1946. I had started that letter with the words 'My dear parents'. She went on to say that our dear Papa had fallen in battle, in Minsk, in September 1944. My mind could not seem to take this in. My father – already two years dead – and I had not known – had never considered the possibility that he might not survive.' Again Kurt paused and I waited.

'I remember going out of the hut and walking to the

furthest line of barbed wire. I lay down on the ground. It was very cold; soon it was dark. I guessed that I had missed evening roll-call, that there would be trouble, but I could not go back into the hut. After a time the big searchlights were switched on and I knew that the guards were looking for me. In the end it was one of my own *kameraden* who found me. The British gave me three days on bread and water for absenting myself from roll-call. Until then,' he said, 'I had not really minded my prisoner-of-war time. It was a fact of life that could not be altered. The war was over. One day they would have to let us go. But the news of my father's death changed my whole way of thinking. Freedom is a state of mind, and now I knew that I had been a prisoner long before the British caught me. I had been locked away and under orders since the day in 1940 when the telegram had come for me to report to Kiel, to join the *Kriegsmarine*. I began to think about my childhood, growing up in Mechtenhagen, about my parents; how sweet the life was that we had together. If there were bad days I could not recall them. I remembered only sunshine; gathering mushrooms and blueberries in the forests; walking with my father on Sunday afternoons; the bicycle that was a present on my sixteenth birthday. He was a quiet man, my father. A very good man. The last time I saw him we were both on leave together. He was convalescent, still walked with crutches. A gun-carriage had rolled across both his legs and broken them. He was ordered back to fight in Russia while he still needed sticks to get around – I try not to remember him like that.' He sighed. 'I carried my mother's postcard everywhere with me; even when the pencilled words were all rubbed off, I still kept it in my pocket. And now, oh how I wanted to be free! I began to watch the English gentry and the farmers as they rode out to hounds on winter mornings. I asked the camp guards about fox-hunting, about the beautiful mounts that they called hunters. I longed to sit again astride a stallion. Such horses, they told me, were bred and trained on local farms. At about that time the rules were changed; trusted prisoners were allowed to leave the camp and live-in with a farmer and his family. I thought about it. I spoke no English, but I could milk cows, work with horses, do any job around a farm. It would be a kind of freedom. No more barbed wire, no roll-call.'

I had said, 'So that is why you came to Hobart's. Why you were so bitter, so angry, when I first met you. I wish I had known then, about your father.'

Kurt's son had learned about his father's death only minutes after the event. Martin had heard the news in the early hours of a January morning, the words crackling out from the radio transmitter of a police car which had come to rush him to Kurt's bedside.

He was told, regretfully, in a hospital corridor, that his mother had for many hours refused to supply the name and address that would have enabled the doctors to summon him sooner.

I finished the sandwiches and soup; there was no reason for me to linger in the pub, and yet I made no move to leave.

It was called the Fox and Hounds. The bar-room walls were hung with sporting prints and hunting horns. From my table by the window I could see the long length of the tidy village street. A few late lunchtime drinkers chatted quietly beside the bar. The payphone stood in a corner near the door. I counted up my small change. Time was when my temper had flared swiftly; the years had slowed my potentiality for anger to a dull burn. I lifted the handset, dialled the sequence of numbers that would connect me to London. My request to speak to Hepzibah again received the stock and breezy answer. 'I'm sorry, she's not back yet, and I'm not sure when she will be.'

I stared at an old print on the wall which showed a strangely elongated white horse leaping over a dangerously high hedge. I braced myself to use the jargon understood by publicity people. I said, 'My publication date is now three days away. It would seem that I have no itinerary of media events, no travel arrangements, and no hotel reservations.'

'We assumed,' said the voice, 'that you would be driving yourself down to the West Country.'

'There and back in the same day?'

'Well – yes.'

'In the first place,' I said, 'I do not drive, and even if I did, this would be a round trip of something like four hundred miles, with a signing session and newspaper interviews sandwiched in between.'

'Oh. Oh well, in that case I'll have to book you a hotel room. No problem at all. What about your rail tickets?'

'I'll attend to that myself, and bill you for it.'

'Fine! Super! Well, nice to talk to you. We'll be in touch.'

The next bus through the village would take me close to Hobart's farm. I studied the picture of the white horse which would never now reach the far side of the hedge. I thought about my house, the damp smell rising from the cellar, the desk piled high with unanswered letters. The bus stop stood opposite the pub; I could see people gathering beside it. I went out to join them.

I did not believe in pilgrimages. The game of 'then' and 'now' was usually too risky. As the road began to climb across the wolds a misty sun appeared between the cloud layers, touching the blur of distant woodlands with a golden nimbus. I loved the drama of the winter skies; was comfortable with a sun that gave light but no warmth.

Memory, if buried deeply enough, can deny almost any truth. It was easy to forget a place, a time, if that was the intention. I had never meant to travel this road, to indulge this very private nostalgia. To contemplate myself when young would be a subtle kind of torment.

The bus halted at a crossroads; a twisting lane led down into a valley. I asked the driver, 'Do you return by this route?'

'Be back this way in half an hour,' he said, 'be sure you're waiting, though. I only come up here on a Monday.'

For the second time that day I stood in a high place; Hobart's farm was still tucked up neatly underneath the hill, Chilton's spread out across the lower reaches of the valley. A narrow lane edged with hawthorn still marked the boundary between them.

Many things were changed. Striplings had grown into mature trees. Hedges had been grubbed-out, turning narrow pastures into broad areas of ploughland. I remembered old gates that creaked on rusty hinges, the dipping unsafe roofs of ancient cowsheds, shabby stables, a muddy track that led up to the farmhouse.

Tarmac had replaced the muddy track; vast Dutch barns now stood in the place of old brick sheds. An expensive cabined tractor moved slowly on the hill behind the house.

A few fields remained hedged and gated. The Home field lay as it had always done, under pasture with a swift brook running through it. The stables, their ancient brickworks now pinned and braced, still leaned dangerously inwards towards the midden.

So when had it begun, my movement outwards towards the wide world? I recalled the urgency of those days and weeks that led up to my departure; the inevitability of it that both charmed and terrified. Sometimes I seemed to be acting in a film or play without knowing the story, or my precise role in it, except that leaving home was my only option.

Arrivals and departures carry penalties and risks. Some things you take with you, some you leave behind. In this isolated valley I had made promises that I could not keep. Because I was young and immature, I had comprehended no feelings other than my own.

I came first to Chilton's on a day in early autumn. Brightly patterned curtains fluttered in the breeze from open windows, freckled mirrors reflected images of chrysanthemums and late roses arranged in brown jugs. The house had a front and back staircase; I was told kindly but firmly that the front stairs, carpeted in blue, were not for my use. The stairs which led up to my bedroom were uncarpeted and narrow. I was to feel like a Victorian housemaid every time I used them.

My bedroom was large. It had a tiny sliding window which looked out on a steep hill crowned with trees. The stone floor was bare except for sheepskin rugs thrown down like stepping-stones between bed and dressing-table and wardrobe. A candle in a blue tin holder stood on a night table. I unpacked the few books I had brought with me: the poems of John Keats, an Edgar Wallace mystery. The book entitled *Keeping Hens in Wartime* I hid beneath a stack of cotton dungarees, together with the liniment and handcream.

My weeks of training brought equal measures of triumph and disaster. The horse was old and crafty. By means of standing on a box I succeeded in putting on his collar and harness; trembling and voiceless, I backed him between the farmcart shafts. It was out in the lane, when I stood high on the cart, reins in hand, that he maliciously took a gateway at too sharp an angle. The gatepost split and fell. I lay winded on the ground beside it. The decision was made, reluctantly, by my employer that I should use the tractor in future.

Once shown the steering wheel, the choke and brake, I drove as recklessly and fast as the engine would permit. My period of training ended and, by this time, I was suffering the extreme exhaustion predicted by my mother. I was woken at five every morning by heavy knocking on my bedroom door. My first task was to light the range fire with kindling I had chopped on the previous day. Only if the kettle boiled quickly could I drink a cup of tea. It was expected that I would have mixed twenty buckets of poultry-mash, filled the water-wagon, started up the tractor and left the yard by six o'clock.

Breakfast was at nine, lunch at one-thirty; supper was a mug of cocoa, homebaked bread and a wedge of Stilton. The food was plentiful and good; of a quality unknown to an urban population for which, after years of wartime depriva-tion, bread was still rationed and meat eaten once or twice in any week. To begin with I had lost weight. With the onset of the winter weather my appetite sharpened. The breeches and sweater, which had hung in folds on my small and bony frame, now began to fit me in a way that drew whistles from the farm boys. I spent time every evening before the triple mirrors of my dressing-table, observing by candlelight the interesting changes in my hitherto boyish silhouette. Milk puddings, and home-cured bacon, had wrought a transforma-tion never achieved by Virol and the doctor's iron tonic. My hair shone; I had a fresh high colour in my cheeks. Amazingly, I was coming to resemble the land-girl of the Government's recruiting poster.

There came a day when I no longer ached and yawned, and fell asleep at seven every evening. The skin of my palms began to harden over, although the rough wool of service-issue socks would always skin my feet. From the wireless in the farmhouse kitchen came the music of romantic songs from London shows. Gracie Fields sang 'Now is the Hour' and 'How are Things in Glocca Morra?' For the first time I felt strong and energetic. There had been so little in my life that summer, and I had hoped for so much more. The men who worked on the farm were middle-aged, long married. The boys were raw youths. I had dreamed of romance in the greenwood.

At threshing-time the Chiltons and Hobarts combined their workforces. The arrangement was reciprocal, long-standing. My task was to take food and drink into the field twice daily – hot tea in a metal can, thick sandwiches and cake packed in a wicker basket.

The corn-stacks stood in the Home field which lay before the farmhouse. I regretted the need to walk there on my sore feet. I was also resentful that these trivial domestic chores around the farm seemed always to fall to the resident land-girl. I was less than gracious as I doled out sandwiches and poured tea into brown mugs. The two men from Hobart's who sat deliberately far apart from the main team were an added source of annoyance. Any extra steps were painful. If I had dared to ignore their presence I would have done so. And then, as I approached them, I saw that they were deeply tanned, fair-haired and unexpectedly good-looking. My shoulders straightened; I swung the wicker basket, tried not to limp, was glad about the new green ribbon in my hair. As I poured tea into his mug the younger man lifted his chin, pushed the thick blond hair from his forehead and feigned an extravagant, wide-eyed amazement. His eyes were blue and knowing; they matched exactly the colour of his shirt and dungarees. I thought I had seen his sort before, wolf-whistling on street corners. When I offered each man a choice of ham or cheese sandwiches, they shrugged and smiled but did not speak. I walked back to where the other men were seated: there was still tea in the can, food in the basket. From the safety of distance I watched the two who sat beside the far hedge. The cheeky one no longer feigned amazement but looked at me with serious regard; I saw now the golden skin of his bare arms, the many shades of blond streaked by the sun into his thick hair, his long upper lip and high cheekbones, the hard line of jaw and square chin.

I walked back to the farmhouse, and now saw, as if for the first time, that the sun hung low in the October sky; that the air was sharp like new wine, and berries of scarlet hip and crimson hawthorn dripped from the hedges. The valley was beautiful; when I thought about the young man in the blue shirt I felt weak, as if all my bones had softened.

This was, I thought, what people must mean when they talked about falling in love.

It was at breakfast the next morning that my employer, speaking to his wife but looking sideways at me, said, 'Those two German prisoners from Hobart's work very well atop the stack.' He paused. 'As long as we all remember that fraternization with them is strictly forbidden.'

The clock on the sideboard was always twenty-three minutes fast. I remember counting the slices of toast in the rack, reading the text on the framed sampler that hung above the range, trying to work out how long it had taken some long-dead Chilton ancestor to embroider the word PEACE. I accepted a second cup of tea and drank it. It was expected that I would be the first to leave the table. I excused myself and walked, without haste, into yet another golden morning.

I had twenty-three minutes before real time caught up with the kitchen clock. I loaded straw bales on to the trailer, assembled the shovel and scraper required for the cleaning out of hen coops. I drove carefully and very slowly to the high fields that lay furthest from the farmhouse, unloaded the straw bales and sat down upon them. I looked at the hens pecking mindlessly among the grass. Ten minutes left until I got to real time. I picked at the plaster which covered a new blister on my thumb. Yesterday, before I had seen his face, the future had promised hard work and boredom, but without complication. 'Fraternization' was not a word with which I was familiar. 'Strictly forbidden' had a more homely ring. In the years of my growing-up it had been strictly forbidden to show lights after dark in case some German pilot, seeing the twenty-watt gleam from our window, assumed that we were his military target for that night. Also forbidden was careless talk which might assist our enemies, or leaving the house without carrying a gas mask.

Shock has a way of inhibiting predictable reaction. I had wept about the shattered gatepost, cursed the tractor engine when it failed to start. Now I felt very strange, as if my blood had started to flow in a contrary direction. I began to scrape at the soiled boards of the hen house, put clean hay into the nesting boxes, fresh straw on the floor. One level of my mind sought to justify the error it had made. I blamed my employer who should have warned me sooner; I blamed the prisoners-of-war who, by wearing unmarked clothing, had misled me as to their true nature. Reason informed me that I had been wickedly deceived. Emotion confirmed that I loved him, hopelessly and forever.

Threshing was over, the link with Hobart's broken. The October days grew short and cold. My father telephoned every Monday evening. I told him I was well and happy. I still slept the deep sleep of physical exhaustion, climbed unwillingly each morning from the depths of my feather bed to face another empty day. My only human contact was a brief exchange of words with my employer and his family as we sat around the breakfast and dinner table. Gracie Fields still sang 'How are Things in Glocca Morra?'. The plaintive tune, the silly words, seemed uncannily to fit my circumstances. I sang them as I gathered eggs, and measured dry mash. 'And does that laddie with the twinkling eye come whistling by? Or does he walk away sad and weary there – not to see me there?'

I tried to be dispassionate and adult. Four years of convent schooling had taught me more about guilt than of forgiveness. I was, I thought, being punished according to my need.

Hens go to roost only in the grey light of approaching night. My last task of the day was to close each coop against the raiding foxes. I walked through the darkening fields as quickly as rough grass and raw heels allowed. The final hen house stood in a corner beside the dividing lane that led up to Hobart's farm.

Autumn evenings in the valley were drowsy, hypnotic. There was a smell of burning leaves on the rising mist, and the trees and hedgerows were full of tiny rustling sounds, and violet shadows. It was so still that every slightest sound was magnified. The crash of the trapdoors as I dropped and fastened them echoed down the long field. I was close to the lane when I became aware of the watcher by the gate. His stance was easy and relaxed. I could just make out the gleam of yellow hair, and the glint of metal from the shotgun broken and draped across his arm. As I drew closer I saw that he now wore the regulation khaki shirt and blue-patched, dark-brown trousers of a prisoner-of-war. At sight of the gun a shaft of fear sent me running back along the field. He called out some kind of greeting. Shame, and a sense of duty, brought me slowly back towards him. Three hen coops still waited to be closed, and the weapon on his arm was surely used only for pheasant shooting? I felt cold. I pushed my bandaged hands into the pockets of my dungarees, and shivered in my shrunken yellow jumper.

He spoke carefully in a voice that was guttural and very deep. 'Good evening.' If he had spoken to me in the threshing field I would have known at once that he was German.

I said angrily, because I had been cheated, 'I thought you couldn't speak any English.'

'I speak little bit. Understand sehr gut.'

I moved closer to the five-barred gate. Here was no laddie with a twinkling eye, but a serious, mature man. 'You didn't speak in the threshing field.'

'Englishman see us there. Better we not talk. Make much trouble.'

I began to move away, back into the shadows, towards the still unshuttered hen coops. 'I must go now,' I told him, 'they won't like it if they catch me talking to you.'

The bus driver said, 'Well – you don't mind taking chances, do you? Another half minute and you would have missed me. Like I said, I only come up this way on a Monday.' He halted briefly at the crossroads. I looked back towards the lane where Kurt and I had first spoken together. On that night there had still been time for me to draw back. Or had there? Chance ruled my life. I was never good at forethought, at premeditation.

❧

PART FOUR

I TRAVELLED to the West Country on a Friday morning. The book I was about to promote was the longest and the most ambitious I had yet attempted. I had lived with the characters for over two years; and found it painful to leave them when the story ended. The lack of interest now shown by my publisher's office dismayed and depressed me. The new notebook still lay untouched upon my desk. Confidence, I told myself, should not be so easily undermined. But it was. Oh, it was!

I sat in the crowded buffet at Paddington station. The place smelled of damp wool and fried food. The man sitting opposite had bought the all-day breakfast, plus a double pack of doughnuts and a beaker of coffee. His purchases took up most of the space on the small table. I drank my tea and watched his hands. The knife and fork were made of dark red plastic which buckled to near-breaking point beneath his fingers. He worked methodically around the plate, cutting the food into careful, one-inch portions. Fried bread and bacon, egg and sausage, tomato and mushrooms, were sectioned and then coated thoroughly with brown sauce. A newspaper lay folded on his suitcase. I could just make out the single headline word, BERLIN. In the past two days I had avoided all possible sources of world news. The Cellophane crackled from the packaged doughnuts. He placed them on a clean plate and again reduced his food to bite-sized portions, but now he ate and drank alternately. A sip of coffee, a square of doughnut. I began to imagine meals and dishes which would surely pose him problems of organization, like stew and tapioca pudding. I tried not to think about Christina, and the Stasi, and the marchers who demanded freedom. Eighteen days had passed since our return from West Berlin. In that time I had sought, unsuccessfully, to mitigate my anxiety by talking to Roman, to Martin. But reality survived. Memory was wilful. The man who sat opposite consumed the last square of doughnut, licked the tip of his index finger and dabbed up and ate the fallen sugar crystals. From his pocket he pulled a half-pound slab of chocolate, which predictably he began to break into separate squares. I watched his fingers build those squares into a wall of chocolate. I could not bear to watch the demolition process. I picked up my suitcase and walked out on to the platform. I sat down on a bench. Half an hour to wait, and there I was, back in West Berlin on that last Sunday morning.

The Flea Markets of West Berlin cover several acres. Set out on stalls under coloured awnings it is possible to buy, at reasonable prices, furniture and paintings, jewellery and *objets d'art*, old linen and blankets, and various accumulated rubbish. The antique and quality section of the market stands attractively beneath trees. It is a popular Sunday morning venue for thousands of West Berliners.

Melanie bought me a silver ring set with rose quartz. I bought her a copper ring set with tiny turquoise. Together with Martin, Maraid and Ryan we ate apple cake and drank juice, strolled in the sunshine. This was the smiling face of West Berlin.

The Polish market also occupied a wide space, but here the terrain was rough grass, the ground uneven. As we entered the site I saw the parked rows of rusted, patched-together vehicles and vans which had brought the Poles across their border with the DDR.

There were no refinements in this market, no stalls or awnings, no protection against bad weather. Here, the vendors squatted on their heels behind rows of goods laid out carefully on strips of poor quality brown paper. The items for sale were cheap and of a shoddy standard not seen in England since the war years.

Whole families crouched behind the brown paper strips: children and grandparents, nursing mothers and young husbands. They all had the lean and anxious looks of people who have never had a sufficiency of food or shelter, or known contentment.

I bought a chess set that I did not need, bargained a little for it as was the custom, and then felt ashamed that I had dared to do so in the face of such poverty. Some families had brought from Poland small quantities of honey in thick jars. Ryan showed deep concern that they should be forced to sell a commodity so obviously needed by their own thin and undernourished children.

As we left the market I saw a coffee mill, the old-fashioned kind that hangs on the kitchen wall, with a porcelain body and a black metal handle that turns the grinding mechanism. The figure of a wild boar was painted on the porcelain front and the one word KAWA. And this time I did not bargain but at once paid the astonished young man his full asking price.

I wanted to inquire what happened when it rained. Did they still come here? Did they spread their strips of paper over mud and protect their pathetic goods with sheets of plastic? But our only common language was the money that I offered, and which he accepted.

The hotel booked by my publisher was dignified and old; the kind of establishment where shoes, placed outside the bedroom door in the evening, were returned clean and polished on the following morning. My room was small but pleasant;

the bed, a white-painted four-poster, was draped with flow-ered chintz, a vase of pink carnations stood on the dressing table. The degree of heating was, as always in such places, more than I could tolerate. I switched off the radiators and opened wide the window. This town of Taunton, which I loved more than any other place on earth, had meant home and security since my early childhood. I looked out across familiar buildings, the library and museum, their outlines indistinct in the November mist; the glow of street lamps reflected in damp pavements. These were the streets where I had walked long ago with my grandmother, my aunt. I began to anticipate tomorrow's signing session. I had often said that if I could not sell my books in this place, I would never sell them anywhere. Promotion required a confidence I did not normally possess, but here in this West Country town I felt safe and welcome.

I left the hotel room and walked to the bookshop. Copies of the book, attractively arranged on an antique table, filled the window. A display board held my photograph and the announcement that I would be present in the shop on the following morning. I stood there for a long time. Against the fall of dark the lighted window seemed unnaturally bright; the photograph on the display board was that of a stranger. I felt the division in my mind expand, and I was conscious in that moment of Kurt's withdrawal to the very margins of my life. I tried to call him back. Once I had stood beside his grave, had said, 'This business of writing . . . it's of no real importance . . . it's what I do with the small part of me that still functions without you.'

The little red notebook had lain on my desk for almost a year now. I dusted it occasionally but never removed it. I had blamed my inability to write on my publisher's disinterest, the departure of a valued editor, my unsatisfactory domestic arrangements. But that small part of me that still functioned without Kurt had also closed down. What I had once been, and what I had become, were irreconcilable.

I don't know how long I stood before that bookshop window. For several terrifying minutes the split in my mind became complete. I seemed to hang in a dark and windless void where Kurt had no presence. Mind no longer spoke to mind.

I have no memory of walking back to the Castle Hotel. In the same state of almost total absence I unpacked my weekend bag, cancelled dinner for that evening, refused an offer of early morning tea and newspapers. The only armchair in the room stood before the television set. I sat down and gazed at the blank screen. I remember thinking that perhaps this was what people meant when they talked about a mental breakdown. The events of recent months lay scrambled and heavy on my mind. Thought itself was incoherent. At some point I leaned forward and pressed the TV switch, but the voices and figures had no meaning; one programme merged into another.

The cacophony of sound that preceded the nine o'clock news brought my gaze back to the screen. As the Brandenburg Gate came slowly into focus I leaned forward to the OFF switch. And then I saw the crowds weeping, and laughing; long columns of East Germans were pouring through the checkpoints quite unhindered by the border guards who stood silently by, looking sheepish and bewildered.

The people came in Trabants and Ladas, or on bicycles; mothers pushed babies in prams, fathers carried toddlers perched shoulder high. They came on the U-Bahn, in taxis.

'No trouble,' they told the interviewer, 'we have passes that allow us to travel freely for six months.'

Young people said, 'We want only to look at the West –
not to stay. The important thing is that for the first time in
our lives we are free to do so.'

The euphoria was tangible against the cold night air. Faces
reflected astonishment and disbelief; men passed weeping and
speechless before the interviewer's microphone. Women cried,
'A miracle! We have wanted so long to be free!'

On top of the Wall a crowd of young people wielded
hammers and chisels. *'Die Mauer muss weg,'* they chanted.
'The Wall must go.' The pictures were coming live from
West Berlin. I knew it was happening there but could not
quite believe it. Less than three weeks ago I had seen the Stasi
lurking on Unter den Linden and in the Marx-Engels-Platz;
had seen their armoured waggons stationed at street corners. I
had believed then, in spite of Martin's optimism, that it would
all end in bloodshed and still heavier repression.

The breaching of the Berlin Wall had taken place in the
early morning hours. Even as I caught my train and travelled
southwards, the unimaginable had happened. At a press conference given by Gunther Schabowski of the Politburo, the
announcement was made suddenly, awkwardly, and almost
as an afterthought at the end of a day's business. 'All citizens
can now be issued with visas for the purposes of travel or
visiting relatives in the West. This order is to take effect at
once.'

'And what we are witnessing now,' said the BBC newsreader, 'must surely be unprecedented in our lifetime!' He
smiled, uncertainly, not quite sure how this rare delivery of
good news should be handled.

I thought about Christina and her family. The twenty-eight
years of their imprisonment was ended. I felt the division in
my mind pull gradually together. Slow tears that came with-

out sound restored me to my whole self. Kurt was returning from the margins of my life. I felt his presence all around me.

The pictures from Berlin continued to roll. The smiling newsreaders introduced BBC correspondents who spoke from the Brandenburg Gate, the Bernauer Strasse.

My thoughts were with Christina, Melanie and Ryan. I rang Martin's number, but there was no reply. I longed to dance and sing and share with them the joy of this night. I dialled West Berlin and when I spoke to Melanie she told me that she had also wept on seeing the TV pictures. Tomorrow, she and Ryan planned to visit the new crossings.

I switched off the television, sat down in the chintz chair and gazed at the blank screen. Pictures came into my mind, black and white, a little jerky but very clear.

Other times. Other people. Spring 1945. And now I witnessed again a private viewing once forced upon me by an old man who had seen the fall of his city to the Mongols, the Russians.

Crates and bunkers filled with dead and dying. Bodies heaped up to the sills of windows. People clawing in the rubble to retrieve the bodies of their dead children. Women leaping out of second-floor windows to escape the rapist soldiers. Mud and machine guns. Hand grenades and knives. The continuous boom of the gun that Berliners had nicknamed the Stalin Organ. The blackened stumps of the *Gedächtniskirche*, the Church of Kaiser Friedrich. The holes instead of doors and windows. Kurfürstendam a corridor of flame. The stench and smoke that had denied the springtime.

It was not a night for sleeping, and yet I slept long and deeply. My first move on waking was towards the television set. The news from Berlin still preceded all other world events.

At Checkpoint Charlie, where I had stood only weeks ago with Martin and Maraid, teenage girls threw flowers at embarrassed border guards. An elderly lady, on hearing the good news late at night, had run from her house to the checkpoint, and revealed now to the interviewer the flannel nightgown she wore beneath her winter coat.

In three East German cities, the Communist Party bosses had committed suicide. In the first five hours of the opening of the Wall, a million people had crossed over into West Berlin. On Potsdamer Platz, close to the built-over ruins of Hitler's bunker, bulldozers were at that very moment creating yet another crossing point through the six-inch, reinforced concrete.

I turned up the sound a little, so that I might bathe and dress and still hear the commentator's voice. I put on a plain grey dress with a deep white collar, fastened the coral brooch and earrings that were my good-luck pieces; still the jubilant people came walking and driving into West Berlin. The transmission ended. I switched off the set, and as the image faded I thought about the notebook lying on my desk. The need to write, which had been absent for many months, was now compulsive.

A signing session in a bookshop is rather like a first night in the theatre. If people come, the experience is wonderful beyond belief. If they stay away, the embarrassed author cowers behind a stack of unsold books, and swears never to be persuaded again to this particular folly.

My recent novels had been set in Taunton and the Blackdown Hills. I walked down to the bookshop to find a small group of readers already waiting for me. I signed my name and answered questions, being necessarily evasive when asked about my next publication. At the end of the morning the bookstore owners declared their satisfaction. On my way back to the Castle Hotel I bought a a new small red notebook.

I should have returned home on Sunday morning but a physical lethargy I could not explain held me fast in Taunton. It was not an unpleasant feeling, but rather like the languor after a high temperature of some duration has fallen back to normal. I avoided the dining room and the hotel breakfast. I retained the room for a further night at my own expense, leaving it only to buy a selection of the Sunday papers and a supply of Mars bars and potato crisps.

I hung the 'Do not disturb' sign on the door, and angled the TV screen so that it was visible from the four-poster. News readings were extended. By switching channels I obtained an almost day-long viewing of live transmissions and programmes of discussion and evaluation from London and Berlin. As I watched I absentmindedly ate junk food and made notes. The red notebook filled up quickly; I hunted for and found hotel stationery in the dressing-table drawer; I wrote on dinner menus and laundry lists, obligingly printed only on one side. The chintzy room seemed an unlikely setting in which to view the fall of Communism in the DDR.

I thought about Roman; imagined the long length of him folded on to one of Serena's Laura Ashley sofas, watching these same pictures, his dark head resting on squashy flowered cushions. I thought about Jasper whom I still suspected to be at risk from some source; but not from Roman. Policies of non-interference could lead to private agonies of mind in which one worried, but without proof.

In Berlin many shops had opened on this phenomenal Sunday morning. The banks were dealing with long queues, handing out the *Begrüssungsgeld*, the one hundred Westmarks of 'greetings money' allowed to each East German visitor.

Kurfürstendamm was blocked with cars, with people window-shopping. They smiled, a little ruefully, when interviewed. 'Here is everything we have ever longed to buy, if we only had sufficient money.' A young shop assistant, aware of the world's cameras trained upon her, said, 'In my whole life I have never seen anything like this. The people think they must spend their hundred marks as quickly as possible, the way they do in the DDR. In case we run out of supplies!' She laughed at the impossible thought. 'Oh, but it's magical. Such a day, such times!'

On Potsdamer Platz the children collected chippings as souvenirs of the Wall. In sweet shops they gazed bemused at the unprecedented choice spread out before them.

Cameramen filmed scenes that would be shown repeatedly throughout the world. There were cameos: unforgettable, emotive pictures. On the windscreens of illegally parked East German cars, the traffic wardens of West Berlin were leaving a banana instead of a parking ticket. Border guards from either side were caught by the camera, unawares, chatting companionably together after twenty-eight years of angry confrontation. And in the background, lifting machinery continued to haul away sections of the Wall.

It was, said the man from BBC television, the most fantastic street party the world had ever witnessed. He waved a hand towards a section of graffiti-daubed concrete swaying high above him. The building of the Berlin Wall, he said, had in fact commenced on a Sunday morning, although he himself was too young to remember the event.

But I remembered it, as vividly as if I had been present on the Bernauer Strasse or Potsdamer Platz.

*

The Saturday night of August 12th, 1961 had been warm and humid. The scent of linden blossoms drifted on the air of the Unter den Linden and was carried on the breeze through the Brandenburg Gate.

The citizens of the city crossed from east to west, and from west to east. They visited cinemas, went dancing, spent the evening with relatives and friends. Little, if anything, was said about the latest political unrest. They had long since accustomed themselves to bad news, as must a population who live in a beleaguered fortress, if their sanity is to be preserved.

It was in the first few minutes of that Sunday morning that the Security Police of West Berlin reported to Allied officers an unusually heavy deployment of military vehicles and personnel in East Berlin. Minutes later, all barge traffic on the River Spree was halted. Reports began to come in that S-Bahn and U-Bahn railway stations had closed down and that passengers were ordered to vacate the eastern trains. Heavy movements of Soviet tanks and armoured vehicles were reported in districts of East Berlin.

At three a.m. precisely on that Sunday in August, an announcement was made on an East German radio station that the border between the two halves of the city was now closed.

On Bernauer Strasse rolls of barbed wire were being unloaded from trucks. As the sky grew light towards the east, the street was completely closed off.

The news from Berlin came to us in England through the television newscast of that Sunday lunchtime. It coincided very neatly, as did so much of the bad news from Kurt's country, with a family crisis for which there could never now be a solution.

For years Kurt's mother had suffered the heart disease that

claimed so many members of her family. A near-fatal heart attack in 1951 had left her with severe angina. In recent photographs she looked well and happy, and letters from her were reassuring. We had grown complacent about her frail state.

The letter from Christina that told of a collapsed lung, pneumonia, heart failure was, therefore, shocking and unexpected.

The summer of 1961 was good; our hay was cut and stacked and the harvest was coming on. Christina's plea that Kurt should come at once to Dresden was the single request that I feared most. On his only excursion behind the Iron Curtain he had come close to permanent detention by the Russians. His recent award of British nationality would not, said the Foreign Office, help him if he should get into difficulties in his country of origin. We had also been told that since our sons had dual nationality, the East German regime could also legitimately claim them. If we should ever go to the DDR and run into trouble, it seemed that I alone would qualify for intervention and retrieval by the British Consul in Berlin.

My private conviction that to travel east was risky was overcome by Kurt's need to see his mother for what might well be their last meeting. I applied to the East German Consulate in London for four visas. If we went, then we would go together. The visas arrived with the telegram that told Kurt of his mother's death. On the day of Frau Baumann's funeral the last loopholes in Berlin were closed.

If the visas had arrived a little sooner, if Kurt's mother had lived a few days longer, we should have been trapped in Dresden, caught behind the Berlin Wall until now.

I travelled back to Leicestershire on Monday. As the train

pulled away from Taunton station I felt the pang of regret that I always suffered; I watched the blue rise of the Blackdown Hills until it passed from view. Further up the line and Glastonbury Tor was green and visible beneath grey clouds. In that same direction the village of Montacute lay golden and quiet in the November morning.

I made the vow to return that I always make at this point of departure, and then turned my face towards the north.

Living alone had made me susceptible in ways undreamed-of in the days when I was a daughter, a wife, and then a mother. There had been a time when to go back to an empty house had meant an hour of rare tranquillity, a time of silence to be valued. I felt shamed by my present thin-skinned neediness, by the fantasy indulged on my return from every journey, that Kurt would be waiting for me at the railway station or in the house.

The phone began to ring as I turned my key in the Yale lock. I set down my bag and grabbed at the receiver. Martin's voice, tight with triumph and emotion, came clearly down the line. 'So what did I tell you!'

'Yes,' I said, 'you were absolutely right to be so optimistic.' As I spoke I wondered if he had felt, on watching the pictures from Berlin, a sense of disappointment not to be there at the Brandenburg Gate.

'A few more days,' I said, 'and we would have seen it all at first hand.'

'I thought that way at first, but on reflection I'm very glad that Maraid and I saw things exactly as they had been since 1961. Those pictures Ryan took of us beside the Wall and at Checkpoint Charlie – they're more special than ever, now.'

We talked for a few minutes. He ended the call with a promise to come over at the weekend. I began to unpack.

The new notebook, bought in Taunton, together with the densely written sheets of hotel stationery, now covered nicely the hitherto bare surface of the desk.

I drifted into sleep that night with the recent TV pictures from Berlin very much upon my mind. In the final conscious moment, Roman's features appeared huge and superimposed upon my personal re-run of last Friday's scenes in the Potsdamer Platz. He accompanied me into strange and troubled dreams.

The morning was fine, the air crisp and cold. Winter had not yet properly begun, there was still the smoky smell of autumn drifting through the park. I walked slowly at first, every joint stiff and aching from too much sitting around in trains and hotel rooms. My failure to recognize as Roman's any vehicle standing in the car park was a disappointment and yet a relief. Even so, I needed urgently to see Jasper.

The Park Ranger from his Landrover nodded me good morning. A solitary man walked an Irish wolfhound. Stags lay at rest among the bracken. The rut was over. Does grazed peacefully in small, companionable groups. Brown leaves were heaped in dry drifts underneath the pollard oaks. The silver surface of the lake was ruffled at intervals by descending teal and mallard. I began to move more easily; the stiffness lessened until at last I was able to step out at a steady even pace. The invigorating cold was pure pleasure. I felt the return of interest, of energy, of involvement. I began to think about my house over which a decision must soon be made. About Martin and the fragility of family relationships. About the writing, begun in Taunton, which might or might not turn out to be a book.

It was as I walked back to the bus stop that I saw Roman

in the café entrance. Dressed from shoulder to ankles in a
voluminous fawn raincoat, his appearance was reassuringly
normal. From his pushchair Jasper began to wave a scarlet
mittened hand. The baby's instant recognition of me made it
impossible to pass them by with a mere smile of acknowledge-
ment, a quick word. Roman raised an eyebrow. 'Hot chocolate?' he asked.

'Why not?' I said, but even as I spoke the serenity I had
found in the Deerpark was lost.

We entered the café and Roman settled Jasper in a high
chair close beside our table. He became aware of my scrutiny
of the child, and pushed back the tumble of curls from the
little boy's forehead. 'Look – no more damage. Not there, or
anywhere.' He paused, then said with deliberate drama, 'The
cause has been eliminated!'

I longed to ask him what he meant, but the chocolate
arrived, with warm milk and biscuits for Jasper. Roman
started to remove the long beige coat. He watched my face
for the inevitable reaction. His suit was made of a soft glove-
leather of brilliant scarlet that only someone with his height
and dark good looks could possibly have worn. A scarf of
striped red and yellow cashmere was knotted gypsy fashion at
his throat. From his ears dangled heavy hoops of old rose-
gold. On his feet, I now noticed, he wore shoes of yellow
leather. His removal of the camouflage coat was made slowly
and with evident enjoyment. I was caught between tears and
laughter for the childish theatricality of him.

'Well,' he asked, 'what do you think?'

'Very – unusual,' I said, 'and very expensive. But you look
marvellous in it.' Seated opposite him across the rustic table I
was more than usually aware of my well-worn tweed skirt
and corduroy jacket. At an adjoining table a party of hikers
chewed silently on cheese rolls, their communal gaze turned

curiously in our direction. As we sipped our drinks I was obliged to study Roman rather than his outfit, and what I saw alarmed me.

The draping of the leather jacket failed to hide the new and frightening thinness of him. He had looked unwell before I left for Taunton, and it seemed to me now, as then, that his sickness was more of the mind than of the body.

His gaze darted constantly back and forth, from Jasper to the hiking party, and downwards into his cup; but never at me. His skin was grey, deep new lines ran from nose to mouth giving him a drawn appearance. But more disturbing than his physical aspect was the barely controlled ferocity of him. It showed in the way his fingers clenched around the teaspoon, his jerky movements and clipped speech.

I said, as gently as I could, 'Something's happened, hasn't it?' I could hear and was shamed by the drag of resentment in my voice.

He heard it too. 'No need for you to concern yourself. My own affair entirely.' But the pain in his eyes was very real.

I looked at Jasper's milky chin, the rounded softness of the little boy, the biscuit crumbs lodged damply between his short fat fingers, and I experienced that lurch of the heart that always came before capitulation. I said, still gazing at the child, 'But I'm already involved. Surely you know that?'

He considered me thoughtfully, seeming to gauge my ability to absorb shock, and evidently rating it as high. He said, deadpan, 'I've disposed of Serena.'

I at once visualized the unknown Serena dead and tied up in a bin bag, dumped in a country lane, her dismembered torso yet to be discovered. I controlled my imagination. Roman's English, almost without accent, was not always accurate as to precise meaning.

'She's left you?' I asked.

'I ordered her to go,' he corrected.

The fine line of difference, I thought, had only to do with Roman's pride. The result left Jasper motherless; and since I appeared to be his sole confidante, it laid Roman's state of mind more heavily than ever upon my conscience.

'So how are you managing?' I asked. We both knew that it was the chain of boutiques of which I spoke.

'Oh, the business side of things is not affected. We leave messages for each other on our respective answering-machines.' He shrugged inside the wide scarlet-leather shoulders. 'It's a relief to have her gone. To know that I won't go home and find her there.' He turned to Jasper. 'He doesn't miss her one little bit. Why should he?'

But how can you know? I thought. Jasper must be approaching his first birthday. He had taken his first steps, spoken half a dozen recognizable words. It was unwise to make such a dangerous assumption. 'He has grandparents, surely?'

'Wintering in Spain. They have a villa in Torremolinos. I wouldn't let them have him for half an hour.'

We drank our chocolate and did not look at one another. In the silence I heard the scrape of the hikers' boots across the tiled floor, the rustle of their nylon anoraks as they prepared to leave. Jasper said in a sad voice, 'All gone now,' and it seemed to me an appropriate comment on his own situation. For I was forced finally to admit that this tense and twitchy young father in his sad clown's outfit was in no fit condition to have sole charge of so young a child.

I said, knowing that I should regret the words as soon as they were spoken, 'I'll help you with Jasper. I'll give you my telephone number. Let's keep in touch.'

His relief was so obvious that I felt guilty. Colour came back into his face. He said, 'I'm beginning to feel hungry. How about you?' He ordered hamburgers and buttered toast for Jasper. I watched the lines in Roman's face grow less marked; he looked across the table at Jasper and me with eyes that no longer gazed exclusively inwards on his own troubles.

He said, conversationally, 'Good news from Berlin!'

'Yes,' I agreed. 'It's still difficult to believe.'

'I watched them on TV – those East Germans.' He smiled. 'The children's clothes are great fun. Colourful and cute. A sort of Hansel-and-Gretel style that I might adapt for our next winter collection. But as for the young adults, they have no sense of fashion. Just jeans, and more jeans. Stone-washed, out of date, old-fashioned.'

I said, 'Scarlet leather suits and handmade shoes are in short supply over there, except perhaps among the hierarchy of the Communist Party. Modishness will not have been a priority for people, most of whom have never even seen bananas.'

'All right,' he conceded, 'but you must admit that they are very different. It comes across when they're being interviewed. The young ones – even the city-bred East Berliners – they have no street-cred, they're painfully naive. I feel sorry for them.'

'Do you? Do you really, Roman? Well, I would call that naivety by other names. That innocence, that old-world niceness that you find pitiable has been their most valuable asset, until now.' I was still unsure of how much I could say to him before his boredom threshold was exhausted. 'When I was in Dresden,' I continued, 'back in 1976, I found East Germany to be exactly like the England of my childhood. No transistor radios, no hooliganism. Young people were polite to older people. Older people were considerate and nice to one another. There was no haste, no rush, no aggravation. The crime rate was very low. When we were in Dresden, Melanie, my friend, left the boot of her car unlocked with all our luggage in it while we went into the hotel to check our reservations. She assured me that our possessions would be perfectly safe. And so they were. It helped to balance my anxiety later in the day, when the desk clerk in the Interhotel took my passport and refused to give it back. It also resigned me to the fact that my room was almost certainly bugged.'

'So what are you saying?' Roman asked. 'That the Wall should have remained closed?'

'No, of course not. But these are heady days. At the moment, young people in the East are drunk on promises as well as wine. The euphoria can't last. I only hope that when the reckoning comes they will be able to cope with disillusion.'

'You really care about all this, don't you?'

'When I married a German, his people in a sense became my people.'

'It's not like that with Serena and me. I can't imagine that kind of marriage.'

'How is it with Serena and you?'

'A mess.' He shrugged his scarlet-clad shoulders, and the haggard look was back in his face. Jasper, bored with soggy toast, had squeezed the buttery bread into pellets and dropped them contentedly one by one from the height of his chair. I wiped his greasy fingers on a paper napkin while Roman cleared the floor of hazard.

I repeated my offer of release. 'Let me have him for a day. Or even two days. Give yourself time to think, to sort things out. Go and see your wife. Talk to her.' I could hear myself sounding like an agony-aunt in the tabloid press. 'Promise me, at least,' I said again, 'that if you really need help, you will ring me.'

From an inside jacket pocket he pulled out a small black diary and a pen, and wrote while I dictated my telephone number. I felt a pang of unease. 'It's unlisted,' I said quickly.

'I don't give it out to many people. It makes for a more peaceful life.'

'Oh, thanks.' His voice was edgy. 'Well, I promise I won't call you unless it's very urgent.' I should have reassured him then, that he had mistaken my meaning. But had he? Truth to tell, I trusted him no more today than I had back in those days of early spring when I first met him. I tried to formulate suspicion, but could not. The threat lay at the core of him. Sometimes it flickered briefly in his eyes, edged his smiles. I suspected that his ability to read my mind had grown stronger over recent weeks.

As if to confirm my thoughts he leaned across the table. 'Have you,' he asked, 'ever done something so terrible that you can never forget it, even for an hour?'

He did not wait for my answer, but lifted Jasper from the high chair and walked swiftly away, lifting a hand in brief farewell.

Telling Martin about Roman had never been an option. My son would use words like dangerous involvement, exploitation, unwise association. He would be kind. He would not refer to my advancing years, the possible impairment of my judgement. But we would both know what he was thinking.

He would never understand my feelings about Jasper. I did not comprehend them altogether myself.

❦

PART FIVE

MARTIN drove slowly through villages and farm-land, his hands resting easy on the steering wheel, a pack of cigarettes unopened on the dash-board. A pale disc of sun hung behind wisps of grey cloud, light frost rimed the hawthorn hedges and the vergeside grass. A flight of peewits rose vertically before him, circled once and then wheeled away towards the north. He slowed almost to a halt in the empty lane and watched the flying birds grow small and disappear. It was not until he reached the first streets of the town that he shook a cigarette from the pack and lit it.

Martin had returned from West Berlin in the uncertain state of one who had undergone an experience for which he was unprepared, and with which he did not quite know how to deal. The invitation to accompany his mother had surprised him. There had been a time when they had met only at Christmas and on birthdays; he had taken her flowers on Mother's Day; sometimes they had come upon each other unexpectedly, in the street. If asked to describe her he would have said that her aloofness touched the point of coldness; a self-contained, rather prim sort of woman who dispensed affection towards her children only as a reward for their good behaviour. The time in Berlin, spent in her company, had been his first sustained contact with her in the twenty years since he had married, and because of that contact and its amazing circumstances, something had changed between them. He was not quite sure of the nature of the difference. But something had definitely changed.

He turned into the narrow street where his mother's house

stood. Described in estate agent's jargon as a Victorian cottage-residence, she had bought it impulsively and without consultation, informing him by telephone that her address had changed. Records showed that the house and its neighbour had been one undivided dwelling in the year of 1859. The adjacent lock-up garages had stabled horses in those days. When the garage doors stood open, the original cobbled floors were still to be seen.

Martin switched off the engine. He smoked the final inch of cigarette and surveyed the rotting wood of his mother's sash windows, the peeling paint of her front door, the brickwork which had not been pointed for one hundred and thirty years. He had conceded, when asked belatedly for his opinion, that the place was structurally sound. When he asked why she had bought it, he was told that the house had a 'peaceful feel about it'. If she had since become aware of defects, she had not confided in him.

She welcomed him with a warmth to which he had not yet become accustomed. A plate of biscuits stood ready on the kitchen counter, coffee bubbled in the percolator. He walked into the tiny sitting room and sat down in the leather wing-chair. A faint smell of mould rose up from the cellar; the loose windows rattled in a gust of wind; he laid a hand upon a nearby radiator which was hot only at its base. His mother handed him a photographer's wallet.

'The pictures,' she said, 'that I took in East and West Berlin. I think you'll like them.'

He liked them very much. Those which showed him with his Aunt Christina were exceptional and significant for him. He recalled his instant recognition of her at the Botanischer Garten S-Bahn station; his aunt's resemblance to his father which had been painful and uncanny, and wonderful beyond belief. He valued most the pictures which showed the two of them together, Christina smiling at him with his father's smile, with the remembered Baumann warmth which had been missing from his life for fourteen years. Affection expressed, openly and without reservation, was the unique gift of this German family. His father's love never had to be earned; he had made no demands, had extracted no penalties for bad behaviour. Martin studied his mother's face; the small pale features were difficult to read.

She said abruptly, 'I'm thinking about selling this house.'

'But why? I thought you liked it here.' He began to list the advantages. 'You have the town park almost on your doorstep, and the library just beyond it. The street leads straight into the town square, shopping couldn't be easier for you. Maraid and I have to drive five miles to the nearest Sainsbury's. And anyway, this place has a peaceful atmosphere about it – or so you said.'

'And so it does. And I do like it here. It's just –' Her tone became aggrieved, as if, he thought, the flaws in the house were somehow his fault. 'It's just – well – there are all these small, rather dark rooms, and repairs need to be done, rather urgently I think. I've also started on a new book. I can't bear the thought of builders, all that upheaval. I really don't think that I can face it.'

The unexpected weakness at once endeared her to him. But still he spoke hesitantly, expecting the usual rebuff. 'I could do certain items for you. As for the rest, I can recommend people who will do a good job at a fair price.'

She looked doubtful.

'Look,' he said, 'finding another house and moving to it will be an even greater upheaval. Just talking about it won't commit you to anything, will it?'

She said, 'I suppose you're right, and I don't need to list the obvious defects. I see you doing that every time you come here.' She stood up. 'The kitchen is one of the problems and I can't think how to solve it.'

The kitchen was very long and L-shaped. The working area was light and fitted pleasantly with oaken cupboards. The far end of the room lay in semi-darkness, lit only by a tiny window. Martin looked through the window and saw that this part of the house backed on to a little terrace, access to which was gained from the far side of the building.

'I could knock out this end wall,' he told his mother, 'and put in patio doors. That would lighten this part of the kitchen, and take you straight out on to the terrace. It could be very pleasant in the summer.'

'Yes,' she said slowly, 'yes. I'll think about it.'

'So what's your other problem?'

'I want,' she said firmly, 'a large, light sitting-room.'

He walked about, tapping walls. 'Can't be done,' he said. 'At least not without major reconstruction.' He turned towards the staircase. She followed, a little reluctantly, he thought.

At the front of the house lay two oddly shaped bedrooms.

'You see what I mean,' she said, 'the proportions are all wrong here.'

He tapped at the dividing wall. 'Supposing,' he said, 'you have this wall knocked down? That would give you one large room right across the front of the house, and two large windows to light it?'

Now she looked frightened. 'Knock down yet another wall?' she asked. 'Isn't that a bit extreme?'

He grinned, and tapped again. 'Listen to the hollow sound,' he said. 'That's not brickwork, it's just studding. When the house was built this was one large bedroom. The division was made in recent years.'

She smiled and rapped the wall, reproducing the hollow sound. 'What,' she asked, 'is studding?'

'Plasterboard, mainly.'

'Oh. Well, in that case – but of course – so that's why these bedrooms feel all wrong.'

He heard the rising excitement in her voice. She repeated his words. 'One large room across the front of the house, and two large windows to light it.'

December brought closer the threat of Christmas. I began to watch the faces of small children, who were seeing for the first time the tinsel and lights strung up in the town square. The writing that might or might not become a book took up the early morning hours. I visited friends in the afternoon; shopped for gifts with Eileen in Nottingham and Leicester.

Over two weeks had passed since my last meeting with Roman. I waited for the call that would bring Jasper to me. I thought a lot about the changes to my house proposed by Martin; pictured the end wall of the kitchen replaced by wide glass doors that could stand open to summer mornings and warm nights. I imagined Christina, sitting with me on the terrace.

I telephoned Martin. 'I've decided to go ahead with the alterations you suggested. I would like you to start with the patio doors leading off the kitchen.'

'Right,' he said. 'I'll come over and measure up. Give you a starting date.' He paused. 'Maraid says if you have no other plans for Christmas, perhaps you would like to spend it here with us?'

The telephone rang very early the next morning. Roman's voice, thin with urgency, apologized. 'Hope I didn't wake you?'

'No. You didn't wake me.'

'I have to go to Ashby de la Zouch. On business. You said that you might have Jasper for an hour or two –?'

'But of course. All day if you want me to.'

'No,' he said. 'A couple of hours will be sufficient. He doesn't know you all that well.'

'Whatever you think best.'

'OK then. Supposing we meet at the Deerpark café? We could drive from there to Ashby. I could buy you lunch and sneak away while Jasper's eating. After that, he's bound to sleep for at least an hour.'

'I'll see you at about ten-thirty,' I said.

The road to Ashby de la Zouch held little traffic. The morning had lightened into clear pale skies and the slanted lemon-coloured sunshine that is unique to early winter. Roman had put on gold-rimmed sunglasses and lowered the visor on his side of the car. He was wearing a business suit of dark grey worsted with a white shirt and blue tie. The car was a small grey hatchback, quite unlike his usual style. His smile was edgy, his tone clipped; as we came into Coalville he said, 'Hope this doesn't inconvenience you. Something came up. Needs sorting out at once – today.'

'No,' I said, 'I've been half expecting you to call me.' I turned back to look at Jasper, who sat regal and upright in his special seat. He looked like a miniature royal on a goodwill tour of the Midlands coalfields. He ignored all my attempts to gain his notice and gazed steadfastly at the winding gear and slagheaps of Snibston and Ellistown. I said, 'He's very quiet.'

'He loves the car,' said Roman. 'He's never any trouble when we travel.'

We came into a part of Leicestershire that was unfamiliar to me. We passed through villages with charming names like Sinope, Griffydam and Peggs Green. I talked about the opening of the Berlin Wall, about Christina's plans to visit England in the coming summer; about the invitation to spend Christmas with Maraid and Martin. Roman, mindful of Jasper, drove sedately and with great care, but frustration showed in his fists clenched around the steering wheel, the stiffness of his shoulders. This morning, more than ever, he seemed to be on the very brink of crisis.

The High Street in Ashby de la Zouch is flanked mainly by antique shops and historically notable public houses. Narrow lanes wind off towards the ruins of castle and abbey. There are courtyards with small exclusive shops, and cafés where only healthy foods are served.

Roman found a place that accepted pushchairs and provided highchairs. It was left to me to unzip Jasper from his suit of emerald green nylon. My fingers were clumsy as I shelled him from the one-piece quilted garment. I praised extravagantly the yellow sweater and green plaid trousers now revealed, and Jasper preened and smiled.

Roman handed me a Mothercare bib and I tied the strings; the back of Jasper's neck still bore the tender creases of his babyhood; he smelled sweet and brand new. Roman, suddenly anxious to be gone, slipped a ten-pound note beneath the menu.

'I'll be back,' he said, 'in exactly two hours. Meet me here.'

We watched him stride out into Ashby's main street. He crossed to the opposite side and ducked into an office, the outer walls of which bore several large and gleaming brass plates.

Jasper said, uncertainly, 'Pappi all gone.'

'He'll be back soon.' I spoke firmly while my mind edged around the unlikely but terrifying possibility that Roman might never return, that I did not know the number of his car, or even his surname, and if he had in fact abandoned Jasper, what would I do then? I snatched up the menu and rejected almost every item listed. I looked at the baby's tremulous face and said, 'I wonder if you like chips?'

Jasper seized upon the word. 'Ships,' he shouted, and banged both fists upon the high-chair tray.

'I don't really think they're good for you,' I told him. 'Perhaps if we ask for a poached egg with them?'

For myself I ordered hot milk and a doughnut. Jasper showed such pleasure when the chips arrived that I guessed they must feature often in his diet. I showed him how to dip them into the egg yolk, a trick that was obviously new.

It was not until his meal was finished, the warm milk drunk, that he said again, and this time on a questioning note, 'Pappi all gone?' Tears were not far off, his lower lips trembled.

I wiped egg yolk from his mouth and fingers, lifted him from the high chair, and slid him back inside the quilted suit. 'Pappi,' I told him gently, 'will be coming back quite soon.' I placed him in the pushchair and tucked the blanket around him. I stroked his cheek and whispered what I hoped were words of reassurance. As we left the café his eyelids were already drooping into sleep. As I negotiated the two steps down on to the pavement I saw Roman on the opposite side of the street, emerging from the doorway of the brassbound office, a slender fairhaired girl at his side. They began to walk uphill, she teetering dangerously a few steps behind him on the highest heeled shoes I had ever seen. He turned without a backward glance into the swingdoor of the Rose and Crown. She followed him across the flagged porch. I saw the heavy door swing dangerously back upon her so that she stumbled and then fell. I saw Roman re-emerge, grab at a handful of her long black coat and yank her upright. He pointed at her shoes. She reached up and slapped his face, then marched before him through the swingdoor. As they passed from view I looked down at the pushchair. Jasper was blessedly asleep.

Ashby de la Zouch had grown colder since our arrival. A keen little wind found my feet and fingers. I had dressed unwisely for smartness rather than warmth, not wishing to embarrass Roman. I began to move briskly up the sloping High Street. The café doughnut had been an unwise choice; it lay leaden and undigested along with the unease I felt at the recent scene. Not for one moment did I doubt that the girl in the stylish black coat was Jasper's mother.

The doors of the Corn Exchange stood wide. A handwritten notice said that an antiques market was held there every Monday. I wheeled Jasper inside on a waft of warm air.

The stalls were draped with white cloths and pieces of old velvet, and lit attractively with fringe-shaded lamps. I began to roam among the Coalport and Wedgwood, the polished silver and jewellery cases, the collections of antique bottles and coloured glass.

There were racks of 1920s coats and dresses with matching hats, and crocodile-skin shoes and handbags. There was furniture which might or might not be reproduction. I lingered for a long time beside the book stalls which sold old and rare editions.

Jasper grew restless. His head moved on the pillow, he rubbed his nose and uttered an experimental wail. He came suddenly and fully awake, looked up into my face and crumpled into tears. I forestalled the only phrase he had so far spoken and before he could inquire again for 'Pappi' I snatched up a wooden duck from a nearby stall, and placed it on the pushchair apron. Jasper sat upright; his fat fingers reached for the distraction, he smiled and said, 'Quack-quack!'

'Clever boy,' I cried. I turned back to the stall and saw that the duck held by Jasper was the smallest of a whole flotilla, beautifully carved and inlaid in expensive woods. The price tag which hung about the neck of the largest duck bore a predictably high figure.

The stallholder said, 'He's taken quite a fancy to it.'

'Yes,' I said, and without hope, 'I don't suppose you would sell me that one small duck?'

'I'd like to oblige you – but, as you can see, it's a part of a set.'

I attempted to prise the duck from Jasper's fingers. He looked reproachfully at me, his eyes filling once again with tears. As I managed to free it, he roared more in anger than regret, 'Quack-quack all gone!'

Meekly, and apologetically, I restored it to him. 'I'll take them all,' I told the grinning stallholder.

'Thought you would,' he said. 'You doting grandmothers are all the same.'

I placed the remaining five ducks of the flotilla upon the apron of the pushchair. Jasper, enchanted, crashed them happily together while I wrote the exorbitant cheque.

The folding and stowing of the pushchair, the strapping of Jasper into his rear seat, gave me time to observe Roman. He did not have the look of a man who had felled his wife by means of a swingdoor, or one who had recently suffered a slapped face. He seemed, in fact, calmer, more relaxed than I had ever known him. Perhaps he was one of those men in whom an act of violence released tension. He asked if Jasper had given me trouble, scolded me lightly for the expensive gift of the carved ducks. I said to consider them as an early Christmas present.

As we drove out of Ashby de la Zouch he was humming

contentedly. I, on the other hand, still felt disturbed by the nasty little scene in the doorway of the Rose and Crown. 'You seem pleased with yourself. Did your business meeting go well?'

'Yes,' he said. 'I think you could say that.'

'And what about Serena? Was she damaged when you let that swingdoor crash back into her face?'

The answer, when it came, was slow, reluctant. 'So you saw that, did you? It was all her own fault. Anyway – what makes you think it was Serena?'

'Who else would you dare to treat with such contempt?'

The silence in the car was absolute. Jasper had resumed his mute role of visiting royal. I regretted the words as soon as they were spoken but could not bring myself to say so.

The sharp sunlight of the morning had become diffused behind thin cloud. Roman continued to drive as carefully and sedately as any Sunday driver. He did not speak until we reached the Deerpark café. He said, without warmth, 'Thank you for looking after Jasper. It was a great help.'

I released myself from the seat belt and opened the car door. I said with equal coldness, 'Think nothing of it. It was a pleasure.'

As the car pulled away from the kerb, Jasper waved the fist that clutched the smallest duck.

At the Brandenburg Gate the media of many countries awaited the opening of a crossing-point at this special place. On December 23rd I heard on the news that the barriers were finally removed.

In the days that led up to Christmas I had waited without real hope for a call from Roman. I visited the Deerpark café, studied vehicles standing in the car park. On one rainy afternoon I went so far as to visit the city mall where Jasper lived, and stared up at the flower-sprigged ruffled blinds which hung at the apartment windows. I even entered the boutique and examined, self-consciously, the racks of droopy mud-coloured skirts and dresses, the trays of brassy, Nefertiti-style bangles and earrings, the incredibly high price tags.

Experience informed me that, when worn by young girls like my granddaughter, these garments were fashionable, charming even. But suspended from hangers they looked much as I felt: dispirited and mean.

On the morning before Christmas Eve I rang the boutique and asked if I might speak to the owner. Mr Smith, I was told, would not be available until after Christmas. Roman's choice of English pseudonym would at any other time have been amusing, but I could think only of Jasper and take comfort in the memory of his pleasure in the carved ducks.

My son Paul came to see me Christmas Eve, bringing flowers. The lamplit room was quiet and full of shadows; his ability to recall exactly the small joys of his childhood amazed and consoled me. He spoke of another Christmas Eve, Martin still a baby, and Paul himself an observant and persuasive child who had known for some days that, among a dozen other gifts, the longed-for train set was lying concealed underneath spare blankets in a wooden chest.

'Please, please! I can't wait till morning. I only want the train set now, before I go to bed.'

He had spoken his first words at nine months. At the age of three he was as articulate as any adult.

'No,' I told him, 'Christmas morning is the time for presents.'

'Not in Germany it isn't.' He had stood, feet apart, his cheeks flushed scarlet with a rare defiance. 'Daddy says – he says that in Germany *der Weihnachtsmann kommt* on Christmas Eve!'

His accurate rendition of Kurt's blend of English and German speech was irresistible and touching. I stood undecided halfway up the stairs. To marry a foreigner, I had read somewhere, was to live a life of translation. It was also one of constant compromise.

'All right,' I said, 'but not the whole train set. I will give you one of the signals to play with. Will that do?'

He had nodded, the bright blond hair falling thick and straight across his forehead. When Kurt and I looked in on him, much later that evening, Paul slept with the signal clutched tightly in his fist.

I studied him now. At the age of forty the once blond hair was silver; he had inherited Kurt's wide cheekbones and high colouring, the deepset blue eyes. Like Kurt, he was passionate and selective in his interests. Paul collected Roman artefacts, studied archaeology, the very distant past. In the company of Karl, his son, he fished the Midland rivers. He had grown into a quiet man, solitary rather than unsociable. He and I understood one another. But then, we always had.

Christmas Day was mild and windless. Martin collected me exactly at the time arranged. He drove slowly along empty roads and there was a kind of peace between us. He did not speak about his childhood memories of Christmas which would remind him painfully of Kurt, but of the future, which was safer.

*

Maraid was loving in her welcome. Arm about my shoulders, she drew me into the house, the family. I admired the tree trimmed by Matthew and Liese. I viewed acquisitions new since my last visit; explored the wintry garden; wondered again at the industry of my son who had raised a spacious house from a smallish bungalow. The affection I offered in return was tentative, exploratory, but then, it always had been. Too close was to invite rejection. If I could only relax into complete trust – but control was difficult to break, and the barrier that stood between Martin and me was as wide and high as it had been when first erected on the night of Kurt's death.

On the third morning after Christmas the telephone rang. The voice was female, low pitched, nervous. 'Am I speaking to Mrs Catherine Baumann?'

I knew at once that the caller was Serena. I said, 'I'm Cathy Baumann.'

'I believe you know my husband. His name is Roman. I have to talk to you about him.'

'I'm listening.'

'No. Not like this. I hate the telephone. I need to see you.'

'Why? What's happened? Is Jasper –?'

'Roman has disappeared. He's taken Jasper with him. He was in a very odd state of mind when I last saw him.' She paused to control the panic in her voice. 'You know more about my husband's movements than anybody else.'

I said, 'I know nothing of Roman's movements.'

'Oh, come on! You're his ever-listening ear. You're the understanding older woman, aren't you?' Her tone began to rise on a high note of suspicion. 'He's not there with you, is he?'

'No,' I said, 'he has never visited my house. I saw your husband last on the day we went to Ashby de la Zouch. We had a sort of disagreement. I objected to his treatment of you. I am afraid I spoke my mind about it.'

'Oh,' she said in a different voice, 'oh well, in that case would you be willing to meet me somewhere?'

'Where?'

'I have to be in Nottingham tomorrow morning. I could meet you for lunch. Or perhaps you would rather I came to your house –?'

'No,' I interrupted, 'Nottingham will suit me very well. I'll be waiting in the Market Square. Twelve-thirty prompt.'

'But how shall we recognize each other?'

'Don't worry,' I said, 'I shall know you right away.'

It was the stilt-like heels that from a distance distinguished her among the flock of youthful fairhaired girls who walked more comfortably across the Market Square in their bright suede Dr Martens and multicoloured trainers. I saw her pause beside the fountain. She at first made tentative moves towards several fashionable fortyish ladies as they emerged from the Exchange Arcade holding carrier bags from Jaeger and Rodier.

It was not until she wrapped the long black coat tight about her and sat down on a stone bench that I began to walk towards her. She noted my approach but her gaze was blank, uninterested. She was not the insipid blonde of my expectations. Seen close to, Serena was all gold. Golden skin, golden hair, and wide, slightly tilted, tawny-coloured eyes.

I said, 'Serena. I'm Cathy Baumann.'

Still seated, she began to take in my white hair, my tailored navy-blue suit with matching shoes and stockings; the large square handbag that looks more like a briefcase. She said,

'But you can't be! You look like a social worker. And you're much too old!'

I smiled, and the pink colour of embarrassment rose beneath the golden skin. One slender, steel-tipped heel beat an involuntary tattoo on the paving of Market Square. Serena was nervous. She said, 'That was very rude of me – and stupid. But I'm sure you've been told how I'm all of that, and worse.'

'Let's get some lunch,' I said.

The restaurant was one of those smart little places situated in a mall even more prestigious and upmarket than that in which lay Roman's principal boutique and his family living-quarters. As we entered the mall Serena had gestured towards a dress shop which bore the familiar red and yellow logo.

'We have a lock-up here,' she said, 'just a small one. Rents in Nottingham are sky high.' Predictably, she ordered salad and Perrier water and, since she insisted on paying for the meal, I felt obliged to be equally abstemious.

I prodded the futuristic arrangement of red and green herbage on my mustard-yellow platter. Serena speared rings of onion and peppers but did not eat them. We tried hard not to look at one another. I needed to gauge the quality of her, but her golden aspect dazzled and distracted me. I sought to reach her through compliments. I said, 'Roman once mentioned, quite rightly, that you were beautiful. He also said that he was very jealous.'

She inclined her head in an oddly old-fashioned gesture of gracious acceptance. 'So what else has he told you?'

'Very little, really.' I began to choose my words with care, not wishing to make statements which might sound like accusations. 'He's not a very – well, cheerful person, is he?'

She threw down her fork and the rings of pepper skittered

to the far edge of her plate. 'Not very cheerful? For someone who writes books, you have pretty limited powers of description. But you're bound to be prejudiced, aren't you? You probably find all that Russian melancholy and German angst attractive?'

'No. As a matter of fact I find it intensely irritating. But I feel – have felt from the very outset – that there is something seriously amiss, some underlying problem.'

'Seriously amiss! Underlying problem! My God, you even talk like a social worker! Roman Komanowski is a madman. He's obsessive, paranoid, depressive, and impossible to live with.'

I laid my fork down carefully across a mound of red cabbage. 'He is also,' I said, 'extremely unhappy.'

'And what do you think I am?' she asked.

Observed close to, the yellowish edges of an ebbing bruise were plain to see across her cheekbone, and I remembered the weight of that swingdoor in Ashby de la Zouch.

'Yes,' I said, 'well, that's why I came here. To hear your side of things. I am not your enemy, Serena. This meeting was, after all, at your request.'

'I know.'

'Roman told me how he met you.'

'I'll bet he did! He loves to tell that story.'

'Is it true?'

'Oh, it's true enough. More fool me for allowing him to talk me into marriage.' A sudden rueful smile transformed the almost too-perfect features. 'It's usually the girl who holds out for a wedding ring and that useless bit of paper that goes with it. In our case it was Roman who simply had to make it legal.'

'He wanted a child?'

'As soon as possible. No consultation. His decision.'

A waiter removed our plates of mangled salad and brought

a tray of tea. I busied myself with milk jug and sugar crystals. The teapot dripped a little, as they always do in expensive restaurants. I caught sight of our reflected images in a flanking mirror. We might have been mother and daughter on a shopping expedition: I in my good navy blue that in future I would be bound to think of as my social worker's outfit; Serena, gilded and exquisite, in a designer dress that was the exact colour of over-boiled cabbage.

I said, 'You're not really worried at all about Roman and Jasper. I think you know where they are.' I spoke more sharply than I had intended.

The pink colour came again into her face and then drained away. 'I had to say something, didn't I? I thought you wouldn't see me. I imagined you different somehow – Roman said you were an author – a bit fierce, not too easy to talk to.'

'And now?'

She surveyed me, head tilted. 'I think,' she said, 'you have an unsympathetic image – it's probably the way you look. Anyway – I'm desperate – I can't talk to my parents – and Roman won't even consider seeking marriage guidance.'

'Are you sure,' I asked, 'that you don't mind my involvement in your personal life? After all, I'm not a relative. I'm just a casual observer, really.'

She said, with devastating insight, 'You're not half as disinterested as you make out. You don't fool me, Mrs Baumann. I'd guess that as a rule you're a very cool sort of woman, not the kind who gets mixed up in other people's messy marriages. Roman says it's Jasper who is the main attraction for you.' Her tone grew bitter. 'You're one of these types who gets all emotional about babies and small children. It's because of my child that you keep visiting the Deerpark!'

'Ah yes. Your child. I was beginning to wonder if you had forgotten his existence.'

'I can't help it, can I?' Now her temper flared. 'I can't help it if I'm not the maternal type. Not all women are, you know.' She looked down at her fingers as they shredded the yellow paper napkin. 'I'm not very good with him. I'm clumsy. He makes me nervous. He's only a baby, but I know he doesn't love me. Doesn't seem to like me. I can't even make him smile. I get so uptight when I'm alone with him that I do stupid things. I dropped him twice when he was very tiny.' She halted, and then continued in a quieter tone, 'Would you like to leave now, or will you stay and drink your tea?'

I said, 'That terrible bruise on Jasper's forehead. How did that happen?'

Her voice was so low that I had to strain to hear it. 'I had,' she said, 'this marvellous idea. Let's spend more time together, have little outings, act like a normal family and perhaps we would become one. It was going really well; we bought him a set of plastic circus animals in Lewis's toy department. Then we took him to McDonald's and he had french fries in a paper cone. He really loved that. We had parked the van quite close to the bank. Roman needed to use the cash dispenser before we went home. He handed Jasper to me and said to get into the van. When Jasper saw Roman walk away he began to scream and struggle. I got very nervous – it was difficult to hold him, and people were staring at us. Well – I misjudged the height of the van roof. As I bent down to get into the passenger seat his forehead hit the roof edge – oh God – I thought I'd killed him! He was so limp and pale. The doctor in Casualty acted all suspicious – we'd been there before – twice, in fact. And each time it was my fault.' She bit her lower lip, and this was the first outward sign she had shown of any inner turmoil. 'Roman didn't trust me after that. Things got very nasty. Rows and accusations. He wouldn't leave Jasper and me alone together. He said I was unfit to be a mother.'

Her tawny eyes filled suddenly and unexpectedly with tears that did not quite spill over. I had the unworthy thought that she might wish to register emotion but be unwilling to smudge her careful make-up.

'And to be perfectly honest,' she went on, 'he's absolutely right.'

I watched the brimming tears roll down her face and drip on to her clenched hands. I said, ashamed, 'It's not that you're unfit. You're simply frightened of handling Jasper. It's partly Roman's fault, he hasn't given you a chance.' The sympathy in my voice intensified her weeping.

'You can see why I had to leave him,' she sobbed. 'I was surplus to requirements. I felt so shut out.'

'Yes. Yes, I can see that. And now?'

'We saw a solicitor that day in Ashby. Nothing was resolved. Our Market Harborough shop has living accommodation. I'm camping out there at the moment.' Her gaze became intent. She asked, 'He's not seeing another woman, is he?'

'No,' I said, 'I'm quite sure he isn't. But apart from your marriage problems, Roman has something quite other on his mind. I always have this feeling when I'm talking to him that a substantial part of his thoughts are elsewhere.' I paused, and now it was my turn for the intent look. 'Where,' I asked, 'has Roman taken Jasper? Where did they spend Christmas?'

'I don't know the exact location. He had airline tickets and his passport. When I asked him where he was going, all he said was "to the Circus".'

The meeting with Serena had answered many questions and

posed a dozen others. We parted on a hopeful note. I advised her immediate return to Roman. There was, I told her, no reason why an uncertain start should presage a disastrous ending, and all it needed was her time and patience to achieve the bonding that had not occurred in the first year of Jasper's life. But don't leave it too late, I recommended. A son who grows to manhood devoted exclusively to his father can be almost impossible to reach.

One question remained before we parted. 'How did you obtain my unlisted telephone number?' I asked.

'Oh,' she replied, without a trace of shame, 'I make it a rule to peek in Roman's diary while he's bathing Jasper. It's where he writes up all his secrets. I don't often learn anything important. He's crafty. He knows very well that I can't read German.'

On the first day of the new year I walked the mile that lay between my house and Kurt's grave. I read as I always did the gold-leaf inscription on the black stone:

BORN Pommern JUNE 10th 1921
DIED England JANUARY 2nd 1975.

I was still unable to come here on the exact day of his passing. I filled a vase with water and arranged the hot-house freesias, knowing that they would perish within hours. I stood there for a long time and watched the sun swing lower in the western skies. As I turned to go I felt Christina's presence with a clarity that was startling.

The sunsets of winter are extraordinary and few. I returned to the town through an afterglow of colours that shaded from crimson into soft pink, to lemon and the palest turquoise, and then downwards into the violet dusk of the early January evening.

I walked very slowly. I thought about Serena and Jasper; about Roman who wore an earring that bore the stamp and style, as did he himself, of the tribe of Zinte gypsies; Roman, who was lithe and limber, who had seemingly flown out at Christmas to an unknown circus destination: who wrote his most secret and personal thoughts in the German language.

On this New Year's day the only café sanctuary open was McDonald's. I needed to sit among strangers, to half-hear conversations in which I had no part. I hesitated at the door; the regular patrons of this place were parents with small children, students from the University, young people who wore tracksuits and carried bags marked Adidas and Head. I went in and was served with root beer in a styrofoam cup, and a cinnamon doughnut in a paper bag. The moulded plastic bench proved more comfortable than it appeared. I had chosen a corner-placing close to the wide plate-glass window. The music, unobtrusive and already out of season, had Johnny Mathis still 'dreaming of a White Christmas'. There were, thank God, no sentimental songs that celebrated New Year.

Kurt loved the television films that showed rivers and mountains, the vast tracts of wild land found in Texas and Wyoming; and the beautiful horses, most of all the horses, ridden by the cowboys and Indians in these Hollywood extravaganzas. We had watched such a film on that first evening of the New Year of 1975.

The heart attack had come upon him without warning. As the film credits climbed the screen he had risen from his armchair and walked into the kitchen. He had that secretive withdrawn look that meant pain. He concealed it from me when he could. But pain does not go away by itself. Angina pectoris had become his master. It obliged him to move slowly, squeezed his chest, commanded obedience, respect. It was parent, teacher, *Wehrmacht*. We both knew that one day it would destroy him.

From the kitchen I could hear the clattering of cups and cutlery. These were his regular self-appointed duties, this setting of the morning tea-tray, the breakfast table. When the silence had lasted a full three minutes I called his name, but he did not answer. As I entered the kitchen he began to fall forwards. I caught him, eased him down into a chair, held him in my arms for comfort, not knowing then that this was to be my last loving contact with him. Minutes later, and he was in the excluding charge of ambulance attendants, nurses; and a doctor who had needed to telephone five hospitals before a bed could be found for a coronary case. No beds being available in the local hospital, he endured the thirty-mile dash to the City Infirmary, the oxygen mask, the stops and starts. He was wheeled through a casualty department full of drunks and addicts. The thugs, the hooligans and the innocent bystanders were waiting in line for running repairs. His stretcher was wheeled at speed, because heart failure rated priority. I sat on a metal chair while the addicts moaned and the vomiting drunks fell around me. No bright lights here, no clean tiled floors, no white walls. This was the condemned wing of an outdated Victorian hospital, soon to be replaced by new red brick and gleaming plate-glass. In the meantime the nurses worked with inefficient lifts and beneath flaking plaster. After thirty minutes by the clock on the wall, he was taken to what I assumed to be Intensive Care.

The nurses' sitting-room was shabby. Lengths of orange cretonne were draped across the armchairs in an attempt to conceal their greasy coverings and broken springs. A scarred table held a dented metal ashtray. A strip of dirty matting

made a hazard for unwary feet. I could not bear to sit down
but paced the six steps between door and window. Over an
hour had passed and no one had spoken to me – I had been
stashed like an untidily wrapped parcel in a left-luggage office.
I was frightened – more frightened than I had ever been. For
as long as I lived I would remember this awful little room,
each minute like an hour, each hour a day.

A youth in a white coat came to see me. His gaze wavered
and bounced off the far wall. He said, without conviction,
'We're doing what we can.'

The nurse was altogether different. Cap perched on her
short blonde hair, belt cinched around the waist of her white
cotton uniform, she was all briskness and barely concealed
contempt. It was many years later, when the knowledge failed
to comfort me, that I learned she could not have been the
Ward Sister I had taken her to be, but a recently promoted
Staff Nurse, left in sole charge over New Year of a number
of critically ill and dying patients.

She said, 'If I allow you to go on the ward to see him, you
will have to promise not to throw hysterics. I have several
extremely sick patients. I must put their welfare first.'

I promised her that I would not do the thing which in any
case I never would have done.

Kurt's bed, the first inside the door, was lit up like a stage set,
leaving the rest of the ward in shadows. Two very young
nurses ministered to him. A stack of pillows lay on a chair;
one girl slid the metal backrest into the upright position while
the other began to heap pillows up behind him. I had taken a
few steps forward when the backrest, insecurely latched, collapsed with a crash that was awful in that quiet place. Pillows
slipped sideways to the floor. I saw him fall backwards on to

the projections of the bare metal, saw the shock superimposed on features already blue and drawn with pain. I wanted to shout, to strike the nurses from his bedside, knowing that I had delivered him into the hands of inept strangers.

It was at this moment that the screaming started inside my head.

I was dismissed, feeling like an errant child who has strayed into the adults' quarters, back to the orange-cretonne chairs and the cups of tea I did not want, and the cigarettes I could not smoke. Banishment equalled punishment. I resumed my pacing of the dusty matting, shoulders bowed, arms wrapped tight around my aching stomach.

The door opened suddenly, and there she was, our angel of mercy, not a blonde hair out of place, not a crease, not a word of hope. She carried a notepad and pen. She said briskly, 'Do you have any family?'

'I have two sons.'

'I need their addresses.'

'Why?'

'I need to contact them.'

'Why?'

Only now did she pause; only now did she look directly at me, see me as a person. She said reprovingly, 'At a time like this you should have your children with you.'

The scream in my head reached an intense pitch. I thought about Paul and his wife and their small child; about Martin, and Maraid who was soon to give birth to her second baby. I imagined the police, at two in the morning, knocking on their doors.

'No,' I said, and now the reproof was in my voice. 'There's no need for that sort of drama.'

In the half-hour that followed she returned to me three

times. I found her persistence irritating. On the final visit she grew angry. I was forced into a stammered explanation.

'He's had previous heart attacks – our sons were never fetched – if he should see them at his bedside this time – he might think – would think that he was – very ill. I don't want him to think –'

She gazed at me, said nothing, and I could not gauge that look. She said, as she left the room, 'You may hear a commotion in the corridor. I have told the team to stand by in case we need them.'

The significance of her words and tone meant nothing to me. Resuscitation, at that time, was a word with which I was unfamiliar.

She left the notepad and pen on the table, close to my hand. Almost at once an older nurse came in. She said, 'I really think you should let your sons know what has happened.' Her voice was gentle, there was kindness in her face. She reached out and touched my hand and that single gesture convinced me that Kurt's condition was more perilous than I had thought. I at once picked up the pen and wrote the names of our sons and their addresses.

She said, 'You can come back to the ward now.'

'But only,' I said, 'if I don't cry, if I don't get in the way? I can't promise not to do that.'

'You could,' she said, 'stand just outside the door.'

At no time did I believe that he could die, that he was already very close to death. In my mind he was one of the immortals. I stood in the corridor beside the swingdoors; after a time I returned to the nurses' room, and sat down on the orange cretonne. When the footsteps pounded past the closed door I chose to believe they belonged to a team of specialists, come to save him. I heard them leave, slowly and quietly. The blonde nurse came back, a sheaf of papers in her hand. She did not look at me. She said, in a cold little voice, 'He's gone. There was nothing we could do.' She slapped the papers on to the table. 'I sent for your sons, but of course it was too late by then.' She began to fill in the blank spaces on a large form. She asked questions: Kurt's age, his date of birth, his place of residence. 'Your husband's belongings,' she said, 'will be put into a plastic bag. You can collect them from Reception, but not until after twelve noon.'

Her final question was put with a forced belated friendliness; her change of attitude was like a commendation of my lack of hysterical behaviour. 'Did you,' she asked, 'spend a happy Christmas?'

Out in the corridor the first face I saw was that of Martin. Anguished and stiff with condemnation, he halted several paces from me. He said, 'I should have been told sooner, I should have been here.'

I turned away and walked towards the lift. Because of the screaming in my head I did not really hear him. The only pain that counted was my own.

Paul and his family, I learned later, had spent New Year with his in-laws. The police had called at his home address but failed to find him.

Three days into January and I began to worry seriously about Jasper. I had failed to ask Serena where she was planning to spend Christmas and New Year. Perhaps she had joined her sun-seeking parents in Torremolinos. Perhaps she had spent the holiday alone, camped-out in her premises in Market Harborough. More likely, there was already another man in her life, or an old love rediscovered. There had once been mention of a previous relationship. A man for whom she had cared deeply.

I wondered if she had missed Roman; if she had thought about Jasper on Christmas morning? On Friday I weakened. I dialled the number of the city-mall boutique and asked for Mr Smith. A series of clicks, and then I heard Roman's voice raised against the sound of drumbeats.

I said, 'It's me. Cathy Baumann.'

'Cathy! Hello! I was just about to call you.' He paused. 'I need another favour from you. I have an appointment this afternoon with my accountant. Could you possibly stay here with Jasper for an hour? I'd be very grateful.'

The background noise reached a crescendo; some distance from the mouthpiece, but loud enough for me to hear, I heard him call out, 'Jasper – *junge – bitte, bitte, sei ruhig!*' To me he said, 'Serena went crazy. She bought him a drum kit for Christmas – it's his favourite thing since we got back.'

Roman's plea that Jasper should be quiet had been spoken in a way that convinced me that his accustomed language to the child was German. His suggestion that I should come to the apartment to mind Jasper surprised me into silence.

'Cathy?' he said. 'Are you still there?'

'Yes.'

'Jasper has a slight chill. I don't think it's a good idea to take him outdoors at the moment.'

'No,' I said. 'No, of course not. I'll be over later on this morning. Be with you about one. Will that do?'

'Great! We'll be looking out for you.'

I had been prepared for the Laura Ashley flounces, the flowered prints, the antique pine and dried-flower arrangements; the fragrance of pot-pourri. What I had not expected was the ordered state of an apartment which contained a small, ambulatory child.

Roman said, 'I've just put him down for his afternoon nap.

He'll sleep for a couple of hours.' He waved a hand towards a pile of fashion magazines set out on a low table. 'Coffee's perking in the kitchen. There's a cake in a tin.' He shrugged himself into a tan suede jacket, then the heavy front door closed noiselessly behind him. A few minutes later I heard the engine of the Porsche roar into life at the rear of the building.

The sitting-room was tidy, dusted, the cushions plumped. Thick-pile carpet dragged at my feet as I walked across the large square hallway. From behind a door that was not quite closed I could hear small snuffling noises.

Jasper slept between nursery-rhyme patterned sheets and beneath a pale-blue quilt. He lay on his left side, his visible cheek unusually flushed, his breathing heavy. I stood for a long time beside the cot seeing nothing but the sweet curve of his long dark lashes, the tumble of black curls, the amazing physical likeness which he bore to Roman. A tension, of which I had not been conscious, began to relax. But for a feverish cold, Jasper was safely asleep, among the lore of Beatrix Potter, his new drum kit standing neatly in a corner, every surface in the room piled up with plush circus animals. A Christmas gift which must have been from Roman had a prominent place on a tall chest-of-drawers. I moved quietly across the room to view the model Big Top, complete with tiny acrobats and clowns and every kind of circus entertainment; an expensive and elaborate toy, which had been bought more, I thought, for Roman's pleasure, at this early stage of Jasper's life.

The kitchen, large and pine-clad, was packed from floor to ceiling, it seemed, with every tool and culinary aid which had ever been invented. I stood, bemused, and tried to give a name to ancient wooden implements and presses, iron and copper pans, all the 'treen' of which Roman had spoken in such disparaging terms.

I sat down at the stripped-pine table and attempted to visualize Roman and Serena, just two years ago, newly wed and happy, creating their first home together. But nothing I had so far witnessed bore even remotely the stamp of Roman Komanowski. The single imprint he had managed to impose on this pink and girlish bower was a military kind of neatness. I studied the copper pans lined up on high shelves, a precise amount of space between each one. Spatulas and wooden spoons stood at attention in sentry-like storage boxes; knives and cleavers, shining and sharpened, clung in long straight rows to a magnetic board. A mug and a bowl of sugar crystals had been placed thoughtfully beside the percolator. I poured coffee and drank it scalding hot. The apartment, although newly built, had the stuffy claustrophobic air of my aunts' Victorian villas, known to me in childhood. I prowled between sitting-room and kitchen, I looked in on Jasper who did not stir.

At the sound of the returning Porsche I placed myself among the feather-filled cushions of a pale pink sofa. When Roman came in I was turning the pages of a magazine called *Gentlemen's Quarterly*. He went first to the nursery, then seated himself in a facing armchair. He smiled and raised an eyebrow. 'Everything OK?'

'Fine,' I said. 'He hasn't even murmured.'

'He hardly slept at all last night. I got the doctor in this morning. He gave him some syrupy red stuff. He said it would make him sleep.' Roman leaned back against rose-patterned chintz, his skin the unhealthy shade of grey I had seen at our last meeting

'Why don't you snatch a few hours' sleep while I am here?' I said.

He at once sat upright. 'No, no. I'm perfectly all right.'

I went back into the kitchen and poured coffee into two mugs. I sat on the edge of the squashy sofa and watched him drink the strong black brew. I said, 'Serena phoned me. We met in Nottingham. We had a long talk.'

As if I had not spoken he said, 'I went to Berlin. I took Jasper with me. We were there when the Brandenburger Tor was opened.'

'No wonder,' I said, 'that he has such a nasty head cold.'

Roman grinned. 'I'd have bet everything I own that you would say that. But as a matter of fact he caught it from Serena. She was sneezing all over him the last time she came here.'

An uneasy silence grew between us. He wanted to ask about my meeting with his wife. I longed to know what had taken him to West Berlin. Speculative glances passed between us. It was I who capitulated. 'All right, then. Serena found my phone number in your diary. She thought I was some sophisticated forty-year-old looking for a – what's the expression? – toy-boy? My advanced age and my appearance gave her quite a shock.'

Roman's mouth thinned to a straight line. 'She has a nerve. By God, she has a nerve. I hope you told her so. I hope you made it clear that you are my best friend.'

'It wasn't,' I said, 'that sort of conversation.'

'So what did she say?'

I considered. 'Looking back,' I said, 'it's hard to be certain.'

'Ha!' he cried. 'That's typical of her.'

'We talked in a restaurant. She's very unhappy. She shed tears over Jasper.'

I saw his expression change from unconcern to something near distress. The fact that Serena had wept, and in a public place, appeared to upset him more than anything she might have said. He had acquired some nervous habits that were new to me. He plucked, destructively, at the fine beige cashmere of his sweater. One foot rotated endlessly; I fixed my gaze on the soft tan leather cordovan as it made the occasional switch from clockwise to anti-clockwise.

'What were you doing in West Berlin?' I asked quietly.

He became very still. 'I don't think,' he said, 'that is any concern of yours.'

I pulled myself out of the clutch of the pink feather-cushions. I walked to the window, looked down at the window shoppers strolling in the mall.

I said, 'Since you have manoeuvred me into positions where I am obliged to feel concern, I don't think you have reason to be critical when that concern leads me to ask questions.' I returned to the sofa and sat upright on the very edge.

'Now,' I said, 'I will ask you again. Why did you go to West Berlin? And why did you take Jasper with you? To travel with a year-old baby into such a situation and in mid-winter – ?'

'Where I go – he goes. That's understood.' A dull flush of anger crept up the wide flat cheekbones; his opalescent eyes were opened fully now; Roman also sat upright in his chair. 'I took good care of him. He slept all the way to Heathrow Airport. We stayed in Berlin's best hotel just off the Ku'damm. At no time was he cold or hungry. Out on the streets he was perfectly safe. He rode in a canvas sling inside my zipped-up jacket – just as he did on the morning we first met you. He was happy all the time. He loved the crowds and the excitement; and it was Christmas.'

Roman's voice broke on that final word; I saw a sheen of tears film his strange eyes. I felt ashamed, then angry.

'You still haven't told me why you went there.'

'Christ!' he shouted. 'You don't give up, do you?' He stood up, his bony shoulders hunched beneath the cashmere sweater, his hands thrust deep into his trouser pockets. For a moment I thought that he would hit me. My voice also shook a little.

'No,' I said. 'I don't give up. I care about your child, but you already know that. I know you find it difficult to part with the smallest item of information. I have known you for nine months and in all that time I have rarely heard you make a straightforward statement on any subject, save perhaps your business matters. You call me your best friend, and you clearly need someone to confide in. But you don't confide, do you? You duck and weave and make ambiguous statements. You ask me frightening questions which leave other queries in my mind. Like have I ever done something so terrible that I can never forget it, even for an hour? You are sufficiently perceptive, perhaps crafty would be a better word, to know how fond I am of Jasper. I think you exploit my attachment, knowing that however oddly you behave, I will always come running back to the Deerpark. You have gradually drawn me deeper and deeper into your life, and yet when I add up what I know about you it amounts to very little.' I paused and went on in a quieter tone, 'You are sick with a misery of some kind, and I don't believe it to be all down to Serena. For myself, I've had all I can take of your moodiness, your little dramas that are intended to draw sympathy from me. How do I even know if you spent Christmas in Berlin? You could have been in Cleethorpes or Skegness. Or perhaps you were here all the time, lying low in the apartment?'

It was the longest speech of my entire life. Roman looked at me, gape-mouthed, then he strode from the room and returned with a sheaf of papers in his fist. He threw them at me.

'Look!' he shouted. 'See if I'm lying! Hotel reservation, airline stubs. What more do you want? My hand on the Bible?' He returned to the armchair. I leaned back against the sofa cushions. The apartment was quiet in spite of its location; the scent of the pot-pourri was very strong. Roman's face had a crumpled look, his voice came out unwillingly and hoarse. The Middle European accent was very strong now, as if he had regressed to a time when English was still an unfamiliar language.

'It is because I take Jasper to Berlin that you are angry with me, and all this time I think you are my friend, that you have understanding of what I suffer. I take him with me because I must. If I leave him with Serena she may do him damage. Anyway, it is important that he be there even though he will not remember what he saw. I had to be there when they opened up the Brandenburger Tor.'

He rose abruptly and went to stand beside the window. He gestured back into the room. 'I wanted black leather chairs and sofas, you know! I like things to be simple, uncluttered. There's no space to spare when you grow up in a showman's waggon. Functional is the word, I think.' His eyes were losing their opacity; the look he gave me now was grave and open. I began to feel that I was seeing Roman Komanowski for the first time. I exhaled a breath that I had not known was being withheld. It came out as a sigh.

'You told me once,' I said, 'that you were born in East Berlin.'

He nodded. 'On a circus pitch in Teltow, on the night of August 12th, 1961.' He looked down into the mall, and for some minutes he was silent. I thought about his place and date of birth.

He said, 'There was a doctor who always attended our people when we appeared in Berlin. He had gone over to the west side of the city on that Saturday evening to visit his elderly mother. He had travelled on the U-Bahn. By midnight the trains had ceased to run. My birth was a difficult one, so my father told me. My mother haemorrhaged. She died ten minutes after I was born. The doctor who might have saved her was trapped on the wrong side of the barbed wire.' He sighed. 'You could say that the Berlin Wall robbed me of my mother.'

I began to choose my words with great care. 'But you are not German, are you?'

He shrugged. 'Take your pick. On my father's side I had a Russian grandfather and a German grandmother. My mother was *Tzigane*. There were those in her family who spoke Polish, Hungarian, Romanian. She was a dancer. I've seen pictures of her. She was so beautiful —'

'The earring,' I said gently, 'the earring you once showed me. It was hers?'

He nodded. He was as close to tears as I had ever seen him.

'I noticed,' I said, 'that you used the Hungarian word *Tzigane* rather than the German form of *Zigeuner*?'

'A gypsy is a gypsy,' he said, 'in any language.' He made a small ironic bow in my direction. 'But you are surely right; after all, Mrs Baumann, you are the writer, are you not? Words are your business.'

The trivial exchange had allowed him time to recover his composure. A wail from the nursery had him striding for the door, but I was there before him. 'Sit down,' I said, 'and leave him to me! You want him to get used to me, don't you?'

Jasper, scarcely awake, surveyed me from beneath heavy eyelids. The flush had gone from his face; I touched his forehead and found it cool. Recognition flickered briefly. 'Quack-quack?' he asked.

I found the smallest of the carved ducks and placed it in his hand. I stroked his cheek and watched his lids come down, heard his breathing grow regular and deep.

Roman looked anxious and uneasy. He half-rose from his armchair.

'Stay put,' I told him, 'he's perfectly all right. Temperature is down, breathing absolutely normal.' I hesitated. 'He knew me, recognized me straight off. He asked for the little duck. He didn't once ask for his "Pappi".'

A spasm of pain twisted Roman's features, but I felt no guilt.

'Tell me,' I said, 'how it was when they opened up the Brandenburger Tor?'

'You really want to know?'

'I really want to know.'

He leaned forward, placed his coffee mug on a low table, made a fist of one hand and gripped it tightly in the other. 'I find it hard to tell things.'

'Yes,' I said, 'I know you do. But some thoughts are better shared. Easier that way. Too many secrets can be a kind of sickness.'

'I am not a thinking man. I am more for action.'

'Oh yes,' I said, 'like jumping on a plane and flying to Berlin without telling anybody! Well all right – you don't have to inform me of your movements, but friends usually show a little more consideration for each other. Or didn't you know that?'

'I have not had much practice at friendship.'

A dozen sharp replies came to my mind, but instinct warned me to be cautious. I reviewed my new knowledge of him. His mother had died when he was born. He had been brought up by his father, in a showman's waggon, in a circus family. Because of his birth and his mother's death in those night hours when the Berlin Wall was first raised, Roman had invested the city of Berlin with a drama and significance that was obsessive, perhaps even dangerous.

As if he read my thoughts, he said, 'You should not be so surprised about me. You and I are much the same kind of people.'

'Why do you say that?'

'I have read your books.'

'But you told me that you never read novels.'

'So I lied a little bit. I read any book that has the word BERLIN in its title.'

My impulse was to deny, to protect myself, to also lie a little bit. I wanted to tell him that my novels were of the lightweight category, a form of writing almost solely the product of the author's imagination. That what I had written was not necessarily true or what I happened to believe in. But then I looked at him again and realized what it was he wanted from me. I said, 'You knew who I was, didn't you? Right from that first morning in the Deerpark? You knew I had written a certain kind of book?'

He twitched a shoulder. 'Not right away. At first you looked like somebody I might once have met and whose face and name I had forgotten. It annoyed me that I couldn't place you. You could never have been a customer in one of my boutiques. And then I remembered. I had seen your picture often in the local papers, heard you speak once on the radio. I had read your Berlin novel long ago, when I first came to England.' He grinned. 'I checked up on your identity with the people in the café, just to be certain.'

I felt annoyed at the deviousness of him, and then recognized his action as one I might myself have used in circumstances similar to his. Perhaps he had seen me as some sort of link with his old life, a source of information? Whatever his needs and motives in furthering our acquaintance, I must have proved a bitter disappointment. I said, 'I haven't been much use to you, have I?'

He looked away to the far wall, where hung a wide-brimmed straw hat wreathed in dried flowers and draped with long pink ribbon streamers. He almost smiled. 'Like I said, you and I are similar kinds of people. You guard your secrets – I guard mine. One day, perhaps, I will tell something very shocking to you. Then maybe you will not wish me anymore to be your friend.' As he spoke he glanced sideways at me, testing my reaction to his hint of danger. It was a game he had played before, but this time I refused to be drawn.

I said, very slowly, in the mildest, least challenging of voices, 'You were about to tell me what happened when the Brandenburg Gate was opened up?'

His gradual reassembly of himself was a physical transformation which I found fascinating to observe. His rotating foot became still, he uncrossed his long legs, pulled himself upright in the armchair, and leaned forward, his head inclined a little to one side. Most remarkable of all was his changed face. I watched the softening of all his features; the lines etched from nose to mouth almost disappeared, the frown mark between his eyebrows smoothed out so that he appeared youthful and kinder. He did not at that moment look like a young man who had performed some horrific, long-past crime, but like a boy who was recalling some magical occasion put on for his sole benefit, and in the wonder of which he could still not quite believe.

The spate of words came out in a voice I had never heard from him, animated, purged of the usual bitter undertones. He said, 'It rained that day. Cold steady rain out of a grey sky. Jasper stayed snug and dry inside my jacket – I bought a big red and yellow striped umbrella, and hot dogs from a stall. Jasper stained my shirt with grease and ketchup – he spilt Coke on my new trousers. And it was fun, Cathy! He laughed at the flags and got all excited at the music. The British were there, with their military band. They wore scarlet uniforms and marched with a white goat on a long chain. I found a good place for us to stand, a little raised up above the crowds. We looked down on thousands of coloured umbrellas; they showed up like rainbows against the greyness of the great columns in Platz der Brandenburger Tor.

'The crowds were quiet, patient, standing in the rain, answering the questions of the media people about how they felt, what they thought of this historic moment. A new path of asphalt had been laid down. This crossing-point was to be for pedestrians only. The young DDR people jostled a bit for a good position, each one wanting to be among the first to make the crossing.'

He paused, reliving the experience, searching for the words that would explain the way he felt. 'It was a very strange feeling to be back there. To hear German spoken instead of English. I remember my *oma* – my German grandmother – she always spoke to me in her own language. I wondered if she still lived, if she was over there on the Unter den Linden, waiting to walk through with the East Berliners. But it was a crazy notion. I had a lot of those while I stood there. Like thinking perhaps that my mother had not died after all, that she would come walking through this new checkpoint, in her dancer's costume, ribbons in her hair, her arms held out to me and Jasper.' His voice shook a little on the child's name. He attempted a smile.

'As it turned out, it was the new East German bossman, Hans Modrow, who came through first with his entourage; a smallish man with silver hair and a calm face, wearing a blue raincoat. I saw him meet Helmut Kohl, the West German Chancellor, an amazing figure, larger than life, taller than his bodyguards, head and shoulders above everybody else. The crowd started chanting "Helmut – Helmut", and the young men and girls began to climb up on to nearby sections of the Wall.

'Then came the speeches. They said all the predictable things, but Walter Momper, Mayor of West Berlin, made the only remark that sticks in my mind. "On this historical Brandenburg Gate," he said, "hangs the heart of every Berliner." Well, the people liked that very much. Helmut Kohl was visibly moved. I too found it moving. My heart also hangs a little on that place. My mother's grave is not so far from there. No matter where we were appearing, we always came back to East Berlin for the day of August 13th. It is the strongest memory of my childhood.'

He halted, briefly, but I dared not speak. 'Modrow and Kohl,' he went on, 'released a flight of white doves, and the barriers were opened. The people from the east side came pouring through the checkpoint. Their guards were watching them of course, but very relaxed. They leaned on the window ledges of their watchtowers, not a single rifle to be seen.' He sighed. 'Just for an hour or two I had a feeling of belonging. It does not happen very often.' The glance he sent me was defensive; it demanded an understanding he did not quite believe I could be capable of giving.

'There's a part of me,' he said, 'that never wants to settle down. I cannot stay long inside the house. I need every day to walk in open spaces, on grass, and among trees. I cannot take orders, neither can I give them. I am aggressive, angry, quick to raise my fist. In business I am very good. I love to haggle, to bargain, to maybe cheat a little. These traits come from my mother's people. I am truly *Tzigane*.'

'But then,' I said, 'there is the other side of you. The conventional young executive who wears a suit and carries a briefcase. There is Roman the steady citizen who pays his taxes; Jasper's good and patient father; the fellow who loves handmade shoes and designer clothing. What happens to the gypsy then?'

I had said the wrong thing, and just at a moment when it seemed we might have reached a better understanding. Roman rose and walked towards the door and I had to let him go. But there would, I knew now, be another day, another time.

PART SIX

PART SIX

WITH every delivery by Martin of tools and timber, the opening up of my kitchen became inevitable. He took measurements and brought me illustrated brochures which showed the types and sizes of patio doors and we decided that the sliding, redwood-framed type would allow the maximum of light and space. He described the safety lock that he would fit, foretold the transformation soon to be effected. I cleared an accumulation of gardening tools, back copies of *The Times* and redundant shoes, from the dark end of the room. In the rest of the house I did an absent-minded tidying and dusting, gathering up Christmas cards from window sills and shelves and putting them into a drawer because I could never bear to part straightaway with so much stated goodwill. I was standing by the window, duster in hand, and watching the gradual flowering of the street lights when the telephone shrilled through the silent house.

Melanie's voice came clearly across eight hundred miles, but subdued, without its usual lilt, and full of tears. She said, 'I don't know how to say this – I have sad news –' The silence was more informative than anything she might have told me.

I watched my hand which still held the yellow duster begin to dust the telephone table, the lamp, the ashtray, and I knew at once what it was that Melanie found impossible to utter. I said, 'Christina. She died, didn't she?'

'Yes. On December 29th. Postal and telephone communication between us and the DDR has almost broken down. The news has only just reached me, ten days after –'

I said, 'Give me a few minutes, will you? I'll call you back.'

I broke the connection and walked to the far end of the kitchen and looked out from the tiny window on to the straggling creepers and empty tubs of the winter terrace. The Christmas letter from Christina had been cheerful, happily reminiscent; since that day in the Botanischer Garten U-Bahn station the image of her had been shadowy but constant. *'Bis Juni'*, we had promised each other, but even as I planned with Martin the purchase of new garden furniture, a summer chaise-longue, flower beds, I could never quite believe that June would come to pass for both of us.

I went back to the telephone and began to dial the West Berlin number, but before the long sequence of digits could be completed I saw Martin's tall thin outline through the glass panels of the outer door. He came in smiling as he always did, and then the smile faded. He asked, 'What's happened?' and there was no easy way to tell him.

'Christina,' I said. 'Melanie just phoned me. The news has just reached her. Christina died on December 29th.'

'Oh no,' he said, 'oh no.'

We sat in facing armchairs and I was glad that he was there. I could not bear the silence or his stricken face and began to talk in a voice unnaturally fast and pitched too high. I rattled on about the slowness of the DDR postal system, the almost total breakdown of their telephone service. When I finally ran out of words he asked, 'How did it happen?'

'I don't know. I couldn't talk to Melanie – I promised I would call her back.'

He said, 'I planned to start work here tomorrow morning. I'll leave it for a day or two –'

'No, Martin. We'll keep to our arrangement.' He could not know how much I needed his presence at this time – the distraction of voices, brickdust, the sounds of drill and hammer.

There is a kind of therapeutic loneliness that can be lived out only in isolation. The time would come when I needed to be on my own, to mourn Christina, but not yet.

Later that evening Liese called me. The young voice on the wire was sad. 'Grandma,' she said, 'I'm so very sorry. Would you like me to come over – stay with you tonight?'

I told her I was grateful for her thoughtfulness, that I had been half-prepared for bad news from Dresden; that I would be all right. But even as I laid the handset down I regretted my refusal of her offer, and still could not bring myself to ring her back and say so.

Once more I dialled the Berlin number, but there was little more that Melanie could add. 'Manfred,' she said, 'will be writing to us, but it may be some days before post arrives from Dresden.'

The January morning was unseasonably mild and still. I stood beside the fridge and watched the electric-powered bricksaw wielded by Martin cut into the end wall of my kitchen easily, like a hot knife through butter. As the bricks began to fall, I experienced a pang of guilt at the destruction of so much solid masonry for nothing more substantial than a whim. Wasn't it folly to repair or alter what wasn't broken? And then, as a final section of high wall crashed outwards, the sunlight streamed in. It slanted across the cream-coloured china on the kitchen dresser, touched a copper-coated jelly mould and a stunted light-starved houseplant.

Martin grinned at me through a red cloud of brickdust. 'Jericho!' he shouted.

By lunchtime most of the end wall was a heap of rubble; into the remaining brickwork a redwood frame was now inserted. Early afternoon saw the addition of glass sliding-doors, then came the fitting of a safety lock, and a final coat of wood stain.

When the work was finished, the rubble cleared, the kitchen swept and tidied, I stood with Martin and looked out on to the terrace. Seen now from within the house, my view of it uninterrupted, the square paved area had taken on a new perspective. I said to him, 'Can you stay a bit longer? I could make you an omelette. I have a chocolate cake.'

He said, 'Look at me – I'm covered in brickdust.'

'It doesn't matter.'

'Well – if you're quite sure.'

While he washed his hands at the kitchen sink I set two places at the table, put the chocolate cake on to a plate, the kettle on for tea. I began to break eggs into a bowl and whisk them. 'Thanks,' I said, 'for being here today. For taking down the wall.'

My thoughts were muddled, my meaning vague, but he understood. He smiled. 'I wouldn't have believed,' he said slowly, 'that it could make such a tremendous difference.'

He dried his hands and looped the towel back on its hook, and just for a moment I experienced again that curious timeshift which took me back over thirty years to the farm-house kitchen; Kurt washing his hands before the meal that he called *abendbrot*, the children already seated at the table; the happiness of it. I crashed the omelette pan on to the hotplate, and Martin laughed and said, 'You're still as noisy with the pots and pans. Nothing really changes, does it?'

The firm of builders, engaged when the mood for house improvement was running strongly, proposed to move in on me on a Thursday morning. Final measurements were taken, walls tapped, grave doubts expressed about a patch of rising damp. I was given a typed list of the necessary replacements and alterations. Mahogany sash windows and matching front door were settled upon as being correct for the period appearance of the cottage. The outer walls, they said, were in urgent need of pointing. The cellar, damp and ill-lit, with steep and dangerous steps leading down, was to be the first job of the day. The conversion of the two front bedrooms into one large sitting-room was turning out to be a more complicated project than I had foreseen. I decided not to think about it but laid in stocks of instant coffee, tea bags and biscuits for the builders, and assembled mugs and teaspoons on a large tray.

They came in a lorry and a small van; cheerful young men, overalled and duffle-coated, who knew their business. It had been resolved that the cellar, unused for many years, could be easily blocked off, but before this could be done, airbricks would need to be inserted and the rubbish of several generations would have to be removed.

In the three years of my ownership of the house I had descended the cellar steps on only one occasion. I watched from the kitchen archway as the three young men laid plastic sheeting over my carpets and opened up the cellar door. The dank smell, faint when the door was shut, now rose up and filled the house.

Two wine velvet wing-chairs, their colour just discernible beneath a coat of blue mould, were the first items to emerge. Then came several old-fashioned cream-painted kitchen units, warped by damp, and an ancient vacuum cleaner. There were office files, their boxes already beginning to disintegrate before they reached the lorry; cartons filled with old clothes; stacks of newspapers and magazines tied up with string; jars that had once held home-made wine; a badly rusted lawnmower.

*

By teatime the cellar had been swept clean, the airbricks inserted and the dangerous descent of stone steps neatly sealed off by new boards of hardwood. Tomorrow, I was told, work would commence upstairs on the removal of the studding wall; furniture and carpets had already been removed from the two front bedrooms and stored by Martin. Only the curtains remained to be unhooked. I was halfway up the stepladder when the telephone rang.

Roman said, 'What happened to you? It's a week since you were here. We've been three times to the Deerpark but you never came. Jasper kept saying, "Cassy all gone".'

'I've been busy. I've got builders here. Most of my time is taken up with making tea and coffee and moving things from one place to another.' I paused. 'Does he really call me Cassy?'

'Started a few days ago. He can't quite manage the "th" sound. He's got quite a few new words.'

I said, 'How about "mama"?'

There was a silence. 'Well – no. But he doesn't need that particular one. In the circumstances.'

Neither did you, I wanted to point out, but did not dare to. 'Mama' was a word that Roman himself had never used, and yet he seemed quite happy to impose the same sad deprivation upon Jasper. I said, 'I'll be in the Deerpark tomorrow morning. The builders are quite capable of making their own hot drinks and I would rather not witness the next stage of these alterations.'

Roman laughed. 'Traumatic, eh?'

'I wanted it done, and so far it's all turned out better than I hoped. But I'm longing to see Jasper. I want to hear him call me Cassy.'

'See you in the café, then,' he said. 'We'll be there about eleven.' He paused. 'I'd appreciate it if you could mind him for an hour or two.'

I returned to the stepladder, unhooked the curtains, and folded them away into a cupboard. Grief for Christina, I was now to discover, had a way of catching me at unexpected moments. Briefly, I wept into the dusty yellow velvet for the lost June days in England which she would never see.

I began to think about Serena alone in Market Harborough. I dialled the number of the boutique and her light, slightly breathless voice answered on the first ring.

'Cathy Baumann,' I said.

'Oh – Cathy.' There was disappointment in her tone.

'I've had an idea, Serena. If you don't wish to take it up I shall quite understand. I'm meeting Roman in the morning. He's asked me to mind Jasper for him. I shall be standing near the Deerpark entrance at twelve o'clock. If you want to see your baby without Roman being present –?'

She allowed the silence to grow between us until I asked, 'Are you still there?'

'Yes. I'm – I'm not too sure about this.'

'Up to you,' I told her. 'I shall wait ten minutes.' Then I added, unforgivably, 'I feel sure that you will recognize us.'

The conversation wilted. I tried hard to hold on to the link between us. I said, 'You'll be pleased to know that Jasper's feverish cold has gone.'

'What cold? I didn't know he'd had one.'

'But he caught it from you. When you delivered his Christmas present.'

'I haven't seen Jasper for several weeks. The toyshop arranged delivery of that drum kit. It's at least a year since I had a cold.'

There was nothing I could say. A sharp little laugh came down the line. 'Roman's lied again, hasn't he?'

'Yes,' I said. 'I'm afraid he has.'

★

The builders returned just after first light. The van and lorry brought five men this time, who confirmed that hot strong tea would be very welcome. They began by spreading grey twill sheeting over the stair-carpet; then sacks of plaster, buckets, several toolbags and an industrial vacuum cleaner were carried up to the two rooms which would soon be one. One of the bedroom doors, it was pointed out, was about to become redundant. I was invited by the foreman to decide which of these exits should be plastered over; as we had both known from the beginning, it was he who made the final choice. As the hammering commenced I assembled the tea and coffee makings and a tin of biscuits on the kitchen table, put on walking shoes and raincoat, and left the house.

In this warm and quiet winter, snow had not fallen and night frosts were light and rare. People talked a lot about a hole in the ozone layer, and the greenhouse effect. Those who favoured sun and heat seemed to view the prospect of future tropical winters with great delight. Even I was mildly thankful for these pleasant January days which permitted a slow walk in the Deerpark with a small convalescent child. I remembered, uneasily, Roman's state of mind at our last meeting. But the longing to see Jasper overcame my apprehension. From the café window I saw the neat grey hatchback pull into the Deerpark car park. In the time it took for Roman to extract Jasper from his seat and walk to where I sat, there was opportunity to observe that father and son were once again kitted out in identical outfits; as they approached I could see the fine detail of their one-piece suits, made of silvery waterproofed material, with matching peaked caps, and on their feet scarlet and silver trainers.

Jasper came into the café walking, still a little unsteadily, and with both hands outstretched to aid his balance. There was a faint but healthy colour in his face; the glossy curls had grown, they escaped his cap and clung around the edges of its peak. He smiled, revealing eight white and even teeth. Recognition widened his grey eyes. 'Cassy!' he yelled, and stumbled alarmingly in his haste to reach me. I caught him, and lifted him to sit beside me.

While the waitress took our order I had time to study Roman. He looked marginally less tense. I said, while we waited for our soup, 'You're both looking very smart this morning.'

'Photographic session was at nine, for one of those family-type magazines.' Roman's tone was terse, dismissive. 'Serena's idea. She called me late last night. I could have done with a bit more notice.'

'I said, 'So you still work together?'

He looked surprised. 'But of course! As far as business is concerned neither one of us could survive without the other.'

The soup arrived, with biscuits and warm milk for Jasper. I fastened a bib around the child's neck, tying the strings with difficulty across the bulky collar of his suit. I attempted to remove his cap but he held on to it with both hands. Roman grinned. 'He's taken a great fancy to that hat. He even wore it in the bath this morning.'

I leaned back in my chair and ate a bread roll. The soup was hot and good, the familiar surroundings reassuring.

From beneath the silver peak of his cap, Roman's eyes were unusually observant. He said, 'Something's on your mind. What is it?' His voice was quiet, inviting confidences.

I felt grateful for his understanding. On a rush of emotion I prepared to tell him that sad news had come from Dresden, but before my thoughts could change into words he said, 'Look, Cathy – I can see that my problems are really getting to you. You don't have to worry about me. I'll work this thing through. I'll even stop telling you my troubles if that is what you want?'

His self-absorption, predictable as it was, froze me into silence. The moment when I might have confided my own grief passed. I said, as lightly as I could, 'Where would you be if I stopped worrying about you?'

He nodded gravely, still assuming my exclusive interest, and I felt a stab of purest hatred for him. I half-rose, pushing back my chair, and Jasper, biscuit halfway to his mouth, sensed the change of atmosphere. He held both arms towards me; his lower lip jutted out. To Roman he said, 'Cassy all gone?'

I lifted the child and held him close; damp shortcake grazed my chin, then his hands locked around my neck. I said, 'Was Serena present at your photo session?'

'No, she wasn't. She makes arrangements and informs me. I don't want that woman anywhere near my son.'

Appalled by his callous words, all my fury leaked away. I felt my deviousness to be vindicated. I could afford now to be magnanimous; almost, but not quite, forgiving. I said smoothly, 'You can leave him with me until four o'clock.'

'Fine,' he said, 'if you're absolutely sure?'

'Quite sure,' I smiled. I made a shooting gesture at him. 'On your way now, Pappi. We don't need you here.'

The child, in faithful imitation of my gesture, also waved plump dismissive hands. Roman registered surprise at Jasper's action, and not a little consternation. When he left the café he was no longer laughing.

Jasper had progressed in every way since he had last been in my charge. He climbed unaided into the pushchair, careful not to squash the striped plush tiger who, it seemed, had prior rights of space which must be respected. I tucked a small blue blanket round them, recalling that, give or take a day or two, nine months had passed since I had first heard his infant wail from inside Roman's jacket.

The carriageway was empty on this mid-week morning. I heard the church clock strike twelve. From where I stood beside the Park gates I could see the approach of the blue Porsche, hear the spatter of gravel as it slewed into the car park. Jasper was at that receptive stage when any word repeated frequently enough would be seized on and remembered. I considered what Roman might say about my actions on his return, and decided again that I no longer cared. I pointed out the slender fairhaired figure picking a hazardous route on stilt-like heels across the churned-up gravel. 'Mummy,' I said firmly. 'Jasper's mummy is coming. Can you see her?'

He peered obediently from beneath the peaked cap. He wrapped his lips around the new word. 'Mum-mee?'

I wondered if the sound would be as sweet in Serena's ears as it was in mine. I made drumsticks of my index fingers and rapped them on the pushchair apron. 'Mummy bought your drums,' I told him. 'Mummy bought them for your Christmas present.'

He looked uncertain, shook his head, said, 'Pappi – drums,' and I was forced to accept his infant logic. In Jasper's fourteen months of life, most good things had come from Roman.

Serena came up to us on a waft of Gucci number three. I recognized the perfume as one favoured lately by my granddaughter Liese. The cream and black tailored outfit looked incongruous in this woodland setting. She flashed me a tight smile and looked down into her baby's upturned face. She said in a cool little voice, 'Hi, Jas – do you know who I am?'

He looked to me for confirmation.

'Mummy,' I said. 'You remember Mummy, don't you?'

'Oh Christ,' she muttered, 'not mummy! I suppose that bloody silly word is your idea, too.'

'Mind your language,' I said sharply, 'unless you want him swearing like a trooper. He's picking up words very quickly just now. As for this meeting being my idea, well, you didn't have to come here, did you?'

'I didn't know that he was talking. How could I? Roman makes it impossible for me to see him. It's not my fault. You wouldn't believe what Roman threatens –'

'Oh yes I would,' I interrupted, 'and I'm not judging you – well, not too much. What counts is that you're here now.'

'He'll kill us both if he finds out what you've done.'

I smiled. 'Jasper can't tell him, his vocabulary is not all that extensive.' I gripped her elbow, shook her cream-clad arm. 'I'll deal with Roman. What matters is that you keep contact with your son. If you don't make some effort now, you may lose him altogether.'

Serena bent down and prepared to lift Jasper from the pushchair. He resisted for a moment. 'Mind Tiggi,' he warned her. 'Tiggi *schläft*.'

She looked inquiringly at me.

'Tiggi is his toy tiger. *Schläft* is the German word for "sleeps". Roman speaks both languages to Jasper. He's growing up to be bilingual. He's mixing them together now, but he won't always do that.'

Serena lifted her child awkwardly, then lowered him as tentatively as she might have handled a piece of Waterford glass, or a Meissen figurine.

'He's been walking for some time now,' I told her. 'It's quite safe to let him go.'

She did not believe me, but bent down and attempted to hold Jasper by his hand. He would not permit it. He howled his rage and almost fell in an effort to escape. She tried to put

her arms around him but he kicked and screamed until she let
him go. She stood up, obviously shaken. 'You see?' she said.
'What did I tell you? He doesn't like me, never did, never
will.'

Jasper lurched away from us. He left the carriageway and
stumbled uncertainly across the short turf. He found a brown
leaf, bent to retrieve it, and lost his balance. We saw him fall,
saw the surprised look on his face, his instant recovery as he
grabbed up the leaf and struggled to his feet.

Serena watched him, her arms hanging limply, her fists
clenched. Aware of my gaze she stuffed her hands into the
inadequate pockets of the cream suit.

'Give him time,' I said gently. But she turned and walked
away, back towards the Porsche. Faster than I had thought
possible on those crazy heels.

My house, which had been built when Victoria was still a
young queen, now had the look of a building still under
construction. In the five hours of my absence the pointing of
the brickwork, the ripping out of old sash windows and their
replacement, had begun and were part-way to completion.
Inside the house the studding wall had been removed. Electric
wires dangled colourfully from sockets and ceiling. Rubble
had been swept into rough mounds and deposited in corners.
The surplus bedroom door had been removed and sacks of
plaster stood ready to be mixed, to fill in the gap. A coating
of white dust had seeped through the house to cover every
surface. I stood in the wide light room; with the false division
gone it was once again as some long-dead architect had intended it should be. In the early twilight of the January
evening it was possible now to see the rightness of the original
proportions.

The remaining work on the house would, I was told, take

over a week to complete; time in which I could study upholstery and wallpaper patterns, and carpet samples. The
writing, which might or might not become a book, could be
done in the early morning hours. I went down to my desk
drawer and found the sheaf of coloured timetables. Buses to
Market Harborough, I discovered, were reasonably frequent.
And Wednesday was early closing day in that town.

The desire to put life to rights for other people was an
indulgence for which I had rarely the time or inclination. I
had never assumed myself equipped to practise interference,
but now I began to feel an irresistible urge to meddle. I rose
early on that Wednesday morning, and left the joiners and
plasterers making good the door and window spaces of the
draughty house.

Market Harborough turned out to be a small and pleasant
market town. Minus the repetitious chainstores, it had a
number of neat, innovative shops, and a beautiful sandstone
church dedicated to St Dionysius. The boutique which bore
Roman's red and yellow logo was not hard to find. I walked
slowly past the display window which held a single garment,
artfully arranged with matching jewellery and shoes. A small
printed card showed that closing time on Wednesdays was at
twelve noon. I found a phone box and called Serena. I said,
'How are you? I would like to see you. Perhaps we could
have lunch together?'

She began to make excuses.

I said, 'I'm here, in Market Harborough. I'm in the phone
box right across the street. I don't intend to leave this town
until I've spoken to you.'

'You'd better come over,' she said. 'You can wait upstairs.
I'll be closing in half an hour.'

The furnishings of the flat above the shop were expensive,

and paradoxically Roman would have approved them had they been in the city mall apartment. The small sitting-room held a white shag carpet, two black leather armchairs, and a Chinese lacquer coffee table. A black and white photograph, greatly enlarged, was the single picture on the white walls. It showed a fashionable couple, arms entwined, walking through a city rainstorm. The pair looked very much as Roman and Serena must have in the days before Jasper was born.

Serena apologized for the room. 'This stuff,' she said, 'belongs to the previous manager. He'll be sending for it soon.'

'Roman would love it,' I said.

'Yes,' she said, surprised, as if she had never considered his taste in anything. 'I think you're right. He would.'

Market Harborough, I observed, had its share of trendy little eating places. I chose a restaurant that looked long established, and as different from the Nottingham salad bar as it was possible to find. It had pale pink tablecloths, gilt chandeliers and William Morris wallpaper. The set lunch was Canterbury lamb; today's sweet, jam roly poly and custard. I passed the mint sauce across the narrow table, and Serena said, 'This reminds me of Sunday lunch at home. It was always lamb or roast beef.'

I felt reassured; a weekend roast seemed to indicate a former normal home life, complete with caring parents. My doubts about Jasper's globe-trotting grandparents underwent a swift reversal. It may have been the comfort of good hot food and the memory of her own childhood that made Serena more approachable today, less brittle, willing even to discuss Jasper. 'I made a fool of myself yesterday,' she said. 'I don't know what you must think of me, walking off like that, after all your trouble – ?'

'It's not my feelings that should concern you,' I told her. 'It's your child who should be considered.'

Her awkwardness with Jasper had been hard for me to comprehend. It was difficult, looking at her now, to believe that she had given birth, had nurtured a child in the first weeks of his life.

I said, 'Why did you leave them? It seems such an extreme move.' I found it almost impossible to speak sympathetically to her, to suppress my own anger and the lingering suspicion that a former lover might have played some role in her departure from Roman.

She did not answer right away. Then she said, 'I've never really analysed my motives. I sort of acted on impulse. It seemed a good move at the time. Our Market Harborough shop was without a manager, I was travelling every day from home. The flat was vacant.' She paused. 'After Jasper got hurt – got that bruise on his forehead – I really panicked. Roman said I wasn't normal – that I was an unnatural mother – that he and Jasper would be better off without me. But you know all this.'

'I know the mechanics of the break-up; what you and Roman say are the reasons for your separation.'

'There's no other man in my life, if that's what you're thinking.' She spoke quietly and with conviction. 'Roman, I may tell you, with all his faults, would be a very hard act for any other man to follow.'

It was then that I knew, without any doubt, that she still loved him. I said, 'How much do you know about your husband, about his past life?'

She paused, a forkful of roast lamb halfway to her mouth. 'Probably a great deal less than you do.'

'Were you never curious? Did you never ask him questions?'

'Of course I did. To begin with. But he soon made it clear that he wasn't going to tell me. I assumed some horrendous family bust-up – well, you know what these Slavs are like. He didn't want to talk, and so I didn't push it. We had plenty of other problems without his family hang-ups.'

'It could be,' I said, 'those very family hang-ups that are breaking up your marriage.'

'How do you mean?'

'Well, did you know that Roman never knew his mother? That she died when he was born? That he himself was reared by men? That he grew up in a travelling circus?'

'You're joking! No – you're not. So how did he come to tell you all this when he's so close-mouthed with everybody else?' She began to speak slowly, thoughtfully. 'Oh, I see. It's the German connection, isn't it? That book you wrote. He read it a dozen times. It all has to do with Berlin. Berlin for Roman means something pretty awful. Sometimes he screams out in his sleep.' When Serena began to think, even when it was too late, she obviously reasoned to some purpose. 'Makes sense, doesn't it?' she went on. 'The way he is with Jasper. The way he acted when I left them. As if it was no more than he had expected. That women could be relied on to abandon their babies, leave their husbands.'

I said, 'Full marks, Serena! It's taken you only fifteen seconds to come to conclusions that took me months to work out.'

She flushed and looked pleased. 'It's not too difficult when you have the relevant information.' She picked up her spoon and began to trickle custard over roly-poly pudding. She said, 'Roman must have looked a lot like Jasper when he was little. That must have been a pretty rough upbringing for him. Poor little boy.'

'Russians and Germans,' I pointed out, 'tend to be overindulgent with their children. He was probably petted and spoiled by the rest of the family.'

'Yes,' she said passionately, 'he probably was. But look at the hang-ups that he has now. Nothing makes up for the loss of a mother, does it?' The words seemed to generate an echo, to fill the room. Her eyes widened. 'Oh God,' she whispered. 'What have I done – what am I still doing to my own child?'

'You don't need to,' I said; 'it's been such a short time since you left. If you go back now – right away –'

'I can't.' She spoke flatly, without hope. There was nothing to be gained by arguing with her.

I said, 'I'll help you all I can. Now that Jasper is active and walking, Roman finds it difficult to keep business appointments. He trusts me. I might even persuade him to leave the child with me for a whole day.'

'Would it work? He's forgotten me already.'

'Give him a chance – give yourself a chance. You'll never know until you try.'

She leaned across the table, laid a hand upon my hand. We smiled at one another. Conspirators, in league against Roman Komanowski. Women.

The renovations, which had seemed at one point never likely to be finished, came to an abrupt conclusion on a Wednesday morning. The final window glazed, the electrical circuits restored; the skip which had stood in the street for a fortnight, piled high with rubble, was taken away for the last time. I worked through the rest of that day, and the whole of the next one, systematically scrubbing and vacuuming the house. Towards evening, grubby and exhausted, I placed a stool in the exact centre of the new and empty room, and sat in a darkness lightened only by the street lamps.

I wondered yet again why I had gone to so much trouble

to change a house which was for my sole occupation. I thought about my life with Kurt, the way we were with one another. There had been no world for me outside of his world. No friends, no personal ambitions, no future which did not include him. Well, I was trying now, wasn't I? Knocking down walls, letting in light; getting to know Martin. And what would Kurt make of it all, if he could come back to me at this moment, miraculously resurrected?

I moved to the pale oblong of the window. Down in the street a strong wind took an empty styrofoam carton from the gutter and whirled it several feet into the air. Because my doors and window frames no longer rattled I had not noticed the rising of the storm. I remembered the evening last November, the falling of the Berlin Wall, the window of the Taunton bookshop where, because my name had been displayed on a hundred book-jackets, I could no longer summon Kurt back to my mind. The wind, funnelling now through the narrow street, made a sad lost sound. I tried to call Kurt to me; he came, although not with the immediacy I sought, but like a figure seen through the wrong end of a telescope; but there was nothing I could do to bring him closer.

I awoke towards dawn to the sound of roof slates crashing on to pavements. We had moved overnight from bright mild sunshine into hurricane-force winds, sub-zero temperatures and snow. The radio reported power cuts in many places. I found a rarely used and tarnished candelabra, and fitted it with fancy candles, just in case. I telephoned Paul, who said that they were all safe. Martin phoned me and I was able to report no damage so far. A large section of his garden fence, he said, had been ripped out, and now lay on his neighbour's lawn. Even as we spoke the line between us began to crackle into silence, and the lights went out.

The battery-powered radio reported overturned cars, countrywide destruction, rail lines blocked by the debris of the storm. Forty people had already perished according to police reports. I lit the fancy candles which dripped dark green wax, and smelled unpleasant when I blew them out. The day passed slowly. Towards evening, power was restored. At nine o'clock a ping from the telephone announced a restored service. The house grew warm again; at the touch of a switch the lights came on.

The gales abated as swiftly as they had arisen. By Sunday, the Forestline buses, heroic as ever, were running a restricted service. In the Deerpark, hoar-frost lingered in sheltered places, and rime, which had not yet given way to sunshine, still stiffened the brown lace of the bracken. The air had a brittle feel about it; the sun was brilliant between low clouds. A great carapace of ice lay across the centre of the lake. Around and above it there was the constant traffic of wild fowl. I watched them for a long time, but I lacked Martin's skills of identification.

I also almost failed to recognize Serena as she walked towards me. She was wearing the cream and burnt-orange tracksuit which I had thought exclusive to Roman and his son. Cream trainers had replaced the spiky heels; her blonde hair was wound into a coil and secured with pins on the crown of her head, and she wore no make-up. She said, 'I tried your phone but you didn't answer. I thought that I might find you here.'

We walked back together towards the car park. As we passed the Ruin she asked, 'I wonder who lived there?'

'Lady Jane Grey spent much of her life there,' I told her. 'She was married at the age of fifteen to Lord Guildford Dudley. Soon after the wedding she became Queen of England and reigned for all of nine days. She was imprisoned in the Tower of London. She and her husband were eventually beheaded.'

Serena paused to gaze at what remained of the almost royal house. She sighed. 'History certainly puts one's own life into perspective. Poor little Jane! Her troubles make mine seem like nothing, don't they?' She said, 'I want to see Jas. I want to get to know him. I want him to know me. I suppose I have a legal right of access but Roman manages to get around it. I don't know what to do.'

'You could arrange your business matters so that he is occupied for whole days. Then he will be forced to ask me to have Jasper. You and I could go to the zoo at Twycross. We could take picnics. Drive up to the coast.' I paused. 'Jasper does not have enough words yet to inform his father about the company I keep.'

'Do you really mean it?'

'If it's what you want.'

She smiled. 'The storm caused a flood in the Market Harborough shop. That should keep him busy for a day, maybe two.'

'Perfect,' I said. 'Get it organized and let me know in good time what your plans are.'

The storm which had ended the long spell of mild and pleasant weather also marked a change in my slow haphazard days. I found a decorator who hung the walls of my new room with a silky cream-striped paper. A pale carpet was fitted. I rehung the yellow velvet curtains. I discovered and bought chairs and a sofa, loose-covered in a Chinese design of quilted flowers and birds.

Martin fitted shelves into an alcove which would hold my small collection of Victorian glass. We robbed pictures from the rest of the house, and he hung them for me.

In the terrace border that spring I planted roses; I filled urns and pots with fuchsias, put up hanging baskets, set out chairs and table. The early morning writing, which now seemed likely to become a book, still progressed only slowly. The house, as a project, was completed. There remained the conundrum of Roman and Serena.

Our deception of Roman had begun in early February. Flood damage in the Market Harborough boutique had been extensive. Serena refused point-blank to deal with the matter. A disgruntled Roman had phoned me with the usual request. I agreed, being careful not to sound too enthusiastic, to mind Jasper for him.

I met her on a wild March morning at the far exit of the Deerpark. A hire car of undistinguished make and unmemorable colour was parked beneath the overhang of a laburnum tree. A child's seat was fitted in the rear; beside it sat a teddy bear. Serena wore the cream and orange tracksuit, trainers on her feet, and her hair bunched up carelessly atop her head. Now she looked like the young mothers I had seen pushing supermarket trolleys; fetching and delivering their children to and from schools and playgroups. Jasper regarded her with puzzled gravity, but did not utter. He stared at the teddy bear but did not touch it.

Serena said, 'Hi, Jas!' and then proceeded to ignore him. I strapped him into the child's seat. Serena drove fast and confidently. She said, 'We'll take a run across to Market Bosworth. I'm in the process of looking for a small boutique exclusive to children.' From time to time she stole a glance through the driving mirror at her rapt son.

'He's good when he's travelling,' I assured her.

'That,' she said, 'is the sort of thing I ought to know – but I don't.'

We drove through villages called Newtown Unthank and Barton-in-the-Beans. Tendrils of soft blonde hair trailed from Serena's topknot and curled around her ears and across the collar of her tracksuit top. She looked approachable and very young. After miles travelled in uneasy silence, I said, 'How was it in the beginning? You and Roman?'

She slowed, allowing a tractor to come out of a farm gate. We drove on, but slowly now. She said, 'It was never really Roman and me. Like I told you, I got pregnant soon after we were married. He was into fatherhood in a big way. He designed my maternity outfits. He came to those damned breathing classes, actually participated. He was the one who had the backache and the morning sickness while I was feeling fine. He read every book and magazine that he could find on the subject, decided what I should eat, how much rest I needed.' She sighed. 'That pregnancy seemed to go on forever. All he wanted to talk about was baby – baby – baby!'

'Most women,' I said, 'would have been delighted to have such a considerate and involved husband.'

'Considerate of whom? I felt like a piece of machinery which had to be kept in perfect working order until the end product was achieved. I no longer knew who I was. I felt as if I had been invaded. I kept telling him "I'm not ready for all this". I got fat and ugly. For the last two months I refused to leave the flat except for clinic visits. He shopped on his own for baby clothes and all the other gear it needs.'

'What about the actual birth?'

'Oh, he was there in the delivery room,' she said bitterly. 'Where else? I said I didn't want him present. That it was private. But Roman was enjoying himself, wasn't he! Masked and gowned, rubbing my back and fetching me orange juice, encouraging me to pant and rest. You would have thought when it was all over that Roman was the one who had given birth. Oh, he really turned the charm on with the medical staff. Guess who had the baby handed to him first. Guess who got all the congratulations. Had it been a biological possibility he would have breastfed – as it was he had first go at bathing and dressing the baby. When I complained to the nurses they told me that fathers who were encouraged to participate from the beginning continued to be supportive towards mother and child. They said I should be grateful that he was so willing to get involved. But I didn't want him supportive; and nobody gave a thought to my involvement.' She glanced into the driving mirror to look at Jasper again. 'He looked like Roman from the minute of his birth. Roman even chose his name.' She looked sideways at me. 'Do you wonder that I felt cheated? I know I hadn't particularly wanted to be a mother quite so soon, but since I was it seemed unfair that nobody noticed my achievement. Even *my* mother kept on about how useless my father had been when I was tiny, and how lucky I was to have so much help.' She paused. 'You won't believe this, Cathy, but Roman and my mother became jealous of each other. There she was, all set to be Supergran to her first grandchild, and he was equally determined to keep Jasper to himself. In the end I snapped. I got so nervous with the baby that I couldn't cope even on the few occasions when I was allowed.' She struck the steering wheel lightly with her clenched fist. 'It's partly my fault, I suppose. I allowed him to take over.'

'Yes,' I said. 'So how did he manage to persuade you that all this role reversal was a good thing?'

'There was,' she said, 'an article in an American magazine. He showed it to me. It was all about the New Man of the Nineteen Nineties. There were pictures of the New Man shopping in the supermarket, pushing a trolley, an infant in a backpack and a toddler following behind. There were other shots: the New Man cooking dinner, hanging out the washing – waving goodbye to his wife as she trots off carrying her briefcase. People, Roman said, should do the thing to which they are best suited. Well, the inference was obvious. Even I could see that.'

'But,' I said, 'it all went wrong.'

'Oh yes.' There was satisfaction in her voice and smile. 'Bringing up baby was rather more than he had bargained for. And then of course there was all the paperwork from our business. I could cope well with the day-to-day running of the shops, but he was still the buyer. Sometimes he'd be up all night, nappies trundling through the washer, invoices spread all over the kitchen table, Jasper fretful with his teeth. While I,' she said, 'can sleep through any sort of noise. "You're the New Man," I told him, "so let's see just how good you are!"'

I remembered Roman, grey-faced and edgy last summer, walking in the Deerpark, presenting an image of the perfect father. 'He has other problems too,' I said. 'There's something in his past life – but you know that, don't you? You said he often screamed out in his sleep.'

I watched her features change, heard the hard note in her voice. 'I don't want to know about Roman's hang-ups. I have plenty of troubles of my own, the greatest of which is sitting right behind me.'

Market Bosworth was a small attractive town of narrow streets lined with cottages, all lovingly maintained. There were antique and craft shops, but no commercial properties to let. We lunched at a pub where a high chair was found for Jasper. We ate cottage pie and sherry trifle. Jasper watched Serena's every move, but she, carefully and wisely, continued to feign ignorance of his existence.

On the drive back to the Deerpark she said with devastating

candour, 'I really didn't like you when we first met. I've come to see you differently lately. After all, I know now that you mean well.' Her smile was faintly tinged with malice. 'I thought, you see, that you were one hundred per cent in Roman's favour.'

'Since we're being frank,' I said, 'I may as well make my position clear. The only one I really care about in all this mess is Jasper.'

In April the East German Government confirmed that the former German lands which lay east of the Oder–Neisse line were to remain Polish Territory for all time. Reconciliation reached out beyond national borders. In the Volkskammer the Speaker, in an emotional speech, said, 'We ask the Jews of the world to forgive us. We feel sad and ashamed. We intend to open diplomatic relations with Israel, and to offer asylum to persecuted Jews.'

Before departing for his regular Easter slimming cure, Helmut Kohl predicted an economic miracle in the East within five years. But only, he said, if the people worked hard and remained in their own villages and towns. Seven hundred East Germans said, *The Times*, were moving daily into the West.

It was announced that a sum of ten billion pounds would barely be sufficient to improve the East German telephone system. But standard issue handsets were still available in shades of vibrant orange or deep purple.

The man in the East German street was preoccupied mainly by how long it would take to exchange his Trabbi for a Volkswagen.

At the end of June I began to take pleasure in my reconstructed dwelling. I arranged and rearranged the bits of coloured Victorian glass which had, like the house, survived a century and a half of gales and wars. I was less aware this year of the discomfort of bright sunshine and soaring temperatures, for as Martin had promised, the glass doors that gave on to the terrace stood open to the breezes of early morning, the cool of evening. And yet, enmeshed as I was in a construction of half-truths and deceptions, there was an unreality about this summer.

Time passed swiftly. Sunday afternoons were spent in Eileen's garden, a green lawn enclosed by trees and bushes and scented with honeysuckle and the pink blooms of a climbing rose. There was a particular Sunday when we ate lunch beneath the cherry tree, a meal of chilled gazpacho, pâté and French bread, ice cream and raspberries, and I told the story of Serena and Roman, but not as if they were invented characters, imagined and set down on paper, but real people with whom I was acquainted.

Twice, often three times in a week, I collected Jasper from Roman, walked the two miles to the far exit from the Deer-park, and placed baby and pushchair in the drab and unidentifiable hire car. The reconciliation between mother and child was slow and painful to observe. Serena no longer rushed to grab Jasper's hand, to protect him from danger. Her tactics had obviously been thought out; she did not discuss them with me, and I respected her judgement. After all, unsolicited advice had been a hazard in my own life.

I had never known Jasper to be really naughty but, like most attractive children, he was accustomed to notice from adults, to admiration. Serena's coolness puzzled and annoyed him. His chagrin showed up in tantrums, a refusal to walk, to eat; anything at all that would gain her attention. She remained throughout stoical and unimpressed. One day, early in July, in the tiger house at Twycross Zoo, I saw Jasper move close to his mother's side, reach up and slip his hand into hers. Across her shoulder Serena shot me a triumphant smile. The single worrying aspect of the happy outcome was that from this moment on, and without prompting, he began to call her 'Mummy'.

At midnight on the thirtieth of June the Ostmark had ceased to be legal tender. Thousands of East Germans came out on to the streets, to celebrate with beer and fireworks the arrival of the western Deutsche Mark. Border and custom controls between the two Germanies were lifted. Along the former death strip, border guards deserted their posts to celebrate with residents of neighbouring east and west villages.

Helmut Kohl, not noticeably slimmer, warned that the road to prosperity would not be easy. 'Many of our country-men in the East,' he said, 'will have to get used to a new way of living.'

In September Liese came to see me. We talked about her life, the boyfriend of long standing, the recent confirmation of her place as a student nurse in a city hospital on the far side of the county. I experienced the uprush of love that I always felt every time I saw her. Grandchildren are unique, an undeserved gift, and this girl already had a wisdom that I had never gained in over sixty years of living.

I asked her, 'Are you happy?'

She thought about it. 'I am contented,' she said, 'not happy. I don't trust happy. It makes me euphoric – heightens expecta-tions.'

She smiled and laid her hand over my hand. 'Don't worry about me, Grandmother, I'll settle for contented.'

*

The coming together of the two German states was planned for October 3rd. *The Times* of that date read: 'Germany is reborn today, and Europe should rejoice. Reunification has occurred with unexpected celerity, driven by the thirst for justice of a people whose patience simply ran out on November 9th last year.'

On that Wednesday in October the first Lufthansa flight since the Second World War was given permission to land at Tegel Airport.

The British Military Mission in West Berlin would now merge with the Embassy in East Berlin. East Germany's Volkskammer had convened for the last time.

Church services and celebration concerts were held throughout both Germanies. The word which described this happy outcome was *einheit* which, according to my Collins German–English dictionary, meant 'unity'.

Roman had complained frequently that summer of the extra work load put upon him by Serena. By October his temper, even for Roman, was very short indeed.

'Suddenly,' he grumbled, 'there are a dozen things she cannot handle. People that only I can deal with, decisions I must make. It's all deliberate of course. She means to wear me down, to make my position impossible to maintain.' He sounded desperate and pompous.

'Well,' I pointed out, 'it is your business too, remember.'

'Oh, I know all that. But she might show some consideration for Jasper and me. A small child takes up a lot of time and energy.'

'Perhaps,' I said, 'she is doing precisely that.'

'I don't understand you.'

'It's not easy to be an alternative mother, never mind what they say in American magazines. You've admitted that twenty-four hours of every day is a pretty big commitment. In a roundabout fashion, by involving you more in the business, Serena is obliging you to let go. She is giving you a break from Jasper.'

He stared long and thoughtfully at me. He eased himself into the driving seat and snapped on the safety belt. 'You've worked all this out,' he said slowly. 'I wonder why you did that?'

I slammed shut the door. From where I stood beside the open window of the car his head for the first time was on a lower level than my own. The illusion of superior height tempted me to further folly.

'You'll never know,' I said, 'how much I have enjoyed this summer.' I dipped my head so that our eyes were on a level. My irrational fear of him grew less. 'If you're not very careful,' I told him, 'you'll lose everything in life that is precious to you. *Einheit* is the current buzz-word in Berlin. Think about it, Roman!'

We were bound to be found out. Looking back, I am surprised, considering the length and scope of the deception, that Serena and I contrived to meet, undetected as we did, for so many months. Jasper, for whom the whole elaborate charade had been arranged, was fast becoming our greatest danger. As his speaking skills improved, so did the risk that he would somehow alert Roman to the truth that it was Serena who accompanied us on our excursions and not the mythical 'friend with a car' of my invention.

Our greatest safety lay, paradoxically, in Roman's total trust of my integrity. There were times when I felt guilty, but murmurs of conscience were easily stifled when I saw Jasper cuddled in Serena's arms. The bonding which had not occurred in the first year of his life was taking firm hold now.

Even in the few hours they could spend together, Serena had learned to handle him confidently; and gradually his infant allegiance had shifted away from me and on to his mother, which was as it should be.

If I prayed at all, it was to mutter a request that we might be granted a little more time.

In the short dark days that led up to Christmas I met and parted regularly with Serena in a narrow lane that lay behind the café. On that Friday in December we had shopped for Christmas presents, visited a Santa Claus grotto, eaten a lunch of fries and burgers in a Nottingham McDonald's. We drove back to the lane through the fading light of late afternoon. A white mist was rising in the Deerpark, a skein of wild geese just visible above the lake. I thought with satisfaction of my house in which the central heating pump would be purring gently and warmth spreading through the rooms. Thirty minutes must elapse before Roman arrived to reclaim his son. Time and to spare for farewells to Serena, and Jasper's usual meal of milk and toast in the Deerpark café.

It was as Serena bent to release Jasper from his car seat that the child shouted, 'Pappi – Pappi, here is Jas!'

I said swiftly to her, 'Get in the car – close the doors. I'll deal with this.'

I had not noticed the approach of Roman, or heard his footfalls in the lane. I took several steps away from the vehicle, barring Roman's path, forcing him to halt. A Russian saying that he had once quoted to me came into my mind. 'If I had known where I was going to fall, I would have laid a mattress there!'

There was to be no time on that winter's evening for Serena or me to lay a mattress against the shock of Roman Komanowski's anger. As it was, I counted myself fortunate to escape physical attack. I looked up into his face and saw rage of a very special kind; the more terrifying because of his tight control. He said in a cold voice, 'You and I have much to talk about.'

'Later,' I said, foolishly and lightly, as if this was some chance social meeting from which I wished to be excused. 'I'm in rather a hurry at the moment. I'll just get Jasper for you.'

With hindsight I could see that there had been warning signals in his voice and face that morning; this was no impulsive loss of temper, but a passion that had swelled and festered until it filled his heart and mind. Beneath the barrage of his words I remained silent and immobile. There was nothing else that I could do. When he finally ran out of invective I asked, 'How did you find out? I suppose you've watched us?'

'Of course I've watched you, ever since that day when you told me that I might lose everything in life that is precious to me. Until then I believed that you were on my side.'

'And so I was − still am. But being on your side doesn't mean my automatic compliance with all you say and do. And then there is Jasper to consider − and Serena who is Jasper's mother. Yes, you are quite right. I have abused your trust, deceived you, meddled in your life. And I'm glad I did so. Do you hear me, Roman? I AM GLAD *I* DID IT.'

So intent were we upon our personal recriminations that neither of us had registered the soft note of the idling car engine. All at once it roared into life; the vehicle shot forwards, leaving the lane at great speed. The disbelief on Roman's face was comical. I almost laughed. I watched as Serena made a sharp right turn towards the city. I expected Roman to leap for his own car, to pursue.

As if he read my thoughts he said, 'Too dangerous for me to chase her now. Too risky for Jasper.' The words held a deeper meaning than he had intended. He looked down at the empty pushchair, at Tiggi the plush tiger, sitting as Jasper always placed him, with more than his fair share of the blue blanket; and even as I strained to see his face in the last of the twilight, a change came over Roman.

He began to crumple as if all his bones had softened. I had the curious impression that only the slight stiffness of the scarlet leather suit still held him upright. He reached out one hand to the pushchair, the other hand gripped my shoulder with surprising strength. I was reminded of Kurt's final heart attack, the way I had taken his full weight. But Roman was too young and fit for such a seizure – and yet, was this not also a sickness of the heart? He said, 'She's got him now. She'll never give him back.'

'No,' I said, 'she wouldn't be that cruel. She's not that kind of person.'

He looked oddly at me. 'You could be right,' he said.

It was dark by the time we reached his car. He handed me the keys, forgetting that I did not drive. I said, roughly, because I was still nervous of him, 'You'd better pull yourself together. I'll come home with you. You're in no state to be alone. But you'll have to drive us.'

I prefer not to remember that drive back to the city. We rode in silence. As we walked from the car park to the lift that would take us up to the apartment, Roman stumbled and almost fell. I caught at his hand to steady him, and his skin was icy. In the dim light of the lift I could see a sheen of perspiration on his face. I said, 'When did you last eat?'

'I don't remember.' His voice was husky.

'Is your throat sore?'

He nodded. 'Flu,' I said. 'There's a lot of it about.'

At some point in the last days the orderly routine of

Roman's life had broken down. Dirty dishes filled the washing-up bowl; the remains of Jasper's breakfast lay on the kitchen table. On the marble counters groceries spilled from carrier bags; a trail of cornflakes spread across the floor. I plugged in the kettle, found two wizened lemons in the fridge, brown sugar in a bowl, and an unopened bottle of Glenfiddich pushed behind a stack of jars which contained sieved carrots, and prunes and custard. While the kettle boiled I made a swift tour of the apartment.

In the bedroom he had once shared with Serena, only the peaches and cream of the colour scheme remained as a reminder of her occupation. I dragged crumpled peach-coloured sheets and pillowcases from the unmade bed, and replaced them with fresh linen from the airing cupboard. I found extra blankets and two hot-water bottles. I squeezed lemon juice into a glass. The drink I gave him was light on juice and boiling water, but heavy on the whisky. He sat wheezing and shivering among chintzy cushions.

I said, 'I've made your bed and put out clean pyjamas.'

He said, 'I want Jasper.'

'Serena has him at the moment and it's better that she should. You're in no fit state to care for him.'

He sipped the whisky. 'I still can't believe you have betrayed me.' He no longer sounded angry but utterly defeated.

'I didn't mean it to turn out like this.'

He said, as if I had not spoken, 'He'll be terrified without me. She's so careless of him – anything could happen.'

Until now I had never doubted the rightness of my actions. Bringing child and mother together seemed to me to be a logical first move towards the reunification of the little family. If I had thought at all about a final outcome it was to picture Serena, confident and capable with Jasper, returning home, welcomed by Roman, all problems solved.

Extreme anxiety tends to make me flippant. In my morning stint of writing, which was surely almost a book, I had plotted for my characters an outcome which included tender words, the beginning of a new understanding.

I looked at Roman shivering in his armchair. I saw again the hire car speeding past me; Serena kidnapping Jasper on what must have been a sudden desperate impulse.

I said, 'It's most inconsiderate of you both to behave as you have done. In my story you're all set for reconciliation. Now I shall have to change the plot, the ending.'

The telephone chirruped across my words, the sound of it muffled beneath a heap of cushions. I found the cordless phone concealed in the sofa, in some game of Jasper's, together with the painted trucks of a wooden train-set.

Serena said, 'Roman?'

'No. It's Cathy. Where are you?'

'In Market Harborough, of course! Where else? And Jas is perfectly safe and happy to be with me.' She paused. 'What are you doing in the mall? It's the last place I would have expected you to be.'

'Hm-mm,' I said. 'For all you knew or cared I could by now have been dead in a ditch, or nursing a black eye.'

'But you're neither, so that's all right. Look – I'm truly sorry, I never meant to desert you. I just can't bear it when he shouts and swears, and Jas was getting very frightened. I only meant to wait for you at the end of the lane, but once the car was moving I couldn't seem to stop.' In a voice that tried and failed to sound unconcerned, she asked, 'So how is the lord and master now?'

I glanced at Roman. His eyes were closed, his breathing laboured.

'He's ill. In fact, he's getting more sick by the minute.'

'Chest?'

'Yes,' I said, 'it looks like flu.'

'It'll be bronchial asthma. He gets it badly every winter. Never admits it, of course. Bad for his macho image. You'll have to get the doctor in, Cathy.'

'Oh great!' I said. 'And a happy Christmas to you too, Serena!'

'Do you want me to come over?'

'No,' I said, 'he looks horribly infectious. Have you left any night things here that I might use?' I asked.

'Left-hand dressing-table drawer. You'll find pyjamas. There's a towelling robe in the airing-cupboard, and a new toothbrush in the bathroom.'

'I'll manage,' I said, and then asked the question that I had vowed I would not ask. 'Jasper truly okay, is he?'

'You still don't trust me, do you? He's here, right beside me. Come on, Jas boy, tell the nice lady that you're safe.'

I heard a throaty little chuckle, heard him say, 'Talk Cassy?'

I said, 'Hello, Jasper.'

'Jas come home Mummy.' He sounded happy and excited. 'Jas got no 'jamas. Sleep in Mummy's bed, put on Mummy's T-shirt.'

'Gosh,' I said, in a tone as envious as I could make it, 'that must be great fun! Wish I could be there with you.'

Serena came back on to the line. She gave me the doctor's name and telephone number. I said, 'I'll pack up some of Jasper's clothes and toys.'

'Oh – don't bother,' she said, and there was a hint of permanence about her next words. 'I'll buy him new ones.' As an afterthought she added, 'Keep in touch, won't you?'

I returned to Roman who was by this time either sleeping or semiconscious. I removed from his grasp the whisky drink which he had barely sipped. I picked up the cordless telephone and began to punch out the doctor's number.

I started to review my position and count up the people who might be alarmed by my unexplained absence from home. Martin and his family were spending Christmas with friends in Bournemouth. Eileen had already left for London to be with her daughter and son-in-law. Paul had phoned to wish me Happy Christmas and to say that he and his son would be visiting at the end of January. Only my neighbours, who held a key for emergencies of this sort, would need to be informed. I was, I told them, caring for a sick friend, and would they be kind enough to feed the budgerigar until my return.

The doctor was young; too young for me to altogether trust his judgement. He was also built like a rugby scrum-half, which was, in the circumstances, his major asset. He lifted Roman from the armchair, carried him into the bedroom, stripped off the suit of scarlet leather, eased him into pyjamas, and between the blankets. He performed his routine with thermometer and stethoscope, and told me what I already knew. 'Bronchial asthma, aggravated by flu, overwork and undernourishment. I've been telling the damned fool for months past that something of this sort would happen in the end.' He looked at me properly for the first time. 'I suppose you're the mother-in-law?'

'No,' I said. 'Just a concerned friend of the family.'

'Ha!' he said bitterly. 'The family,' and I knew then that he was aware of all the Komanowski problems. The visits to the Casualty Department, Serena's departure. When I told him of the day's events he was not surprised.

'Can you stay?' he asked.

'Yes,' I said. 'Well, I can hardly leave him, can I?'

He looked doubtfully at me. 'I have,' I added, 'nursed my sons through glandular and rheumatic fever. I was rather younger then, I must admit –'

'He's a bit of a handful, this one, when he's sick,' said Roman's medical man. 'If it all gets beyond you – call me. In any case, I'll look in again tomorrow.' He patted my shoulder. 'Warmth and rest and plenty of fluids. He'll be up and about again in a few days. I'll send somebody round with his medicine and tablets.'

When I looked surprised he added, 'Mr Komanowski is my private patient.'

I hardly noticed Christmas. The festival passed in a sequence of days in which Roman shivered and sweated, cursed the doctor and me for our ministrations, and demanded hourly to have Jasper returned to him at once. I came to dread most of all the time between darkness and the early morning hours. Then it was that he experienced dreams, or were they fever-induced hallucinations?

I sat each evening in a small cream velvet-covered armchair, the frilled peach satin lampshade angled so that the light did not shine across his face. I had dragged the chair close up to the bedside. I sat poised to push him back on to the heaped-up pillows, to replace his thrown-off blankets, and force the inhalant spray between his teeth when his breathing became laboured.

There were hours when the peaches-and-cream bedroom was peopled with imagined acrobats and jugglers, clowns and lion-tamers. While his speech roved from Romanes into German I was still with him; when he lapsed into Russian or Polish I was lost. He was, bewilderingly, both man and child, sometimes swearing fluently in a variety of tongues, other times crying out in a voice as soft and infantile as Jasper's. It was in this childish mode that he cried out for the mother he had never known. The culmination of these nightmares always followed the same pattern. Sitting upright in his bed

Roman screamed in German, so often that I could not be wrong in my translation, 'Get up, damn you! Don't lie there like that – stop fooling me, Viktor!' and then in a hushed voice, 'I'm sorry, Papa – sorry.'

On Christmas Eve three parcels had been delivered by an Express service. The enclosed note said: 'Happy Christmas from S. and J. All is well in Market Harborough. See you in the new year.' I unpacked a box which held a Christmas cake, a box of liqueur chocolates, a bottle of Tia Maria and one of cherry brandy. The other packages were wrapped expensively in gold- and silver-coloured foil; mine contained a tailored housecoat of red velvet and matching slippers. The other one, addressed to Roman, I placed on the hall table.

There came a night when Roman's temperature returned to normal. He slept quietly and deeply. His first question on waking was, predictably, 'Where's Jasper?'

'He's safe and well in Market Harborough – with his mother. We thought it best to leave him there over Christmas.' I spoke as if Jasper's return was dependent only on Roman's recovery from flu and assorted complications.

He said, 'What day is it?'

'It's New Year's Day.'

He fingered the ten-day growth of beard. 'You've been here over a week?'

I nodded.

He said, 'I don't remember much about it.' The look he gave me was wary and defensive, his eyes narrowed into slits. He studied my face, searching for hints of what I might have learned about him. He was at that moment more gypsy than he had ever been. He said, in a blaze of defiance, 'When I shout out in my sleep I never talk in English.'

I hesitated, but only briefly. 'No,' I said, 'you never talk in English; you speak mostly in German.'

The significance of what I said brought him close to panic. Before I could turn away he saw the knowledge in my eyes. The faint colour in his face, restored by natural sleep, now leached out to leave a greenish pallor. I sensed his desperation, his agony of mind, and I was seized by a fierce and anxious pity for him. He threw back the duvet, swung himself into a sitting position on the bed-edge, and attempted to stand up. In a cold and final voice he said, 'Thank you for taking care of me. You can go home now.'

For a second or two he achieved his full height, and then the long thin legs began to fold and he fell back into the bed. With his wild black hair and jutting beard he looked both villainous and comic. I plumped his pillows, straightened out the duvet, fastened the top button of his pyjama jacket.

'I'm going to make you toast and scrambled eggs, and a large mug of hot chocolate.'

He said, 'I'm not hungry.'

'If I cook it – you will eat it. Even if it takes you all day.'

His gaze locked on to mine, and neither of us looked away. He began to laugh. And so did I.

Towards the evening, after small meals and long naps, I persuaded him to open the gold-wrapped parcel from Serena. It contained a robe of heavy silk, chequered black and white like a gigantic chessboard. He liked it sufficiently to try it on. I helped his arms into the wide sleeves, angled the cheval-mirror towards the bed so that he might study his reflection.

He said wryly, 'Colours are spot-on, aren't they? It goes with the black beard and white face.'

I said, 'Serena paid a lot of money for that robe. The label is Italian.'

'I know. It's the sort of thing she does. It's her only way of showing love.'

I walked to the window, pushed aside the ruffled blind and looked down into the twilit mall. Late New Year revellers still sang and shouted in the city centre. Guitar music throbbed from a nearby café. I thought about last year's winter sunset, walking away from Kurt's grave and knowing that wherever his spirit dwelt, it was not and never had been in that place. I thought about love and the time that people wasted in bitterness and recriminations.

I said to Roman, 'My husband died sixteen years ago tonight. This is the first year I haven't visited his grave.'

'You should have said! I would have ordered a taxi to take you there and bring you back.' His voice shook a little as if he really cared.

'It doesn't matter. Perhaps it's time I stopped behaving like a Victorian widow. In any case, he's somewhere else. I don't know where.'

'Yes,' he said, 'you and I are caught up in a time-warp. We make great efforts to be normal, to do what is expected of us, but always the past marches close beside us. We walk in step with our dead. We cannot let them go.'

I moved back to the cream chair, which still stood close beside the bed. I sat down and was at once included in the reflected images from the cheval-mirror. We made an odd pair, Roman and I: he, all black and white, slumped weakly against peachy pillows; I, still dressed in the dark blue skirt in which I had been hijacked, and a pair of scratchy lacy tights and a bright pink sweater left behind by Serena.

The apartment had become surprisingly homelike to me in the ten days of my occupation. It was not only the ease with which I now moved and worked in an unfamiliar kitchen, my ability to sleep deeply on the chintzy, feathered sofa. It was the need fulfilled to take care of another person's welfare. By choice the recipient of all that grandmotherliness would have been Jasper. But his place was with Serena. It was Roman who, in these last days, I had finally recognized for what he was. Stripped of his designer outfits, out of his head with a peculiar mixture of guilt and fever, I no longer found him threatening. I smiled into the mirror at him, and he said, 'That first time you saw me in the Deerpark – you knew then that I was a murderer – didn't you?'

There is an inevitability about confession. Once begun, the speaker is compelled to finish. I longed to shout at Roman, 'Don't tell me! Telling only makes it real!' But there we were, caught in the time-warp, just as he had said, and now his mirrored eyes were dark with the horror of his words. It was like watching the tearing of living flesh from live bone. He said, 'When I was seventeen years old I killed my brother. Then I ran away. You could say that I have never stopped running.' These were the words that even at the height of fever he had never uttered, and I knew then that at last we had come to the very core of him. I felt the weight of his burden settle on my mind, and braced myself to take it. We sat in the peach-glow of Serena's lamps; the mall was quiet now, the revellers departed. The story he was to tell was the strangest I would ever hear. As he started to speak I recalled that this was the exact time, sixteen years ago, when Kurt had slipped away from me to an unknown destination, the hour when the tides of the earth turn and life is at its lowest ebb.

He began awkwardly. 'Some of this you know, but I will tell it anyway.' As always, in times of stress, his accent was pronounced.

'I come from circus people. A long way back they were

dancers, performers of music, gypsies. In the recent generations they had, as you say, managed to get their act together. And the State recognizes the talented; there is in Russia a Circus School.' His lips stretched in the rictus of a smile. 'They were good, the old ones. My grandfather was a strongman, my German grandmother was an acrobat and wirewalker. My father was a clown. But Viktor and I, and our sister Anya, we were trained to be an aerial troupe. There are three performers in a trapeze act. One is the catcher, the other two the fliers. The catcher has three ways of holding the flier: by the leg, the wrist, or the ankle. We mostly used the wrist-to-wrist technique. The catcher must be very strong, reliable, of steady temperament; he must not drink spirits or smoke tobacco. Most of all his concentration must be total, for the lives of the fliers are in his hands. We were already one of the top acts, but my father was worried. I was tall and still growing. The best and safest aerialists are small men. There was another problem. I was discontented. Nobody notices the catcher; he just hangs there, head down, arms outstretched. It was Viktor, the flier, who was fêted. He was brilliant, dedicated; he was also disciplined. He had passed through the Circus School. People showed him great respect. It seemed to me that he had everything – he had even known our mother.

'My father was worried. He talked to me about joining an equestrian act or a team of jugglers. He must have known that it was unsafe to keep me with Anya and Viktor, but because he was a kind man and I was the youngest, he had not yet found the courage to remove me from the act. And so it happened, as it was bound to. In a second, in the blink of an eye.' Roman moved uneasily against the pillows; his hands were trembling.

'Two days before it happened I had been interviewed for the Circus School. Physically I met all their requirements. I had a strong physique, good looks, a perfect sense of balance. Psychologically I simply would not do. My temperament, they said, was flawed.'

He paused and clasped his shaking hands together, twisting his linked fingers as if he could crush out their guilt. The tension in the room was almost more than I could bear. At no time did he look directly at me, and now in the silence his gaze met mine, but only through the cheval-mirror.

He said, 'You have to understand about circus. It is a kingdom, a separate world, international. Only in England does it count simply as an entertainment for the children. In Russia, in Poland, Hungary, Romania, it is an art form. Even in the time of the tsars, the circus paid no taxes. Circus has its own laws; it is in many ways a closed world. There is never a language problem; I first spoke in English when I was three years old. In our company four of the grooms were Englishmen; also there was a clown from Lancashire whom I called "uncle".'

As he spoke, Roman unclasped his fingers. He placed his hands upon the satin surface of the duvet. He said, 'We were pitched on the outskirts of a large West German city. Circus performers of our high class were permitted, like virtuoso pianists and violinists, like dancers of the ballet, to travel beyond the borders of the eastern bloc. There was, of course, the occasional defection, but most of us had families. We had all heard the stories about retribution.' He halted and when he spoke again the timbre of his voice had changed. He sounded younger, almost adolescent. 'I wanted to frighten him, that's all I meant to do. I wanted to show him that he could not perform without me. At least that is what I told myself. But there is a rule in circus that partners in a dangerous act should not appear together if there is bad blood between them. Viktor and I had exchanged some bitter words that night. I climbed the ropes with no clear intention in my mind; he stood poised on his trapeze bowing to the crowd, and then turned to me with that usual look of perfect trust. And in that moment I knew exactly what it was that I could do. Anya was not involved in this first *passe par-dessous* of our act, she stood behind him on the perch. Down below my father waited, as he always did, to hear that slap of hand on wrist that means the flier's safety.

'The body of a flier travels at tremendous speed. It is not possible for him to see the catcher's hands, to make a final adjustment. All I needed to do to give him a fright, or so I thought, was to fumble the catch a little bit. Just this once I would be a fraction too high in my position, so that his fingertips brushed mine before I dropped down to make the final secure wrist-hold. It was a lunatic plan. He fell – hit the edge of the net – I knew before I reached the ground that something terrible had happened to Viktor.

'My father knelt beside him. He held my brother's wrist. He looked up at me and there was no mercy in his face. He said, "His back is broken. You let him fall. You tried deliberately to kill him." He spoke in an old argot used by the Zinte people. Only Anya and I, among that crowd of onlookers, understood his meaning.

'I ran back to the waggon I had always shared with Viktor. All around the walls hung his spangled costumes, the posters that advertised our act. I do not recall any pause for thought. I gathered up the treasures that were mine: the jewellery left me by my mother and grandfather, the heavy gold neck-chains and bracelets, the broad rings set with sapphires and diamonds. The single silver earring, the one you recognized as being Zinte, was already in my ear. Its twin was still hooked in Viktor's earlobe. Aerial acts are very superstitious; the earrings had always been our good-luck mascots.

'I changed into a dark suit and a raincoat, and covered my head with a soft-brimmed hat. In the car park I hitched a lift with a young German couple. I explained that my car wouldn't start, that I urgently needed to get back to the city. I sat in the back of the car, the brim of my hat pulled as low as it would go. I need not have worried. They talked about the accident and never looked in my direction. Nobody ever recognizes the catcher. On the road we passed ambulances and police cars, their sirens screaming. One hour later I walked into a German police station and asked for political asylum.

'Oh, they investigated me. I spent the next six months in a prison cell. My brother, they said, was on a life-support system, but in my heart I believed he was dead. But they finally accepted, on my father's sworn affidavit, that the fall had been accidental. They also accepted that, in my country of origin, mistakes such as mine would be dealt with severely. In the end, and perhaps because my grandmother had once been a star of the German circus, they allowed me to stay in their country.

'I moved to West Berlin, and discovered that for a multi-lingual catcher of a flying-trapeze act, there are very few jobs open, and no other circus would ever employ me. But I was good-looking in a way that was to suit the fashions of the nineteen eighties. The sale of a ring or two put some D-Mark in my pocket. I got on to the books of an agency that hired out photographic models. I did a few TV commercials, a lot of magazine work. In 1981 I came to London.

'As a model I had been highly paid, but I knew my limitations, and fashions change. I began to improve my skills in written English. I took a course in business studies.

'Two years later I met Serena – and the rest, as they say, is history.'

*

In the morning I telephoned Serena. 'I need to see you, urgently.'

'How soon?'

'This morning.'

'I'm pretty tied-up here. There's Jas; and my January sale begins today.'

'It won't wait.'

'What's wrong? Is it Roman? Yes, of course it is. It's always bloody Roman. I knew it was too good to last. Well, I won't bring Jas back. I've made my mind up. I can't part with him now. It's not fair of you to do this to me, Cathy!'

I said, 'All I'm asking is a meeting. I can't talk freely here, he'll be out of the bathroom any second now.'

'Oh. He's on his feet again, is he? No wonder you're worried. Look – if he's that much better and it's so important, you can come to me. Get a taxi – I'll pay the driver. See you!'

The flat above the small boutique smelled of chips and Johnson's Baby Powder. The white shag carpet was patterned now with the stains made by a small and adventurous child. The black leather furniture felt sticky; piles of unironed laundry were heaped on the coffee table. An enormous Christmas tree, complete with baubles, still stood in a corner. Jasper, grubby and plump, played absorbedly with toys, none of which were representative of activities of the circus. He smiled a little uncertainly at me, struggling towards a connection that might be painful for him. Recognition widened his eyes. He said, 'Pappi –?'

'Soon,' I said. 'You'll see him soon.'

Serena had lost some of her fashionable patina. Her hair needed washing. She also bore the evidence of Jasper's breakfast preferences. Egg yolk had left its mark on her black velvet slacks; Ribena had stained her shirt of pure white silk.

She exuded the kind of happiness the existence of which I had quite forgotten.

We sat in facing armchairs. 'Well?' she asked. 'So what's the panic?'

I said, 'I want you to think carefully before you answer. How much do you really care about Roman?'

She said, 'You're talking life and death stuff, aren't you? Of course you are. You wouldn't bother for anything less.' She sighed and gazed thoughtfully at Jasper. She said, 'I love the man. I suspect he isn't worth the way I feel about him. But nobody's perfect.'

'There are extenuating circumstances – of a most grave and serious nature. At this moment he is in danger of going over the edge. He is physically exhausted from the recent illness, but the balance of his mind is in even greater danger. He needs you, Serena.'

'Did he send you here?'

'No. And he must never know about this conversation. Last night he talked to me about his early life. I think if you go back he will tell you about it. This much I will say, Jasper needs two parents. And there is something else; when Roman was in Berlin for the opening of the Brandenburg Gate, he thought he saw a man – a man he had mourned as dead for the last thirteen years. It is important that we trace that man, Serena.'

She returned to the mall two days later. Within an hour of my arrival home I received a huge bouquet of yellow roses, and a card which said, 'Thank you for everything – Jasper, Serena and Roman.'

In the weeks that followed I made no move to contact them. From time to time there would be a phone call. I would talk to each of them in turn. They were well and happy. They still argued; well, who didn't? Roman had told his story to Serena. Together they were taking steps to trace a man named Viktor Komanowski.

The writing, which had amazingly become a book, had an unfinished feel about it. I was also finding, after my deep involvement in the lives of others, great difficulty in climbing back into my own life.

❥

PART SEVEN

A YEAR had passed since the call from Melanie that had told me of Christina's death. That grief, muted and overlaid by the events of recent months, still ran deep beneath the surface of my feelings. But I also counted up the good things that had happened: the understanding I had reached with Martin; my regained ability to write; the restoration of both his parents to Jasper. And always, there were my grandchildren, undeserved and loving, each one of whom was special.

As winter edged cautiously into a cold, wet spring, my thoughts turned back towards Berlin. I walked in the Deerpark to which Roman never came any more. I missed Jasper. But the absence of father and child reassured me, as could nothing else, that the Komanowskis now functioned as a family. The phone calls, and they were increasingly infrequent, came always from Serena. She reported Jasper's progress; there were, she said, already several hopeful leads in their search for information about a man named Viktor Komanowski.

But it was in April, when the letter containing the enclosure arrived from Melanie and Ryan, that I felt the spin of the wheel which brought me full circle, back into my own private world of unsatisfied seeking. 'We are planning a trip into Poland, to visit Mechtenhagen. As you probably know, this village was the birthplace of Christina and Kurt. If you would like to come with us, we would love to take you there.'

Melanie had also sent me transcripts, in both English and

German, of something written by Christina, found recently by Manfred among papers left by his mother. Dated in the spring of 1952 it was, said Melanie, set out in the form of a rough draft of a letter, written to the schoolmaster who had taught in the little school at Mechtenhagen.

I switched on the desk lamp and settled down to read. It was a testament both of courage and horror; but understated and controlled.

My Dear Teacher Habek, and Frau Habek,

At last my promised letter comes. Wholeheartedly I thank you both for your extensive letter. Now I will tell you as briefly as possible about the time after 1944.

This terrible time started for us with the death of my father. Soon after we had received this news, all letters ceased from my brother Kurt. Our last words from him said that he was near Calais. Towards the end of November 1944 a printed card arrived telling us that he was a prisoner-of-war in England. A small brightening in the clouds. His first letter from England did not arrive until July 1946, it began 'Dear parents'. So Kurt learned about the death of his father two years after the event.

My husband Ernst was wounded. He had a bullet in his lung. Until December 1944 he was in Dirschau, but had to return to the fighting line shortly before Christmas. On February 7th 1945 he wrote to me from Upper Silesia, and that was the last letter I ever received from him because on March 5th the Russians came and all connections were cut.

Very early on Sunday March 4th the Trechler farmers came through Mechtenhagen with heavily laden waggons. We could not yet quite believe that the situation was that serious, although we heard every day of the terrible refugee misery on the main road from Greifenberg to Stepenitz, and had sometimes seen the bitter and frozen people.

The von Riesbach family had also prepared some waggons in which we might escape, but then the decision was made that we should all remain in Mechtenhagen – otherwise, what was to become of the cattle? On Sunday many French prisoners-of-war came and stayed overnight in the barn. In the east we saw everywhere the glow of fires through the night from Sunday to Monday. It was frightening and I didn't go to bed anymore. We heard no sounds of shooting, but on Monday a few single soldiers came through the village, some very young men with anti-tank weapons, and then at midday the first Russian tanks came.

These first soldiers were reasonable and friendly, and we prayed that it would stay like that. Then we did a very stupid thing. Every piece of clothing, especially men's and summer clothes, we buried in the ground.

About five o'clock that day, the infantry came. It was quiet enough in our house but in the school, in the house of my mother-in-law, and at the Kannenbergs, hell was let loose! All at once the order went around that we should leave the village with hand luggage only. My mother took the pram with Manfred in it. He was not yet a year old. I took my bicycle, hung with all sorts of things from the handlebars. Having got as far as the Hoppner house I ran back and collected a bucket, a blanket and some bread and lard. My mother-in-law and some of our neighbours took cover between pine trees.

The rest of us went through a field towards the Rehhagen. There, Frau von Riesbach arranged to have a straw hut built which would give us cover for the first few days. Many refugees had their horses taken from them; the horses from the Estate were also taken away.

Frau von Riesbach and her two children were not allowed to leave the farmyard. Melanie was tortured a lot. It was later that night when all three of them reached our hut in a state of great exhaustion. On Thursday morning the von Riesbach family left our company, as they felt that their presence among us was a threat to the people of Mechtenhagen. On Friday Frau von Riesbach slashed her wrists and those of her two children. They were given first-aid by the Russians, and then cared for by the people of a nearby village. But in that village, although the taps of the distillery had been opened to prevent the contents falling into the hands of Russian soldiers, all had not leaked away before the armies arrived. And now, the devil was up in that place! Through the excessive consumption of alcohol, human beings had turned into wild animals.

In our straw hut it was very crowded, including many refugees who travelled on again the next day. We cooked coffee in buckets, obtaining water from a small ditch. Our circumstances were terrible. We could not have stayed there long; the children could not be cleaned, and there was no milk for them.

On the following Tuesday the houses and barns of Karlies and our aunt Marie had been burned down. We had seen the fire. Towards the evening an angry Russian and a German came to us, and forced us to give our rings and watches. We were then made to return to Mechtenhagen.

Back in the village we were overcome with fear and horror. The streets were filled, half a metre deep, with scattered clothing, bread, meat, sausage, flour, bedding and dead animals, all mixed up together. Amid all this the surviving pigs and chickens sought their food.

All the stables were open and the animals gone. Chaos was within the houses. In our house the radio lay smashed in the living-room doorway. All drawers were tossed upon the floor. On the 13th of the month the men of the village were taken away to drive cattle. On the following day we women were ordered once again to leave Mechtenhagen. We were supposed to go to Baugard, but once in the forest we took a turn to the right towards the Herrenweg, where we hid among low trees. We had sufficient food with us, and found a wonderful brook. Even the children were tired from so much fresh air.

We stayed in that place until a day when the air began to throb and rumble, and we guessed there was heavy fighting towards Stettin. Some German soldiers visited us and advised us to be quiet. The shooting began to come towards us from the railway line, so we fled back again to Mechtenhagen. As we came across the fields towards the barn we saw two hundred German prisoners being marched away under Russian guard. We did not dare to stay in the village, but walked from one place to another, being moved on always by the Poles. In the middle of April we came back again to Mechtenhagen.

As we came out of the forest we could see that our village was now completely changed. Everywhere something white was hanging. Many sheds had been built. It looked really terrible. Quite a number of Russian regiments of soldiers must have been quartered there. Almost all the houses were changed into rough sleeping quarters, with stoves ripped out, doors lifted off their hinges and bed linen nailed to the walls. Between Kiekbuschens' and our cowshed stood cupboard after cupboard, the doors in use as bridges over the puddles. Our couch was in the schoolhouse attic, our sofa was in the Ludtkes' house, a sprung feather mattress at the Langes', and similarly all the furniture of each family was scattered about the village.

During the day we all stayed within our houses. The nights were traumatic. We young women had to jump out of the windows and hide in the garden or field, or stay overnight in the hay loft. Mornings and evenings there was an endless stream of Russian carts transporting timber from the sawmill, to a place where many barracks were built at the edge of the forest. There was not a single cow left in the village. The ten cows we had driven home from the meadow were all stolen from us in the night. It was a terrible, restless time.

At the beginning of May the Russian soldiers came and took all the women, boys and girls to work on the railway line, taking up and loading the rails. At the beginning of June German prisoners-of-war came and took over our work and we were able to return home. Frau von Riesbach and her son were separated from us at about this time, but Melanie stayed with us.

Mechtenhagen was, in the meantime, under Polish occupation. Only one soldier from our village ever returned home, and he came on crutches. His father and the shepherd came back later.

The years from 1945 to 1947 were full of restlessness, worry, hunger and distress. We had to work from dawn till dusk, in heat and frost. There was no mercy; not much to eat and little money. The Russians were still quartered in a neighbouring village.

On the 25th of June 1947 we were finally driven out of Mechtenhagen, being allowed to take 40 kg of luggage with us. We were transported to Stettin and from there to Dresden, where we have remained.

Since the August of 1945 I had developed large holes in the shin of my left leg, with terrible pain at night after all the standing during the day. In winter time the wounds became black because of the cold. I went into hospital in Dresden, and after eight weeks the leg had healed. But as we had hardly anything to eat at that time, very few vegetables and potatoes available, and insufficient of everything, I went out gathering remnants of the harvest, and soon the new skin on my leg was damaged again. I had two more stays in hospital, but now, thank God, the wounds are closed.

My brother Kurt is in England. He married there in 1948, and was released from prisoner-of-war camp, then came to an area near Hanover. He visited us here in Dresden, and stayed one week. He remained in Germany until November 1948, and then returned to England with his wife. They have two sons, one is two and a half years old, and the other is six months old.

The von Riesbach family are now living in Berlin. Melanie has been living for the past two years in England, where she is training to be a nurse.

The transcript ended; I laid the typed sheets on the desk and thought how Christina's words were more poignant, more expressive of the shame and horror of war, than anything I had ever read. I thought about Mechtenhagen; the way Kurt had described it, a kind of paradise never to be regained. He had not been able to return.

I re-read Melanie's letter: 'We are planning a trip into Poland, to visit Mechtenhagen . . . If you would like to come with us, we would love to take you there.'

Since the opening of the Berlin Wall had caused the military flight paths to the city to be abolished, I was able this time to avoid the confusion of Heathrow or Gatwick, and fly from the smaller and quieter Birmingham Airport. As I booked my flight and packed a suitcase I became aware, quite suddenly, of a bone-wearying exhaustion; a surfeit of pressures which I could not identify, and did not in any case know how to relieve. Conscious of an unusual physical frailty I sought to make the journey easy. I booked an overnight stay at the airport hotel, ate a bar-meal of sandwiches and soup, watched a little television, and slept until roused by an early morning call.

We lifted off out of pouring rain and into high winds; to land two hours later in drenched and overcast Berlin, where Melanie and Ryan were waiting for me.

On previous visits I had come in autumn, in winter; but Berlin in May time, even in this cold reluctant spring, had a charm that made my heart lift. On Mechner Strasse the acacia trees were in full green leaf. There were primulas and pansies in the window-boxes, tulips and daffodils in gardens. This particular return to Germany had a strong feel of preordination; it was to be like no other I had ever made.

On that first night I slept for a full eleven hours and awoke with a feeling that in some deep essential region of the spirit the process of repair had already begun. I did the things I had always done on my first morning in Berlin. I collected Deutsche Mark from the Berliner Bank, gazed in shop windows; eased myself gently into another language, into an environment that was very different from my own.

The café on Handel Strasse had changed into its summer decor. The blue velvet curtains had been replaced by drapes of heavy lace. Little white vases held pink carnations. As she took my order the waitress lit a fancy candle, and placed the candlestick of cut glass in the exact centre of the pink table-cloth. I found the small attention very pleasant, and smiled at the memory of the uncivilized paper-bags and plastic cutlery of McDonald's in England.

Out on Hindenburgdamm the morning traffic was as heavy as ever. Cyclists sped by the café window, riding on their special area of pavement, young mothers wheeled pushchairs; the very elderly walked in close-linked couples, supporting one another. It was all the same, and yet in one respect only it was very different. Christina would not be arriving this time at the Botanischer Garten U-Bahn station.

Back in the apartment we sat companionably and long over lunch, making plans and studying maps. In mid-afternoon the rain eased, and a drive through the city was suggested.

We drove out of Lichterfelde and passed for a time through neighbourhoods and streets that were still familiar to me, and so I hardly noticed when Ryan turned the car towards the east, to Teltow and the new crossing-points which had been created in the more rural districts of Berlin. But then I saw for the first time the shabby houses which, since the removal of the Wall, now stood revealed and curiously naked, with their sagging roofs and peeling plaster among a no man's land of mud and weeds. For twenty-eight years this district had been concealed from Western gaze by concrete and electrified fences. Now, all that remained in this place to show where the Wall had stood was row upon row of redundant sodium lamps, their wires torn loose; and the narrow tarmac-runs along which the East German guards had driven on their frequent inspection patrols. The watchtowers, Ryan told me, had recently been dismantled and removed. Only one remained, and he stopped the car so that I might get out and take a photograph of it as it lay collapsed into the mud, its grey metal supports bent inwards like the legs of some sinister and dying insect.

Away from the patrol-runs we saw several buildings under repair. In recent months the old and charming houses had been given new coats of paint and stucco. Shops and cafés now displayed highly coloured advertisements for Marlboro and Pils. Here, too, the first green haze of spring lay upon the trees and hedges. There were flowers in the gardens, and the cherry trees were in full bloom. I stood with Ryan in the cool damp afternoon and he pointed out the signs of the ending of the long separation of East and West Berlin, scars which were already healing over beneath fresh growths of grass and the wild flowers of springtime. For Melanie and Ryan, who had witnessed the opening of the Wall and its gradual removal, the creation of new crossing-points, the reunification of this country, the changes had come so rapidly that these raw and open spaces in their city were still a matter for conjecture and discussion; for hope and fear.

For me, newly come from England, and in spite of information gained from media reports, the shock of these strange, almost ghostly gaps in the city's fabric was even more difficult to absorb. The shadow of the Wall, the remaining detritus of the border-crossings, still lay across Berlin like a stain which would not wash away.

As we drove through areas that had once abutted on to the no man's land created by the Wall, I saw a house half of which had, long ago, been demolished to accommodate a watchtower. There was a street, one side of which had stood on the west side, the other in the eastern sector, with the Wall running through the middle. The western houses were attractive, with fresh paint and window-boxes, and Audis and Opels parked along the kerbside. On the east side of that same street, the Trabbis and Wartburgs stood before stained and grey apartment blocks of crumbling stucco and rotting woodwork. I took my photographs and wrote my notes, and we stood together beside the car for a quiet moment, three people – one German, two English – each one a product of our separate history, our generation. I studied Ryan, and began to suspect in him an emotional involvement with this country and its people that was equal to my own.

In the morning we drove out to a place called Guterfelde, and found among fields of growing corn a monstrous moonscape of the broken reinforced-concrete slabs which had once comprised the Berlin Wall. The removal of this strange debris from many miles of city streets had caused a disposal problem which looked unlikely to be solved. We picked our way among the broken watchtowers and the flutter of damp office files, towards a reconstituted section of the Wall, reared-up and quite undamaged, as if to demonstrate for this last time its redundant slogans and brilliant graffiti.

These sites, which lie in open country around the city of Berlin, are known as the Graveyards of the Wallstones.

That evening we ate a supper of fresh salmon baked with lemon slices, and served with salad and creamed potatoes. My appetite, which had been poor for many months, suddenly returned. We watched the TV weather forecast. The weather over Poland had been cold that day, with snow and rain. Tomorrow promised cloud and showers. In the kitchen, Melanie began to assemble flasks and sandwich boxes. We would need to make an early morning start.

The forecast of bad weather over Poland seemed likely to be accurate. We drove out of Berlin under grey skies; as we came on to the autobahn a spatter of raindrops hit the windscreen. The date was May 7th, but the temperature belonged to winter.

I was comfortable and warm in the back seat of the car, the cameras and picnic bags piled up beside me, a new red notebook in my jacket pocket. It might have been a day trip to a place of interest, an excursion not to be missed in an itinerary of foreign travel except that, for me, this journey I had never expected to make had its own unique importance; and because of the memories, the experiences of life, the expectations which rode with all of us, I felt myself to be separated, fixed in an isolation which affection and familiarity could not quite bridge.

It was in the mature years of his life that Ryan had first heard the name of Mechtenhagen. I wondered if it was true for him, as it had been for me, that 'he who marries a foreigner lives a life of translation'. In the nine years of his marriage to Melanie, lived in West Berlin, Ryan had acquired a comprehensive knowledge of the city's political situation, its distant and more recent past. He was also familiar with the von Riesbach family history, and was aware of the significance of Mechtenhagen. But what about his feelings? I would, I thought, never dare to question him, and although I was sure he did not suspect this, there was still much about Ryan that overawed me. Behind the charming smile, the wide forehead, there was a brilliant intellect, an analytical and probing mind. He was a man of broad and comprehensive interests, and yet, even in his most passionate involvements he seemed to display a slightly clinical detachment; the timbre of his voice remained steady, his features unrevealing. From my seat in the rear of the car I studied him through the driving mirror, in the way that I had once watched Martin; and with as little understanding. For Ryan and Martin were Englishmen, and the only man to whom I had been close in all my life had been a German.

On that drive up to the Polish border my thoughts were jumbled. I began to think about this country of which I had heard so much throughout the years, and knew so little. I had read the kind of book that is available to any student of European history. How, in 1943, there had been a conference in Teheran between Churchill, Roosevelt and Stalin, at which the future of eastern Europe was decided. The Polish boundaries were to be moved to take over the German states of Pomerania, Silesia, and part of East Prussia, including the city of Breslau and the free port of Danzig. These lands which lay east of the rivers Oder and Neisse were to be stripped of their German populations and inhabited by Poles. And so it happened. Told in the flat unemotional prose of an English historian it had sounded so simple; no more than the moving of coloured pins upon a map. But I remembered Christina's testament of horror; the atrocities which had been practised on a rural population of women and children who had themselves committed no crime.

I leaned a little to the right so that I might see Melanie more clearly. She sat, the map of Poland spread before her, the smooth cap of her pale blonde hair curved inwards to frame features that had hardly changed since that day in 1965 when she had visited Kurt in England. I began to remember the letter she had sent him, and his reaction to it.

The letters from Germany had never brought good news. Over the years I had learned to distrust the Dresden postmark, but this one was stamped WEST BERLIN. I turned the envelope over and read the name on the flap. 'From somebody called von Riesbach,' I said as I handed it to Kurt. He read the letter through twice but said nothing, so I took the single sheet from his hand and began to read for myself.

Dear Kurt,
   We were very sorry to hear of your illness. Christina, as you probably know, writes regularly to us. She has applied for permission to visit you but has been refused. Therefore, as I shall be visiting friends in England at the end of May, Christina has asked me to call to see you. If this is acceptable to you, will you please let me know as soon as possible.
   M. von R.

Kurt had looked amazed and embarrassed. 'I want no visitors here,' he said firmly, before I could comment. 'I need to be quiet. The doctor says so.'

'But surely this one woman can hardly disturb you. Unless she is some old flame you would rather not meet?'

He grinned. 'You couldn't be further from the truth. Melanie von Riesbach is several years younger than I am, and way above me in the pecking order. If she had even so much as looked my way her father would have horsewhipped us both.'

'My God,' I said, impressed. 'What is she then, some kind of a princess?'

'You might have thought so,' he said bitterly. 'She comes from an old and aristocratic family. The word *von* is the equivalent of Sir or Lady in your language. The von Riesbachs owned the village of Mechtenhagen before the war. In a way, they owned all of us as well.'

I asked, 'What do you mean?', intrigued at this notion of twentieth-century serfdom.

'If you wanted to work – you worked for von Riesbach. If you wanted to eat, have a roof, keep your pigs and chickens, your strip of grazing, your vegetable plot – you bent the knee, and looked cheerful while you did it.' Kurt moved to a chair near the fire and held out his cold hands to the blaze. 'I hated von Riesbach. When I was a boy I quarrelled with him: a pretty risky thing to do in that situation. If I remember correctly I threw some potatoes at him. I thought he would drop down dead from anger: he used his riding crop on me.' Kurt paused and drew his breath in sharply. 'After that my parents were forced to send me away from home, to work for another employer. I came back only at weekends. I never forgave von Riesbach for that.'

I asked, 'A pretty big noise in the Nazi Party too, I suppose?' I thought that I had a clear picture now of this lord of the manor, this *Junker*. Uniformed, jackbooted, hung about with medals and old duelling scars. Grinding the people of Mechtenhagen beneath his spurred heel.

Kurt looked astounded. '*Ach* no! Von Riesbach was never a Nazi. He worked and spoke out against them. You must

understand that he was a powerful man in our district. Politic-
ally we were all influenced by him. He was once arrested
and held for a time.'

I said, 'So he was not altogether a bad man.'

'Well,' Kurt admitted, as if the idea was a new one, 'he was
certainly anti-Hitler. He was conscripted and sent to the Front
though, like everyone else.'

'And after the war?'

'He lost everything. He lives now in a flat in West Berlin. I
think he works for the British Control Commission as an inter-
preter.'

'But why is your sister so closely involved with these
people?'

'Christina was *Kindermädchen* to the von Riesbach children.
There were two of them, Melanie, and a younger child, a
boy.' Kurt sounded rueful. 'Myself – I never could understand
her attachment to them. Christina really loved that family –
especially Melanie. But it looks as if the von Riesbachs have
kept in touch with the village people. Christina has mentioned
in her letters that they write and send parcels: give what help
they can.'

'That doesn't sound too despotic.'

Kurt held out a hand, palm upwards, offering me reasons.
'The Frau von Riesbach was a truly good woman. Kind and
thoughtful.' He shrugged and his lips turned down at the
corners. 'If I was to meet them now, after twenty years, it
might all be different.'

I said, tapping the letter, 'It seems as if you will have to
meet their daughter. For your sister's peace of mind at least,
this Melanie von Riesbach will have to come here.'

I had my private doubts about this visitor from Berlin but I
suppressed them beneath a welter of housewifely duties. I

prepared a bedroom; planned meals several days in advance; and put out my best pink towels in the bathroom.

I had never met an aristocratic German. I was not quite sure of the form.

When the train pulled into Kingsbridge station, I saw an attractive woman coming down the platform, carrying her own suitcase. There was something about the expensive cut of her short blonde hair and the style of her pale blue suit that shouted 'continental'. The guest had arrived.

After the first uneasy skirmishings it was clear that the lady from West Berlin would be easy to please. She was quietly grateful for the offer of a hot bath after her long journey. She would not expect hotel service, monogrammed silver, haute cuisine. Melanie von Riesbach had praised my roast lamb and mint sauce, and rhubarb crumble. She settled down by the fire like any Mechtenhagen *kamerad* from the good old days in Pommern. Kurt was at ease. I could feel his pleasurable relaxation in my own facial muscles.

Aristocrat or proletarian, it made no difference; conversations between East Germans always took the same route. 'What happened when the Russians, the Poles –?' I left them to their reminising.

When I returned the atmosphere had changed between them. I paused beside the sitting-room door, unwilling to enter. I heard Melanie say, 'My mother cut my wrists and then her own. We woke up in a makeshift hospital several hours later. A Russian was sitting beside my bed; a boy who spoke a few words of German. He was very angry with me. He pointed at my bandaged wrists. "You not believe in God," he scolded. "If you believe in God you not do this bad thing."'

There were livid scars underneath her wide silver bracelets, and now Kurt could see for himself that Melanie, the *Junker's* daughter, had also suffered.

After four days and nights spent with my family, the lady from West Berlin had departed.

'She came first to England in 1950,' Kurt told me, 'to train as a nurse in England. Imagine that – a nurse, a von Riesbach! She took SRN – pretty good, don't you think? To pass her exams in a foreign language.'

I smiled at his changed direction. 'You seem to have altered your opinions about these von Riesbachs?'

He had spread out his hands, palms upwards. 'War,' he explained. 'War changes people.'

It was noon when we drove up to the collection of drab buildings that marked the border-crossing. We joined a line of waiting vehicles that was shorter than expected. Within the hour we were through, and crossing the bridge that spanned the River Oder.

The autobahn on which we travelled was well-maintained but bumpy. I asked Ryan if the Poles had built it and should not have been surprised when he said that this was Hitler's highway – laid down in the 1930s; the route along which the Russian armies had advanced in 1945 on their way towards Berlin – for I had seen this road many times before on black and white cinema news-reels, and now I had a sense of travelling back into my own past; of reliving experiences that were not my own.

The air seemed colder on this side of the Oder; grey-black clouds were massed to the north, but rain no longer fell and now the road signs were in Polish; I saw the marker for GDANSK which had formerly been DANZIG. I struggled with the spelling of the city called SZCZECIN which had once been STETTIN. I realized that these two place names comprised my total knowledge of the Polish language.

We picnicked in a lay-by. Melanie had brought flasks of thick and warming leek-and-potato soup, crisp rolls and cartons of salad. We ate with appetites made keener by the piquant nature of our location. But for the infrequent passing of a military vehicle or shabby van, the autobahn was empty.

Silences between old and close friends can be allowed for, understood. There were questions that I longed to ask but could not voice. We drove on, moving north and eastwards towards the Baltic coastline and Mechtenhagen; and now it seemed to me that Melanie grasped the Polish map a little tighter with her left hand, while the index-finger of her right hand traced uncertainly the coloured line that would bring us to our destination, and I wondered about the cost of private anguish, the risk involved in remembering old horrors. I wanted to reach out to her but could not. I sat mute and watchful as we drove deeper into silent landscapes where the forests stretched away to the horizon.

There came a moment when Ryan made a right turn, and I saw that we had left the autobahn for narrow country roads. The Polish place names here bore little or no relation to their former German titles; the village streets were empty of people. We passed an occasional battered tractor, the driver of which made a thoughtful study of our Berlin number plates. We travelled slowly over sealed roads that were in reasonable condition; but the houses were shabby, as were the buildings of eastern Germany and East Berlin; drab, as they were bound to be in an economy where cement and paint were luxuries rarely to be obtained.

Melanie and Ryan had made this journey once before in the clammy discomfort of torrential August rain. Their solitary contact in Mechtenhagen at that time had been welcoming but nervous, unsure of the wisdom of a meeting with people from the West. That visit, which had promised much, had been no more than a brief exchange of greetings, a slow drive-through; a stirring of memories which might have been better left undisturbed.

Spring was very late this year in Pommern. A few trees were still leafless, but the fields were green with crops of winter corn. The road began to slope upwards; great stands of pine, silver birch and aspen stretched away on either side. Water from melted snow and recent storms lay on low ground and in rutted tracks. We came abruptly off the smooth surface of tarmac and drove on to damp, packed earth uneven with potholes.

Ryan said, 'Did all of this land belong to your family?'

'Yes,' said Melanie, 'six thousand hectares.' Her voice was low and full of pain and I knew that her anguish did not come from the loss of material possessions, but from the passing of a way of life, an era that would not return.

I thought about the Polish people who had been brought from their homes to populate a country that was foreign to them. Forty-five years on and their occupation seemed still to be uneasy in this land which could hold no family memories for them, no blood ties of the kind that are especially precious to a rural population. They had re-consecrated the German churches to their Roman Catholic faith, set up shrines to the Virgin Mary in wayside grottoes, but there was no sense of true belonging.

Of the original number of thirty houses which had clustered around church and school, only twelve remained. We drove slowly between them, and Melanie pointed out the gaps, named the family dwellings which, in the war and since, had burned down or fallen into ruin.

Our Polish contact had been informed by letter of the

expected time of our arrival. We were greeted with an enthusiasm that came close to affection. The anxiety shown towards Melanie and Ryan on their last visit had quite disappeared. We were invited into the house to drink tea; as we entered, the music of guitars and synthesizer drifted out upon the cold moist air of afternoon, and I assumed that, somewhere within, a radio was playing.

The living room of the Polish house was simple and homely. Religious pictures hung beside the mounted antlers of stags long-dead. The house was very warm, heated from a tiled stove of a type rarely seen in western homes. A black and white television set had its special place on a corner shelf. The guitar music came from an adjoining room and Melanie inquired about its source.

'My sons,' said our host, and we paused to listen. 'They are rehearsing for tonight's performance.'

They were playing a slow and haunting melody that for me held a quality of heartbreak. The young men began to sing a Polish love song, the arrangement and style of which was reminiscent of the best of Lennon and McCartney, and the sound of their voices in this place and situation brought me close to tears.

A walk through the village was suggested. I looked at Melanie and saw the hope flare in her eyes, and I was happy and yet fearful for her. As we left the house the music followed us, and I knew that the unbearable sweet-sadness of it would haunt me whenever I remembered this day, and for all my life.

When we came to the Baumann house I paused to photograph it: a squat and solid building, its stucco stained and grey, the white paint of its windows peeling. I began to remember Christina's testament of the April of 1944, imagined the furniture dragged from this place, the looting and burning, the terror of the women and their small children. I had expected to recognize Kurt's home from pictures I had seen, but it stood without significance like a stranger.

Melanie walked with our Polish friends; Ryan and I followed at a little distance. As we came level with them, Melanie turned to us and said in English, 'So they have returned.' She spoke softly, in a tone of awe and pleasure; we followed her gaze upwards, and there in the enfolding branches of a high tree we saw the pair of storks atop their nest.

The return of the storks from Africa, to their nesting sites in Mechtenhagen, had been a fable told often by Kurt to his young sons. He had described the intricate construction of the huge nests, and how the sparrows would build among the lower layers of the straw and sticks. For Paul and Martin, the story of the storks had held a quality of magic.

'They always arrived,' said Melanie, 'on every March 21st. In the war, and for a long time afterwards, so I am told, they never came. It was considered to be lucky for the community among whom the storks chose to make their home. Perhaps the good days will come back to Mechtenhagen.'

Ryan and I paused beside what remained of the tiny stone-built church. Here it was that generations of Baumanns had been baptized and married, and buried in surrounding ground. The doors and windows, the pointed wooden tower had long since perished; the tallest wall to remain standing was now only shoulder-high. We stood among the fallen stones, the bindweed, the nettles and the ivy, and I tried to imagine an aisle, an altar, a choir singing; the young Christina and Kurt, solemn-faced at their Confirmation Service. I looked back to the house where they were born and saw how church and school and home had all been in close view of each other. It explained so many things about him, preferences and beliefs, that, because my terms of reference were different, I had

277

never understood. How could I have visualized a life so isolated, so concerned with principles of day-to-day survival; of a people set apart and folded inwards one upon another, among the silence of these forest tracts?

Melanie and her escort had moved ahead of us, and Ryan and I began to walk a little faster. As we came up to them I saw Melanie pause and skip a step or two; a movement that indicated pure joy. Our guide was leading us towards the *Hof* – the former home of the von Riesbach family; the Great House in this tiny village.

It was no longer the country residence of a cultured family but a working farmhouse. The former lawns, gardens and apple orchard now housed chicken-runs and makeshift sheds. A dog on a long chain barked fiercely at us as we passed. The raised tree-shaded terrace, where *kaffee und kuchen* had been taken on summer afternoons, was a repository for implements and buckets, its concrete surface cracked, its tubs of bright flowers no more than a memory held in a young girl's mind.

As we walked away, she said in English, 'I hardly recognize any of it – but then, why should I?' Melanie spoke in the muffled tone that holds back tears. Ryan spoke quietly to her; I didn't hear the words but I heard the compassion in his voice; and I knew then how much he loved her.

As we walked away she pointed upwards to the little dormer window that marked her childhood bedroom; she stood for a moment underneath the one remaining apple tree. She said, 'My father planted this, in 1939.'

We said our farewells to the kindly Poles who had permitted our intrusion into their lives. We drove away, passing once more the house where Kurt was born, the school he had attended, the church where as a child he had been taught to believe in a loving God; and I had no sense of his presence, or that he had ever dwelt there.

The road that led away from Mechtenhagen sloped gently downhill.

Melanie said, 'In 1945, when things were very bad here, and this route was blocked with army vehicles and refugees, I was sixteen years old. I came every night with the district nurse and we tried to help the awful suffering of the people.' Her words had the effect upon me of a window opening.

'A nurse,' Kurt had once said wonderingly of Melanie, 'a von Riesbach?'

And so this, I thought, is where and when her mode of caring, her generosity of spirit, her sweetness, had begun.

The skies to the north and east were lighter now. The strange unseasonable weather had a tint of primrose shading over from the west. I began to imagine haytime in these meadows, Kurt and Christina working with their parents. I looked around me and knew that these fields and trees were much as they had always been; that what I saw now had once delighted Kurt. And all at once I felt a leaping joy, a kind of exultation that had been absent since the hour he died.

Throughout that day I had fought a sense of urgency, knowing that I no longer had the youth and energy to conjure magic. But now the magic stood all around me. 'The May-time is the sweetest in my country,' he had said, 'when all comes green.'

Ryan slowed and then halted beside a rutted track that led away into deep forest. I began to walk across the depth of rotted leaves and slippery pine needles, between the scarred bark of old trees and the trembling greenness of young leaves.

I moved slowly and certainly towards a clearing where the light of the pale mid-afternoon filtered only dimly. I halted and stood very still. A little wind passed across my face, ruffled my hair and touched my lips. And I knew then that I had found Kurt.

I parted from Melanie and Ryan two days later. We sat in the red and yellow décor of Tegel Airport and said the usual things: 'I'll call you – safe journey – stay well until we meet again.'

But there were no words that could ever express or explain the unity of love that had grown between us in these few days; our personal and private *einheit*.

We, who had each one married a foreigner with all the risk and danger that entails, had learned from one another how best to go on living our lives of translation.

❥

Epilogue

THE year turned slowly towards autumn. Birds began to gather in the hedgerows and in tall trees. In Leicestershire the final legal stubble-burning by English farmers took on the significance of rural last rites. From the heights of the medieval Deerpark Cathy Baumann watched with her son Martin as the dark smoke rolled out across the shorn fields.

She recalled the springtime in Berlin and Poland, daffodils flowering among the last of the winter snows; the Polish love songs played and sung by the young men in Mechtenhagen, the nesting storks, the forest clearing where she had found Kurt.

From June to September time had been suspended, and summer lost. Martin had driven her to distant hospitals, had waited for her in crowded outpatient departments while scans were taken, and consultant surgeons pronounced verdicts and informed her of decisions about her health. It was Martin who, on a Monday in August, delivered her to the surgical ward for an operation; his was the first face she recognized on emergence from the anaesthetic. It was Martin who moved into her house, who stayed with her through the time of convalescence. In the evenings they had eaten Chinese take-away meals and watched sit-com television. They spoke about his childhood, the teenage years, his closeness to his father. As they talked she sensed the change in him and in her own self; the relationship was no longer that of mother and son, but of equals, friends. All walls had been demolished. Now she watched the white birds swoop and dive about the lake. For the red and fallow deer the rut was almost over. A few more weeks and she would see the pollard oaks tested by November gales. At the thought of winter following she felt the old thrill of anticipation run along her veins, quickening her blood and breath. She turned to Martin, took his arm and smiled. 'Let's walk,' she said, 'before the light fades.'